"Where is she?" He raised his sword toward the abbess.

The sight of her abbess threatened was enough to spark Amée's fiery temperament, which she struggled with daily to control. She stepped in front of the sword. "I am Amée Évreux."

"You?" The warrior looked at her with barely concealed horror.

Amée raised her chin defiantly. "How dare you enter this holy place with weapons raised?"

He smiled, a flicker of respect crossing his features, and sheathed his sword. "Princess Gisela sent me."

It was a mistake! It had to be.

"I am to be wed to Christ," she whispered. Even as she said the words, she knew her father had broken his promise. The ghost of hope, a life free from her father, disappeared with her misty breath.

Jorund stepped forward, his calloused hand brushing the hair away from her face. The raven curls she usually kept tightly bound beneath a novice wimple and veil flowed around her. In less than a month her hair would have been roughly shorn, and she would have taken her vows. The restrictions and chains of her life as Lady Amée Évreux cast aside. Ahead only spiritual peace and obscurity.

Not the hell her mother suffered. Not marriage.

"No," the man sighed, as if he pitied her. "You're going to be wed to me."

LUCY MORRIS

—

A Nun for the
Viking Warrior

HARLEQUIN
HISTORICAL

HARLEQUIN®
HISTORICAL™

Recycling programs
for this product may
not exist in your area.

ISBN-13: 978-1-335-40748-1

A Nun for the Viking Warrior

Copyright © 2021 by Lucy Morris

This edition published by arrangement with Harlequin Books S.A.

For questions and comments about the quality of this book,
please contact us at CustomerService@Harlequin.com.

Harlequin Enterprises ULC
22 Adelaide St. West, 40th Floor
Toronto, Ontario M5H 4E3, Canada
www.Harlequin.com

Printed in U.S.A.

Lucy Morris lives in Essex, UK, with her husband, two young children and two cats. She has a massive sweet tooth and loves gin, bubbly and Irn-Bru. She's a member of the UK Romantic Novelists' Association. She was delighted to accept a two-book deal with Harlequin after submitting her story to the Warriors Wanted! submission blitz for Viking, medieval and Highlander romances. Writing for Harlequin Historical is a dream come true for her and she hopes you enjoy her books!

Books by Lucy Morris

Harlequin Historical

The Viking Chief's Marriage Alliance

Visit the Author Profile page
at Harlequin.com.

Chapter One

*St Scholastica Nunnery, Kingdom of Northmannia,
formerly part of West Francia, 912 AD*

'We won't let the heathens take you!' Sister Gabriel cried, almost hysterical. She gripped Amée Évreux's arm painfully tight as they watched the wooden door shake with every strike of the battering ram. The sound echoed through the stone walls of the nunnery as if God Himself were knocking at the gate.

Except, of course, if it had been God Amée wouldn't have been so fearful.

The abbess had refused the men entry as it was the middle of the night. They were obviously Norsemen and she'd been concerned for the safety of those within the cloister. Unfortunately, the men seemed unwilling to wait until dawn to speak with them.

Despite her own fear Amée gave her friend a comforting touch on the arm. 'The door will hold—it's been there for nearly a hundred years. It won't fail us—not in our time of need.' She tried to hide her shivering as she looked at the rest of her frightened sisters, offering what she hoped was a reassuring smile. They all looked at her as if she were mad.

Maybe she was?

An image of her distraught mother ripping up her father's clothes came to mind and she briskly rubbed her arms for comfort as well as warmth. It was no wonder she was cold. She wore only her shift and the boots she'd hastily pulled on when the abbess had hauled her from her bed. Another friend passed her a blanket and she wrapped it around her shoulders with a grateful smile.

Abbess Berthild frowned at the trembling double doors as years of dust was shaken from its weathered hinges. 'It will hold… At least until morning. Once their tempers have cooled, I'm sure they will be more reasonable in the light of a new day. There is a treaty now. They can no longer behave like animals!'

'What's going on?' whispered one of the novices.

Sister Gabriel was helpfully quick to explain Amée's impending doom. 'His name is Jorund Jötunnson and he has come to take our poor Amée! He looks like the devil himself. As tall as a mountain and as broad as the sea!' She made the holy sign with a quivering hand. Amée couldn't blame her for being afraid. They'd all—in one way or another—seen the fury of the Norse as they'd burned through Francia. Bringing death and despair to all who stood in their path.

Was that why they were here?

Surely not. It was well known the nunnery had nothing of value, and why had the warrior asked for her specifically?

She tried to remain optimistic for the sake of her sisters. But each bang on the door was another blow to her equanimity. Would her own defences eventually crumble? She clutched the blanket tighter as her heart thundered louder and louder in her chest like a runaway horse.

Sister Gabriel continued—oblivious to Amée's crisis of confidence. 'He is one of Jarl Rollo's men. He says Amée has been promised to him! Abbess Berthild has refused him entry until he can provide proof of this from our King.'

Everyone's eyes turned towards Amée.

She looked up at the abbess. 'Maybe I should go out and speak with him? It would be wrong to put you and the others at risk. Besides, maybe it's a misunderstanding.' How she prayed it was a misunderstanding! Otherwise, the future she'd worked so hard for would be lost. She smiled brightly. 'Princess Gisla will know the truth of it…'

Bang!

'And he can't possibly refuse to speak with his overlord's wife…'

Bang!

Her voice trailed off with each continued knock to the door. 'She will understand and sort this whole mess out.'

Bang!

'She considers me a friend. I was her companion for many years at court.'

Bang!

'All will be well. I'm sure of it. A few calm, reasonable words with the…'

Bang!

'…the man, and he'll understand.'

Bang!

The abbess sniffed. 'Absolutely not.'

The doors creaked and groaned.

Wide-eyed with horror, the sisters and novices of the

nunnery watched as the oak began to bow under the strain. For many of the sisters, this was not the first time a Norseman had broken into their home. But with the recent treaty—which granted land and Princess Gisla's hand in marriage to Jarl Rollo in return for protection against raids—they'd prayed those days of torment were behind them.

Apparently not.

With a deafening crack, both the hinges and the thick oak bar gave way. The double doors splitting and then falling to the ground like overripe figs.

The women lurched back in fright and a few of the serfs ran into the shadows seeking a place to hide. Several Norse warriors dressed in leathers burst into the cloister. Dropping the tree trunk they'd used as a hastily cut battering ram, they drew their swords and approached slowly with predatory intent, glistening with sweat and barely concealed rage.

'Where is Amée Évreux?' shouted the giant at the head of the group. He was the tallest man she had ever seen. She had to look up at most people, but he may as well have been sat on a horse for the way her neck had to bend backwards to see him clearly as he approached. He was battle-scarred, with a half-head of dark blond hair thickly coiled on top and braided down his back. The sides of his head were closely shorn, as was his face, revealing a strong jaw.

But it was his piercing blue eyes that cut down all her optimism and hope. They were as sharp and as deadly as the sword in his hand. There would be no negotiation, no reasoning or bargaining, with this man. Her knees became soft and she stumbled back a step.

'Enough games!' He snarled, his teeth almost wolf-like

as shadows danced across his menacing face. 'If I will not have your hospitality, I will have what I came for!'

He's terrifying!

Amée watched him approach and her vision contracted. All else forgotten as he prowled forward with fierce masculinity. This man was all-powerful, and even worse, he knew it. The irritation cooled as he looked around at their pale faces, but he didn't look ashamed of what he'd done—he looked…*beautiful.*

She blinked in confusion at her odd twist in thought, but it was true.

He was beautiful, in his own raw and wild way. In the same way Amée might admire a hawk swooping in for the kill or the flash of lightning. She shivered as she realised her fanciful notions were once again clouding her judgement.

How many times had her father beaten romantic notions out of her mother? Too many times to count…too many to bear.

She clenched her jaw and sucked in a deep breath to wash away the distracting ideas that swam freely in her head.

She had to focus on the facts.

He was a heathen raider who had no respect for God or women, only for blood and gold.

The enemy.

He raised his sword towards the abbess. The steel shone bright in the flickering flames of the sconces surrounding the entrance hall. 'Where is *she*?'

The sight of her abbess being threatened was enough to spark the fiery temperament Amée struggled daily to control. She stepped in front of the sword. Unfortunately, because of her short stature, it still pointed above her head at the abbess. So, her gesture appeared futile. Regardless, she spoke with as much imperial command as she could muster. 'I am Amée Évreux.'

'*You?*' He looked her up and down with barely concealed horror.

Amée tried not to take offence—after all, why should she care what this beast thought of her? She raised her chin defiantly. 'How dare you enter this holy place with weapons raised? Even your leader, Rollo, has converted to Christ. He cannot condone such actions.'

He smiled, a flicker of respect crossing his features, and sheathed his sword. 'I think you do not know the Jarl as well as I do, Lady Évreux. It's good to *finally* meet you.' His voice was a distant rumble of thunder that sent a shiver down her spine.

Her eyes narrowed. 'Perhaps not, but I am a dear friend of his wife, Princess Gisla. She would never approve—'

'She is the one who sent me.'

It was a mistake! It had to be.

Amée felt the blood drain from her face and she clutched the blanket tighter around her shoulders. The chill of the forest air rushed in after their intruders, bringing with it the cold dread of familial duty she'd hoped was long forgotten.

'I am to be wed to Christ,' she whispered. Even as she said the words, she knew her life had changed forever in some terrible way. Her father had broken his promise. She was his chattel and always would be. The ghost of hope, a life free from her father, disappeared with her misty breath into the midnight air.

Jorund stepped forward. His arm ring shone in the candlelight as he reached with a calloused hand to brush the hair away from her face. The raven curls she usually kept tightly bound beneath a novice wimple and veil flowed around her in thick sleep-mussed waves. In less than a month her hair would have been roughly shorn, and she would have taken her vows. The restrictions and chains of her life as Lady Amée Évreux cast aside. Ahead only spiritual peace and obscurity.

Not the hell her mother suffered. Not marriage.

'No.' He sighed, as if he pitied her. 'You're going to be wed to me.'

Jorund stared at the young woman in front of him. *Why did she have to be so damn...small?*

At first, he'd dismissed her as a child. Wrapped up in a huge blanket, with little worn-out boots peeping through the pools of rough wool gathered around her. But when she'd confronted him with a tilted jaw of defiance, he'd recognised her for what she truly was.

A beautiful noblewoman...albeit a very small one.

He tried his best to smother his disappointment. What had he expected? A giant like himself? Hardly likely amongst the Francia nobility. Yet there was strength there: she had the pitiful arrogance of a wolf pup that thought it was much bigger than it actually was.

He'd met her father very briefly at the signing of the treaty, and even after that short acquaintance he knew Lothair Évreux was as much of a trickster as Loki. No doubt it was why he'd been so slow and vague in his correspondence. Lothair had probably hoped she would have already taken holy orders before Jorund could find her. At least she didn't appear anything like her father, the opposite, in fact—emotions and thoughts washed across her face without guard or pretence. It was refreshing.

His heart softened a little knowing how vulnerable she

felt. But he could not give her hope. They would marry and he would have Évreux. His chance for a peaceful and respected life. A nervous bride would not stand in his way. She would learn he wasn't the callous brute he appeared...eventually.

He shifted on the balls of his feet with a frown. He certainly felt like a callous brute at this moment.

'You have no jurisdiction here, you heathen brute!' snapped a strange woman from the side with a shrill voice and panicked eyes. He frowned and stared her down. It was odd that she'd used such similar phrasing to his own thoughts. The woman shrank into the shadows with a pitiful squeak.

So be it if they were afraid of him. Maybe he could get out of here quicker. He did so hate the Christian churches with their depressing images and draughty halls.

Why was he here? he asked himself again for the hundredth time. *Because Princess Gisla begged her husband to grant her this favour.*

Rollo would do anything for his beautiful bride. And Jorund would do anything for Rollo, who'd been more of a father to him than the wretched worm who'd sired him.

'The treaty has been signed by your King. The land between the River Epte and the sea, as well as the Duchy of Brittany, belongs to Jarl Rollo. It includes Évreux, the land gifted to me through our marriage.'

Amée's bitter voice interrupted him. 'If it is Jarl Rollo's land now, then why do you need my hand in marriage to rule it? Take it! It is mine only in title. I have not been there since I was a child, when *your people* first ransacked it.'

Her eyes spat fire as she spoke and he had the uneasy

feeling his wife would not be as accommodating as Princess Gisla was to Rollo.

'Because your Princess has commanded it,' he answered with a shrug. It was true. The land was his by right, nothing could take it from him. But the Princess was determined to mix the blood of both their people in as many matches as she could arrange between the Norse and the Franks. She and Rollo wanted an enduring peace, and who could argue against that?

Amée began to choke on her words of denial, her breath speeding up with fear and panic. 'No, I can't... My father has given me permission to take holy orders... I'm to live here now...peacefully...and put aside my duties as a lady of the court. I... I...' She looked at her abbess for guidance and was met by the sad shake of the woman's head.

'Your father now agrees with the Princess and has retracted his approval for you to live here.' He gestured at the damp walls of the cloister with disgust. He would provide a better home for her than this. 'I have a missive from him that confirms it.'

Jorund took out the scroll from his tunic but didn't bother to offer it.

The abbess let out an exasperated hiss. 'Why didn't you mention this earlier? I would have granted you admittance if I'd known you had her father's written permission!'

Jorund handed her the parchment. Eagerly she broke the seal and unfurled it. There was a reason why he hadn't initially provided the scroll when he'd first reached the stone nunnery. He'd been cautious because he couldn't read it—neither runes nor the written words of the Franks. It didn't matter to him that he couldn't read.

However, he didn't fully trust what the document actually said, especially as it had come directly from Lothair rather than Rollo. For all he knew, it would give the bearer permission to kill him and his warriors. But after breaking into the dismally fortified building, he'd quickly realised there were no archers or defence of any kind within the crumbling old walls. He had no reason to fear a counterattack.

He noticed Amée was staring up at him. A slow dawn of despair spread across her features. Big eyes, soft brown with flecks of gold within, were perceptive and glinted with barely concealed emotion. For all of her bluster and confidence, she was afraid, and that sat badly with him.

Unconsciously, he shifted his weight from side to side, a nervous habit from when he'd learned to fight as a child, constantly checking and rechecking his ever-changing balance. He bristled with irritation at the way she took the smallest of steps backwards, as if she were afraid of what he might do.

Was marrying him such a terrible fate? Maybe it was to her, he admitted.

A bit of reassurance, then.

He turned and waved forward the nervous priest he'd dragged along from Rouen. 'I have brought a priest to perform the marriage ceremony. It will be a *Christian* ceremony. He washed me at the same time as he did Rollo. Didn't you, Augustus?' He slapped the man on his back good-naturedly, but the man was as light as a bird and would have fallen on his face if Jorund hadn't quickly righted him.

Instead of looking reassured, Amée paled.

There was an awkward silence that lasted several of her gasping breaths and then she shouted, 'No!'

The sudden burst of passionate refusal echoed around the arched hallway and rebounded at him with a hollow sound.

He stared at her dumbfounded. What could he say to that? He'd not expected her to be happy about the sudden change in her circumstances, but he'd expected her to at least accept both her father and the Princess's decision.

'Amée…' said the gentle voice of her abbess.

But she shook her head and took a further step back. 'No!'

She took another step and then another.

'I won't!'

Then she turned and ran.

Chapter Two

Amée ran down the colonnade from the nunnery's gatehouse back towards the dormitory. Above the courtyard the full moon illuminated her way, as well as the occasional torch in one of the alcoves to her right. She didn't know where she was running to, or what she could possibly do to end this nightmare. She only knew that she had to get away from him, and the doomed fate he represented.

Marriage.

A future of servitude and misery. Bound to a man not of her choosing, who did not care whether she lived or died, so long as the land of her home was his.

She would never survive it, and that knowledge only made her boots beat harder against the stone.

So, she ran. Desperate to find some dark corner to hide in. Some hole where he would never find her. She knew it was madness to run. But at this moment she felt as if she were a child again, and so she did what she had always done when things went badly.

Hide! Hide! Hide!

The word beat inside her head with the rhythm of her feet and the pounding of her heart. Was it her heart, or another pair of boots following closely behind? A very large and heavy pair of boots.

Jorund!

The jerk on the blanket pulled her backwards as he grabbed it from behind. A little stumble, but she quickly released it and carried on running as fast as she could.

Unfortunately, she didn't get far. His hand grabbed her shoulder and firmly turned her to face him. Then another arm wrapped around her waist and dragged her into a shadowed alcove.

Running was fruitless. She was no longer a child.

With no place to hide she found herself falling in on herself. She began to tremble, unable to catch her breath. Panting and gasping as if she were in the throes of drowning. Her hands clenched so tight, she knew by the prick of pain on her palms that she would have welts afterwards.

I must look mad.

But the futility and stupidity of her actions never helped when she felt like this. They only added to the storm inside her head until she lost herself in a sea of panic. No longer a woman but a wild animal. Her breath was short, fast and painfully laboured. Misery and torment stretched out before her and she felt like a frightened rabbit caught in a noose.

She twisted to get out of his hold, but it was like fighting against the earth and sky. Pointless.

'Stop it! Are you mad?' Jorund barked out.

She whimpered, mortified at her own weakness and fear.

The Norse abhorred fear. Would he kill her out of sheer disgust?

She stared up into the hard lines of his face and her knees buckled beneath her. She would have crumpled to the floor if he'd not held her tight.

Jorund said something harsh in Norse and then gently tucked her under his arm as if she were a fruit basket. He walked over to a nearby bench positioned against the cloister wall.

It was usually a place of quiet spiritual contemplation, where the abbess might console a novice...where, in fact, the abbess had spoken to Amée about her own doubts only a few days ago.

However, tonight she was sat on a giant warrior's lap being cradled to his barrel chest as if she were a child. She blinked against the hardboiled leather in disbelief. He smelt of sweat, horse and forest pine. His big hand cradled her head as he pressed her against his beating heart and...*hushed* her.

If Jorund had broken out into song and danced across the cloister, she couldn't have been more surprised. He hadn't struck her yet, and seemed to have no intention of doing so. His touch was gentle and careful, which was such an unexpectedly pleasant change that she found herself sinking into his warmth.

She'd never been held like this by a man before.

The strength and power should have been terrifying, and yet, it was strangely comforting wrapped around her like this.

'Enough,' he said quietly, as if he weren't talking to her any more but to the panic within her. Commanding the sea to part so that she might find some way back. 'Breathe in,' he said, drawing in a deep breath of his own. 'Breathe out.' The air rushed from his lungs in one long deliberate breath. He kept repeating his words and actions until she dimly became aware that he was encouraging her to do the same.

His body in contrast to hers was relaxed. He was still a mountain of hard muscle but he'd not lashed out at her as she might have expected when he'd caught her. Instead, he seemed to be the calmest she'd seen him since he broke into the nunnery. Undisturbed to find himself sat on a bench with a frightened woman trembling on his lap.

She sucked in a breath, unable to hold it for as long or as evenly as he could. It took a long time, but eventually her breathing eased as she focused on his words and the calm depth of his voice. His eyes as bright as sapphires in the darkness of the alcove captured all of her attention and her fears sank into them.

He smiled. 'Good, all will be well. There's no need to be afraid. Breathe in… Breathe out.'

Strangely, she did feel better. She was no longer trembling at least. Soothed and encouraged by his confidence. The warmth of his hand as it rubbed her arm was like a soft caress. Up and down, in time with his slow breath. He was like an anchor tethering her during the storm. She was no longer lost, no longer afraid.

As she finally gained control over her emotions, she realised three startling facts all at once.

Firstly, she was only wearing her thin linen nightshift and boots.

Secondly, she was being cradled by a Norseman who had just broken into her nunnery and demanded her hand in marriage.

And lastly, and most disturbingly of all, she liked this closeness.

She did not want to leave his embrace. She was neither cold nor frightened. In fact, she almost felt…safe and… warm. Something she'd not felt in years. A part of her never wanted it to end.

* * *

Jorund stared at the woman in his arms as a slow blush crept up her face and neck. Her breathing, which moments ago had been filled with terror, was now relaxed.

Fear no longer clouded her eyes. She was herself again.

'Thank you,' she whispered, her voice husky. Desire sparked in his belly and the gold flecks in her eyes only fanned the flames. Was she looking at him with…longing? His arms instinctively pulled her curvaceous body ever so slightly closer.

'You're welcome. Why did you run?' he asked gently, not wishing to frighten her.

The blush deepened. 'I…I…never expected…this.'

Did she mean marriage in general, or marriage to a man like him?

Either way he could understand her distress.

'That is understandable. Change can be frightening. But it doesn't always have to be a bad thing. Fate and change are what make life interesting.'

She thought for a moment, a tiny frown creasing her brow, adorable in its innocence. 'Maybe…'

His hands ached to touch her. He appeased the desire by gathering up a piece of her linen shift in his hands and rubbing the coarse fabric between his fingertips. It was an area near her thigh and the light from the torch above their heads illuminated the outline of her rounded flesh beneath. The heat between his legs rose and ached. He became light-headed imagining how much softer her skin would feel…like Byzantine silk. 'You will see. All will be well,' he uttered.

After a moment of silence, he raised his eyes to hers. Warm dark eyes stared back at him with hope and she gave him a tentative smile that stole the breath from his lungs.

Warmth spread through his chest—not only lust, but something far more powerful and rare.

Hope.

Hope, for the end to his loneliness. That he may be able to bury the darker side of his soul that yearned for vengeance. Live in peace and nurture the lighter side of himself that wished only to protect. To have a family and an honourable life.

Granted, her reaction to their future together had initially been...unfavourable.

Very unfavourable, in fact—she'd practically drowned in her own fear, after taking only one look at his awkward, brutish body. She'd fled as fast as her legs could carry her.

But maybe it was just the shock of it all? She was calm now and seemed open to him. She'd not moved from her position as another woman might have done. Maybe she welcomed his touch? After being sheltered in this lifeless place, a young woman with a passionate heart might even encourage his touch...by, say, remaining in his lap?

His eyes roamed over her body. Wondering if he dared to kiss her.

Without the blanket covering her, he could see what his body already knew. She was most definitely not a child. Short, yes. But her legs were strong and sturdy, her bottom and hips fully curved, accentuating their feminine shape. Full breasts pressed against the linen of her shift, her nipples tight against the fabric in the torchlight.

He looked to her face for permission. Her pupils were wide, her mouth lush and slightly parted. He could see a mixture of confusion and desire in her expression, as if she didn't understand her body's reaction to him.

If she kissed him now, offered herself in any way, he

would happily pleasure her here and now, regardless of her God's anger at the insult.

Who was he to deny her anything?

Testing the waters, he smoothed his hand up her thigh, drawing her closer. She softened into him, moulding herself to him unconsciously chest to chest. Her curtain of ebony hair tickling his exposed arms and neck.

Uncertainty made his throat dry and his heart quicken.

She'd proved brave before, maybe he could tempt her to be brave again?

He leaned closer, until their breath mingled. Fresh soap, linen and a hint of drowsy lavender filled his nose. Clean, fresh smells in contrast to his no doubt dirty well-travelled sweat. It reminded him that he was in no fit state to be seducing maidens.

He leaned away, and as if they were tied together by an invisible ribbon she followed. The shift in her posture pushed his stiff manhood against her hip. Her hand dropped absently touching the unexpected obstruction and he groaned.

He meant his next words as a compliment…*he really did*. 'Careful… I may take you up on your offer.' Unable to resist, he flexed his hips to emphasise and—if truth be told—further enjoy her touch.

Her eyes looked down at her hand in bewilderment. The outraged gasp as she jumped off his lap was confirmation enough that she'd not realised what she was doing.

'I thought it was your sword!' she cried, looking both horrified and confused at the bulge in his leather trousers.

He snorted in amusement at her innocent words. But instead of replying he focused on adjusting his clothing to ease his discomfort. When he looked up, he immediately felt guilty for laughing at her. She'd wrapped her arms around herself in a protective stance and her lips were trembling as if she were trying not to cry.

He stood and took a step towards her. She backed away, the fragile ribbon that had connected them moments before severed by his stupidity and lust.

A righteous storm began to boil within, as the darker side of him reared to the surface.

Tonight had been a long night after an even longer week. Frustration and tiredness easily getting the better of him. As soon as possible, he needed to get away from this depressing place and begin the life he'd craved for so long.

Enough words! He'd already spoken more in the last hour than he'd spoken in the past week with his warriors, and he was still no further ahead in his plans. He was a man of action, not a negotiator, and especially not a seducer of virgins. As his time with Amée had unfortunately proven. He'd been stupid to think she would have walked into his arms so easily.

She took one fearful step back and then another...

'Amée, I *swear*!' he shouted, causing her to jump as if he'd struck her. He struggled to control and soften his voice... And failed. The next words that came out of his mouth were no better than a hissed threat. 'I *swear*, if you run from me once more, I will not chase you. But I *will* lay waste to this place until nothing remains but rubble. You and your sisters will have nowhere to go, nowhere to hide!' His patience was gone.

'Please...don't.' Her voice trembled.

'We will marry tonight and then travel to Évreux,' he said briskly. He felt wretched doing it, but charm had never been a skill of his.

Brute strength and ruthless command? Yes. But not

charm. It would be better to not let his fragile hopes get in the way of his future.

Better for her.

She stared down at her boots as they peeped out from beneath her shift. Then she nodded, defeated.

His stomach filled with bile and self-loathing.

Chapter Three

'It's probably for the best,' said Abbess Berthild, with a pat of Amée's arm as she helped her dress and gather up her meagre possessions.

'He's a brute!'

The abbess paused for a moment, as if considering the description, and then shrugged. 'They all are, my dear.' Then she popped Amée's comb in her sack without any further hesitation.

She wasn't sure if the abbess meant the Norse or men in general. She had the uneasy suspicion it was the latter.

Exasperated she turned away to take one last look at the dormitory in which she'd slept for the last year. To think she'd thought she would never leave, and yet here she was, having her sack packed for her. Preparing to take her marriage vows instead of the holy orders she'd planned.

She had to marry him.

That had been certain even before Jorund had threatened to lay waste to the nunnery. But now she had this as a further incentive not to climb out of the dormitory window and run into the forest. What else could she do? She had to protect them. Never would she let innocents suffer in her place.

However, she was a little disappointed that no one else appeared to be concerned about her personal sacrifice. She'd hoped for some outrage at least. Perhaps for the abbess to shed a few tears? Possibly even clutch her arm and beg her to refuse the match. To not martyr herself to the Viking lord for their sakes.

Amée could never have imagined the abbess would so calmly help her pack. Had everything she'd done since her arrival been for nothing?

'*How* can you say that it's for the best? I was meant to take holy orders! Surely there's something we can do? Petition the King or His Holiness? Ask for more time? He can't abduct me from my holy vocation!'

The abbess gave a loud and long-suffering sigh. 'My dear, I know you mean well. But I have to say I am not surprised that God has intervened—'

'It wasn't God! It was a giant *Viking* who broke down our door!' she cried, no longer caring if she appeared disrespectful. The whole situation was disrespectful... *to her*!

'Well, he's graciously paid for the repairs, and even paid the village blacksmith a generous sum to improve the hinges and locks. So, we'll actually end up with a better door—' The abbess paused at the horrified look on Amée's face. 'That's beside the point... Amée, you have been a most diligent and *enthusiastic* novice. Your skills organising the education of the novices, as well as the management of the larders, has been outstanding. But I'm afraid I have always had misgivings as to whether taking holy orders was really the best path in life for you. You have had doubts about your vocation—' The abbess raised her hand, cutting Amée off before she could deny her statement. 'And those doubts cannot be brushed aside, no matter how much you may wish to. I do not think a life of servitude and quiet contemplation is right for you…and there is no shame in that. Jorund seems a reasonable man…if direct…and what our land needs is protection and peace with the Norsemen. Maybe that is your true destiny.'

Amée stayed silent throughout the abbess's speech. She wanted to rage against it, but a deep and shameful part of her knew the abbess was right.

She'd made a terrible novice, not through lack of trying.

Oh, how she'd tried!

But it was like asking a rooster not to crow. She could never be quiet when she needed to be. Her prayers were always distracted, and she'd been scolded thousands of times for fidgeting during lauds. She excelled in teaching and organisation, that was true, but she lacked the faith in her calling. Part of her had always longed for… more. She'd hoped that her spirit might quieten over time, and she would eventually find the peace and wisdom she craved.

But marriage? And to a man who would no doubt treat her no better than her father? A man who would make demands and expect respect while offering none.

Except he *had* been kind to her, if only for a moment, when he'd helped her calm down. Then… She still wasn't sure what had happened. He'd been holding her, easing her nerves, and then…and then she'd been lost in his sky-blue eyes and gentle touch. And then she'd…

Oh, heavens!

Her face flamed with embarrassment, quickly followed by outrage. It was an accident and he'd laughed at her, mocked her innocence! She hadn't realised a man's body did that, and her palm burned with the memory of his…hardness.

Amée shook her head—she shouldn't be thinking about that.

'Are you well?' asked the concerned abbess. 'You look feverish… Maybe you should have something to eat.'

'I'm fine! It's just a little warm in here.'

The abbess looked around at Amée's draughty dormitory and frowned. 'I see. Well, your betrothed was quite insistent that you marry before you leave. Although why he can't wait until morning is a mystery. His documentation from your father appears legitimate.'

The abbess handed her the scroll, and Amée read it thoroughly. She knew her father would always be careful to protect his own interests first.

Sure enough, Amée found it.

The first page was a missive in her father's hand confirming the details of the contract on the second. The contract was between her father and King Charles, the Frankish King. It detailed specific requirements regarding her marriage, and the passing of Évreux from her father's control to Jorund's.

If she did not produce an heir after two winters of marriage, then the property would return to her father, bypassing even Rollo.

How had her father managed that?

And…more worryingly, what did he intend? Amée thought back to her last audience in front of her father. She'd timed it well. Recently remarried to a much younger woman, Lothair had been optimistic about his new life and the prospect of a male heir.

So, Amée had requested an audience and wailed about her sudden fervent 'devotion to God' and her newfound calling for a more spiritual life. The truth was she'd been desperate to leave his tyranny, as well as the royal court. She knew the type of men he considered allies and she feared he would eventually choose one of those simpering toads as her future husband.

Had he believed her devotion to God? Had he presumed she would have refused the match with Jorund?

Possibly, although she doubted her father thought her *that* strong-willed. She'd managed to outwit him a few times over the years, but she'd never dared outright defiance. She knew it was always a fruitless exercise.

She offered the scroll back to the abbess, who shook her head. 'Keep it. It's almost the only thing left that's yours. I'm afraid all your other belongings were sold not long after you arrived.'

She remembered the fine clothes and jewellery she'd arrived in. She'd not missed them; in fact, it had been liberating to remove them. No longer a lady with familial responsibility. No longer Lothair Évreux's daughter. She'd been so happy to give up those roles that day. 'I remember—we were able to fix the barn roof when we sold them.'

The abbess smiled fondly at Amée's reply. 'You will be missed.' Then her face clouded with worry. 'Are you aware of what happens in the marriage bed?'

Amée nodded quickly. 'Yes, of course!' It was still a little vague in her head—'putting a key in a lock,' she'd overheard at court—and after feeling Jorund's hard bulge she was beginning to understand it a little better. Regardless of her unanswered questions, there was no way on this sweet earth that she was going to talk to the abbess about it.

The older woman seemed as relieved as she did and gave a brisk nod. 'Good. Good.'

They left her dormitory and after a short walk arrived at the nunnery's chapel and found Jorund and his warriors resting there, still wearing their weapons, oblivious to the significance of the place.

The abbess cleared her throat and every man in the room turned towards them. Including Jorund, who took her breath away with his bright blue eyes. They ensnared her and held her like invisible chains. She was unable to break the connection or even think clearly, as she remembered the touch of his hand on her thigh, his breath against her lips… She sucked in a shaky breath.

He walked forward to meet them, and she swore the floor trembled with his every step.

What was to become of her?

Jorund found his wedding to be very dull and unnecessarily long-winded. He'd asked the priest more than once to hurry. But it hadn't made any difference; it still hadn't ended even as the dawn began to creep across the stone floor.

The monotonous droning language of Amée's religion had put more than one of his warriors to sleep, including his second in command, Valda, who slept slumped over her shield on one of the benches at the front. He envied her ability to sleep whenever and wherever she willed it.

Despite the approaching day it was still dark, and the torches had done nothing to improve the grim atmosphere of the chapel. With its stone altar and hard wooden benches, it was a cheerless room. At least his men could sit. For half the ceremony he and Amée had

had to kneel on the stone floor while the priest waved and chanted above them.

He'd thought it was all over when he'd sipped the wine and eaten the nibble of bread offered, but apparently that had just been the start of the tedious ceremony. Then they'd had to stand and face one another as the priest continued talking endlessly. He sighed bitterly, earning a glance from his diminutive bride. Was that censure flashing in her gold-flecked eyes? He hoped so—her earlier terror had put him in a bad mood and he'd rather face her anger than her fear.

The priest held out the ring Jorund had acquired for his wedding to Amée. More religious words from the priest followed, and then he was asked to repeat strange words as he held the ring over each of his bride's fingers, starting at her thumb and ending with her ring finger. He must have said the words badly as the abbess behind Amée rolled her eyes more than once.

Loki take him! He wanted this nonsense to end. Rollo had insisted the marriage be witnessed in the sight of their God. He'd have preferred a Norse wedding ceremony if he were honest, where they could exchange weapons as well as rings and vows. He could run for his bride, make a blood sacrifice and drink the bridal ale until they were both so merry they'd fall into bed together for days of lovemaking.

Do something!

Christian ceremonies seemed to be a lot of solemn listening to priests and doing very little. To him, it went against the natural order. Weddings should be a celebration of an alliance. This depressing affair was more like a funeral.

He looked down at Amée's tiny hand as he threaded

the ring on her finger. The jewellery was far too big and the garnet jewel hung limply against her knuckle.

'I'll get it resized,' he said, and she looked at the ring forlornly as if it were a shackle.

The priest then held a cloth over their heads and said yet more words. It was lucky Jorund was kneeling; otherwise, that part would not have been possible. Making vows in a language he did not understand did not sit right with him. But apparently it was an essential part of the ceremony. Finally, the priest declared, wiping the dripping sweat from his forehead with relief, 'It is done. She is yours.'

Not exactly the most comforting thing to tell a bride, even if it were true.

Amée sighed unhappily and Jorund threw the priest such a savage look that the man's knees buckled and he had to stumble away.

Jorund took her jewelled hand in his as he first stood and then helped her to her feet. It was so fragile and small that it irrationally angered him. He found her overwhelmingly attractive, but her vulnerability worried him.

Practically, he would have preferred a more robust woman as his bride. One who was both physically and emotionally strong enough to live with a big beast like him. A shield maiden possibly, someone like Valda— who if he didn't think of as a sister he would have married a long time ago.

Regardless, he never would have chosen someone like Amée. A tender flower he was afraid to crush if he held her too tightly. But he wanted her, desperately, and could not even try to deny it. He wanted her softness and gentleness in his life. Her innocent touches not tarnished by war or darkness.

Something pure and honest.

How he longed for simplicity. The traditions of his ancestors ran through his mind and in a sudden act of madness he found himself speaking the old Norse vow. He translated it into her own language so that she could understand. 'We proclaim ourselves as one flesh and one spirit, and pledge from this day forward we will take the responsibilities and enjoy the privileges of being one.'

She blinked up at him. Her head tilted in confusion and something else…something that made a flame of hope flicker in his chest.

He cursed his hot temperament silently.

Already he'd betrayed her with a promise he couldn't keep.

They would never truly be one.

He was too broken for someone as gentle as her.

And yet…she was his wife.

How should he proceed? All he wanted was a fresh, new life. But could he hide his past from her? He feared he was too big and obvious to hide anything. Too brutish and clumsy, lacking in any refinement she might expect in a husband. He'd practically been born on the battle-field, had been a warrior since he could stand, had seen terrible things at far too young an age—that had been mainly his father's doing.

His father's influence on him was the hardest shame to stomach. He'd only run with him for a short time as a child, but those days haunted him still. He should have at least tried to stop the awful crimes his father committed, or returned to his mother's shield maidens. But he'd only seen thirteen winters and had had the heart of a pitiful child seeking approval and love from a man who deserved neither.

Thankfully, he'd found the wisdom to leave quickly, but his father's atrocities would follow him for ever, like a shadow comprised of the dead.

He'd learnt of his father's passing only recently. Ragnar had had his throat slit in his sleep by warriors under his own command. Some squabble over the distribution of their silver. He imagined his father had tried to steal from his own men and had fallen under their wrath. A pathetic and pitiful death at the best of times, made somehow more shameful because Jorund had barely blinked at the news. He only wished he'd had the courage to kill Ragnar himself, but the idea had been too sickening, and he'd lacked the courage to do it.

Maybe it was his father's influence that held him back?

No matter how much he wished it wasn't true, his father's foul blood ran in his veins. There would always be the risk that he could become corrupted by power and cruelty like his father had before him.

The idea of that frightened him more than anything in this world or the next.

But he would try his best to keep Amée safe and happy, that was all he could really promise her: that he would try.

Maybe eventually she could grow to respect him... Like him even?

The colliding thoughts of his past and future forced him into action and he took one step closer towards Amée.

He bent down and kissed her. A long press of the lips that she stiffened beneath but didn't shy away from, which was a victory in itself. The smell of soap and lavender filled his senses and he pressed closer, wrapping his arms around her small frame. Unable to help himself, he lifted her up off her feet so that he could bring her to his full height, squeezing her bottom to press it more firmly against his aching groin. She gasped and he took the opportunity to slide his tongue into her mouth. Deepening the kiss into what he really craved.

Acceptance.

She was so innocent she did not respond to the tease of his tongue. She gripped his upper arms tightly, but she allowed his kiss and did not turn away. He would need to be patient before he took her to bed. But he allowed himself this one taste of passion. It would have to satisfy him until he had her permission to do anything more. Which, he suspected from the shocked way she'd touched his erection earlier, might be a while away and after some persuasion.

His men cheered, and when he finally raised his head from his new wife's plump lips he saw that the priest looked faint and the abbess was scowling. He placed Amée back on her shaky feet and took her hand in his, shocked by the intensity of his own lust. 'We leave immediately,' he said gruffly.

He only hoped the ferocity of his feelings would ease with time. It was probably because he was so close to achieving his goal. Once they were safely back and settled in Évreux, he would have his duties to focus his restless energy on.

Eventually, she would accept him, and once she was heavy with his child, they could live together in peace as the family he'd always longed for.

Chapter Four

Amée said her goodbyes to her fellow novices, young oblates and the holy sisters as quickly as she could. Hugging each one in turn and wishing them future happiness and peace. She wished she could have said more, but Jorund seemed eager to leave and she worried she'd caused enough problems with her new husband already. His expression darkened further and further as she worked through the crowd. But she refused to be dragged away from her home before she'd said goodbye to everyone.

This was her farewell, not only to the people, but to the life she might have had. The life she'd slowly carved out for herself, with simpering smiles and practiced devotion in front of her father.

This was meant to be her reward, her sanctuary, and she'd embraced it fully. Even if her heart hadn't been as faithful to God as some of her sisters' were, she'd tried.

Now that was all gone, washed away with a broken promise.

Memories began to flood back. The bruises on her mother's face and arms. How her mother's fragile heart had shattered every time her father rejected or scorned her in his many thoughtless ways. By joining the nunnery, Amée had thought to escape that hopeless misery of an existence.

If anything, her future looked even bleaker than it had at court.

A Viking for a husband! How could God do this to her? She'd tried so hard to be good.

Yes, sometimes her thoughts had become distracted in prayer, and she was prone to chatter, but it was never intentional or malicious.

Jorund was walking towards her, and by the look on his face he was losing patience with her yet again. She gave the abbess a quick final embrace, and then hurried to her horse, her sack of clothing clutched to her belly with both hands.

It was the smallest of the horses gathered, and nothing compared to the huge stallion Jorund rode. But it was still much larger than the donkey she'd ridden to market. It was light brown with darker brown markings over its flank, which looked almost like a crescent moon. She approached it cautiously.

How on this sweet earth would she get on it?

She yelped as two hands gripped her waist and lifted her high in the air. Whoever it was deposited her on the mare's back quickly and with surprising ease.

It was Jorund, of course it was Jorund. He seemed to enjoy lifting her up at every opportunity. Heat flooded her face as she remembered the last time he'd picked her up was to kiss her…passionately.

Well, if he thought to intimidate her by picking her up at every opportunity, he was sorely mistaken. Yes, she'd made a fool of herself before, but that had been in a fit of panic. She was calmer now, soon she'd remember how to hide in a world ruled by powerful men.

She awkwardly tried to grab the reins, which was not easy as she still held her sack. Silently he took it from her and tied it to the back of her saddle.

'Thank you,' she said begrudgingly, unable to fight against her manners. But he was already gone, walking away with the commanding air of a born leader.

The village carpenter and blacksmith were working on the doors to the nunnery and after pausing to allow them to pass they went back to work. Her friends gave half-hearted waves before they, too, went about their duties, as if Amée's departure was of no great importance. She supposed she'd only lived there a short time in comparison to some of the nuns and novices... But still...

Had any of them been a true friend? The sudden pain of that thought pricked at her eyes and she sniffed back the tears that threatened to fall.

She'd never felt more alone.

With a sigh she patted the horse's neck and bent down to whisper in its ear. 'You and I shall be the best of friends, yes? You're going to be gentle and good with me, and I'll be gentle and good with you. I'm going to call you...Luna.'

She sighed as she rose up. There was a reason why she'd chosen a monastic life, above that of a wife and lady. She didn't want to live every day with her emotions and thoughts caged. Obligated to serve and please another, who cared nothing for her—if he was anything like the power-hungry men of the court.

A part of her, a distant, childish part of her, longed to be loved. When she first arrived at court, she'd tried desperately to make friends, to show her father she could be the perfect lady. But the ladies had made a mockery of her efforts and she'd quickly realised there was no place for her there. Gisla had been kind to her, but the rest of them… Well, she'd given up trying to please them in the end. She'd spent her remaining years dodging the court vipers, eventually finding the courage to forge her own path to independence.

She'd learnt quickly that she could never be the dignified, elegant lady people expected of her. But her life from now on would be one long struggle to conform to that role. It wasn't what she'd hoped for, but it wasn't unexpected either—she'd just thought she'd successfully avoided it…until now.

If her father hadn't agreed to the nunnery, then she would have been married off far sooner, and she'd have faced the same fate. She glanced at the brawny figure of her husband as he swung up and onto his gigantic horse… Well, maybe not the *exact* same fate.

What she wanted to know and couldn't quite work out was—would this be better or worse than a man of her father's choosing?

Jorund's strange vow in the chapel had been almost… *romantic*.

He'd spoken of marriage as if it were a partnership built from mutual respect. An old Norse marriage vow, she suspected. Did that mean Norse marriages were more equal? She dismissed the idea immediately. The Latin sacrament spoke of a similar devotion between man and wife in marriage, but it didn't mean it was true in life. He was probably only reminding her that he was a heathen and had no respect for her Christian values.

She looked down at the huge ring on her finger. She'd lose it if it remained there. She untied the wooden cross at her neck and threaded the ring on the string. She'd wear it around her neck… Until she didn't need it any longer.

Their party began to move. Jorund took the lead. Several warriors surrounded her on both sides, like a cage. Maybe he thought she'd bolt again? But that was ridiculous; she'd taken the sacrament of marriage. She was bound to him now. A prickle of awareness ran down her spine as she stared at Jorund's broad shoulders up ahead. He wore a bearskin cloak. She'd heard some Norse warriors called themselves 'Berserkers.' They believed they could turn into their spirit animal during battle. Bears or wolves usually, and subsequently felt no fear or pain, their blind fury destroying everything in their path. One of the novices had told her of it, how such men continued to fight despite crippling injuries. She'd described how she'd seen one man die laughing.

The story had given Amée nightmares.

She shivered. The Norsemen were *so* strange. The church called them a plague. They'd arrived in Francia and brought with them a storm of death. Her country, which was once part of Charlemagne's proud and sprawling Empire, was now withering under the strain of constant attack from all sides, and centuries of weak kings. The Norse dressed differently, spoke a different language and held different beliefs, and now she was married to one. Without having any idea of what kind of a man he truly was.

What *was* the role expected of her?

She knew the role of a Frankish nobleman's wife. She'd learned that misery firsthand watching her parents' poisonous union die.

But what was the role of a *Viking's* wife?

She imagined it was very different. That the role of

women was also very different. There were even a couple of females amongst Jorund's warriors—the Vikings called them 'shield maidens,' although there seemed nothing maidenly about them. One in particular spoke with Jorund often. She had fiery hair and hazel eyes that were intelligent and hard, and she walked with a swagger, her long strong arms swinging freely. Amée found her terrifying and fascinating in equal measure.

Amée wasn't strong or fierce. When tasked with wringing the hens' necks for the pot she'd burst into tears and had to beg one of the others to do it. There was no way she could ever go into battle. These shield maidens were also meant to be wanton creatures who worshipped a fertility goddess. Did he expect her to be knowledgeable in such matters?

Because she wasn't. At all.

But did he *expect* her to be? He'd laughed when she'd touched him by accident. Maybe he expected her to touch him? Maybe he expected her to behave like a pagan woman? Heat flushed up her neck as she imagined herself reacting differently to him. Stroking his hard bulge instead of jumping away? He'd groaned at her touch and that was amazing in itself—that she'd been able to make a man groan with desire. It was…exciting.

Maybe, if she'd not been so afraid, she might have let her body sway a little closer to his lips. Would he have kissed her? Like he'd done at their wedding? Pulled her close to his body, taut muscle pressed against her soft breasts, his tongue sliding and stroking inside her mouth as if he were tasting her, consuming her…

No, be sensible, Amée!

Her mind was getting carried away. She shook her head and deliberately focused on the muddy path ahead.

Jorund had married a Frankish woman in a Christian ceremony. He'd spoken in her language since his arrival and had said he'd been baptised in the faith. It was part of the treaty's agreement. The Norse were meant to integrate with and protect the Frankish people. In return they received land and titles.

Besides, if what he'd said as a wedding vow was true, then they were a partnership. He was hers as much as she was his.

Her silly romantic heart fluttered a little at that. She liked the idea of being equally valued. Which was ridiculous considering she knew the true place of a wife, and she doubted it was any different for the Norse—not really.

Something her mother had said came to mind. 'A woman lives with the boot of her father against her neck followed by the boot of her husband. We are only truly free when death comes to claim our soul.' She shivered—those words had always haunted her.

Amée stared at her husband's back for the rest of the morning. Wondering how much heavier the boot of a conqueror would feel compared to her father's.

Before midday they stopped to rest the horses and she ate some of the bread and cheese handed around. Her bottom was aching terribly, but that wasn't Luna's fault. Amée's growing anxiety had caused her to sit stiffly in the saddle and her whole body ached from the strain. It didn't look as if they'd be making camp here. She suspected she would have to somehow climb back on Luna at some point to continue their journey. She sat beside the stream away from the others and chewed her bread and cheese slowly, hoping to delay the inevitable.

Jorund walked towards where she sat and she quickly

looked away, hoping not to draw attention to herself. She shifted her bottom a little trying to get comfortable. She swore she could still feel the impression of the saddle beneath her.

'You're sore,' rumbled Jorund's deep voice as he sat down beside her, his big body blocking the sun and casting her in shadow. It wasn't a question, but she answered anyway.

'A little. I'm not used to riding. We only have the donkey and use him only for our short trips to the market.' She tried to stop the tide of her babbling, but as always when her nerves got the better of her, she continued to talk nonsense. It was probably because she was so tired— she'd missed a night's sleep after all. 'Going to the market isn't a very long journey, and I ride there once a month. But I guess I'll have to get used to it now. Riding, I mean. In Évreux my mother used to ride out to the town and villages regularly... From the fort... If the fort is still there? I haven't been back in years—'

To her everlasting gratitude Jorund interrupted her. Unfortunately, it was to ask her another question. 'Why did you want to become a holy woman?'

Amée stared at him, unsure of what to say. At least she'd stopped pouring words into his great big lap. Would it offend him if she told him the truth? 'I wished for a more...spiritual life,' she said, the lie feeling obvious on her tongue.

'You don't like children?'

She shook her head vehemently. 'I love children!'

I probably can't have them, but I do love them.

Her mother had struggled to conceive for years before her birth, and Amée had been the only fruit of her parents' marriage. It was probably why her father had added it to the contract because he thought her as barren as her mother.

Jorund looked a little relieved at her answer and gave a grunting nod in response.

Unable to stand the silence she carried on speaking. She couldn't help herself. 'Teaching the younger oblates was my favourite duty…as well as playing with the serfs' children. Although that wasn't actually one of my duties.' In fact, it had got her in trouble too many times to count. If she had to choose, she would rather be on her knees playing in the mud than on her knees praying to God. Which was a terribly sinful thought. She almost said a prayer to balance it out. But then realised she didn't have to; she had a different path in life now. It was an odd feeling…almost freeing.

However, she was shaken back to the present by Jorund's next words. 'Good. I want children. The sooner the better.'

She stiffened.

Of course he did!

It was part of her father's agreement to their marriage. And here she was *encouraging* him to bed her as soon as possible! What would he do if she couldn't have any children? She ate her bread, not wanting to fill her mouth with any more nonsense. It was dry and tasteless on her tongue.

His frown returned and he looked at her with that wolf-like tilt of his head. 'Do you not like men?'

She swallowed her bread, unsure of what to say. She thought men were terrifying. But how could she tell him that? And what did that have to do with children anyway? 'I like…all people.'

'*All* people?' His mouth fought unsuccessfully to hide a smile.

She stiffened. 'Yes, if they are good and kind.'

The amusement died on his lips.

Had she insulted him?

Possibly. She doubted Christian values of goodness were seen as virtues by conquering invaders.

'And what makes a person good?' He took a savage bite of his bread, then spoke with his mouth full as he pointed at her with the remaining chunk. 'In your mind.'

'I... I...' Amée wasn't sure what to say.

'Someone humble, perhaps? Faithful? Generous?' He chewed hard between each suggestion as if he were chewing rocks rather than bread.

'I...suppose... Yes?' She wasn't sure where this was going, but she sensed by his suddenly brisk manner that she'd offended him somehow. Although she couldn't imagine what would irritate him so much about her comment.

'Not a killer, then? Or a thief?' he asked, before swallowing. He then tossed the remainder in his mouth, which he destroyed with equal force.

'Well, of course...not...' Her words faltered and fell from her lips too late to take them back. By the sharp nod of his head, she realised her mistake.

'I am not a good person in your mind. I have killed many in battle and stolen land from your King,' he said, finishing the last of his bread in one gulp. It wasn't an accusation, but a statement of fact.

She felt tricked—he'd done that deliberately to make her feel bad! Later, she would wonder where her courage had come from to bait him. But at this moment all she felt was anger at the injustice of her situation. 'I don't *know* you. And it would be wrong of me to judge you without knowing you. *That* would be unkind of me. *That* would make me a bad person.'

He stared at her for a long moment as if he were trying to solve a puzzle in his head, and then he shrugged as if whatever he'd concluded didn't matter anyway. 'You can bring up our children in your faith. But I will deal with their training.'

Cold dread washed through her. She did not like the sound of that—she loved to teach, being restricted from doing so would be unbearable... Unless he only meant their education in warfare...which was something she definitely couldn't teach. How Norse would their children's upbringing be—if she had any at all? 'But it's your faith too, isn't it? You said you were baptised with Rollo. So, your faith is Christian now. Your sins have been washed away.'

He blinked and eased backwards, as if to see her better. 'Washed away?'

'Yes, that's what baptism means. All your sins are washed away and you are reborn.'

Of all the things she'd expected him to do, laugh with derision was not one of them. After a moment he composed himself and explained slowly as if she were a child. 'Reputation can never be washed away. A man's actions and deeds follow him from this life unto the next. No amount of water can take them away. Your baptism means nothing to us.' He frowned at the horror on her face and turned his head towards the bubbling stream beside them. 'Sometimes we say and do things we do not mean. We do it, in the hope that we can build a better life for ourselves.' When he looked back, she was struck by the brightness of his eyes. A richer blue than the summer sky above their heads, and intense with an honest sincerity that touched her heart. For such a brutish man, he had the loveliest eyes. 'Isn't that why you decided to become a nun? To have a better life for yourself.'

She sucked in a sharp breath. 'No! I... I... I wanted a spiritual life!'

'Hmph,' he replied, and with that one guttural sound she knew he had seen straight through her protest to the truth beneath. She had used the nunnery as a way to shield herself from the outside world. He'd seen the truth of it straight away, and she felt ashamed. He'd been honest about what he wanted. Why couldn't she be honest about what she wanted?

Maybe she should try a little harder to get to know him. Who was she to judge his life, when she'd barely lived? She'd said it herself. It *was* wrong to judge people without getting to know them first. She shouldn't presume that just because he was Norse he would be any worse than her father had been.

She vowed to try harder.

Jorund stood, the sun bathing her in light once again. 'Be ready to leave soon. We've a long ride until nightfall. Then we'll make camp.'

Chapter Five

Jorund looked around him at their camp as dusk faded to night. This afternoon they'd made good time and he was confident they would reach Évreux before nightfall the following day. If they rose early enough, and they would, because Jorund had no intention of spending two nights in this territory with a vulnerable woman in tow.

He rolled his shoulder to release some tension. Amée looked exhausted as she dropped off her horse for the second time with a quiet hiss of pain. A pang of guilt made his jaw clench. He'd seen her slowly hunch further and further over her mare until she was practically lying on its neck by the end of the day. She hobbled to a blanket by the fire like a little old woman, her body stiff with soreness and cramp.

Still, it was better that she suffer some mild and fleeting discomfort than have her life put at risk by unnecessary delay.

Raiders still roamed the land.

They'd had to move further towards the main river, which meant this area was dangerous. In fact, all of the land surrounding Évreux was still not secure and therefore hazardous. He'd not raided Évreux personally, but he knew the town had been burned several times, and had seen the evidence of its demise personally. He hoped Amée would not be too horrified by it.

She'd said she'd not seen it for many years. But he knew it would be nothing like the prosperous trading centre she remembered. It would take him a long time to rebuild and strengthen the town's defences against invasion. Not to mention gain the trust of his new people, who at the moment viewed him as an impostor and tyrant.

The nunnery had been deep in the forest a long way from Évreux and its settlements. It had taken several days to find it. No doubt it was why it had stayed safe from attack for so long. Despite it not being officially on his land, he'd already decided to ensure it was better defended once he'd secured his own fort. If taken, the nunnery would make a good stronghold for raiders to camp in and launch attacks against him with impunity.

It was part of Rollo's agreement with the Frankish King. When he'd gifted them land, they'd agreed to rule and protect it—the war bands had to go. Jorund was confident they would achieve control eventually. Rollo was a fierce leader with the loyalty and respect of many warriors and chieftains such as himself. They would make quick work of bringing order to the region, but they were not quite there yet.

Once he'd checked and secured the perimeter of their encampment, he made his way to the fire and the meal his men had prepared. After ladling some stew into a bowl, he sat beside Amée to eat. He tried not to take offence at the way she stiffened and shuffled a little further away. As a big man he was used to people being intimidated by his presence—he just hoped it wouldn't be too long before she got used to him. His earlier conversation with her had only strengthened his belief that she was innocent in all matters sexual. Bedding her would take time and patience, especially as she thought so badly of him.

Maybe threatening to lay waste to the nunnery wasn't the best first step in achieving that? Or telling her that he was a thief and a killer?

He rolled his shoulder again to ease another wave of tension that had followed those unsettling thoughts. He vowed to be more patient in future.

Amée handed her bowl back to one of his men who was gathering utensils for cleaning. She thanked him and smiled. It was the first genuine smile he'd seen from her and an invisible hand closed around his heart and squeezed.

Taking his chance to prove to his new wife that he wasn't a completely heartless beast he grabbed a fur from a nearby pile and offered it to her. 'You should lie down. We have a long day tomorrow.'

She turned to him and took the fur. Running her fingers over the pelt in a caress that shouldn't have stirred his blood like it did.

'What about you? Don't you need to sleep?' Her voice was unexpectedly nervous considering the banality of her question. She didn't lie down, and he could only see half of her face in the dancing flames of the campfire.

'I don't plan to sleep much.'

'You don't expect…' Her voice was a panicked squeak and he leaned closer trying to see her expression better. 'Tonight?'

He frowned. 'What about tonight?'

Her shoulders relaxed a little. 'You don't expect to…? I mean, for tonight to be our wedding night? Do you?'

A low laugh escaped his lips. So, she was worried he wanted to have sex with her?

Well...he did.

That thought sobered him, and his laughter died.

After his disastrous attempt at conversation earlier he'd realised they both needed time. He should reassure her, but instead he found himself teasing, like a childish youth pulling on a girl's braids for attention. 'In front of my men?' he asked, with mock horror.

She made a shocked choking sound and he turned back to his meal to hide his amusement. 'No, I prefer privacy and a soft bed when I'm with a woman.' Unable to help himself he added, 'Well, most of the time...' He glanced back at her and noticed she'd turned pale. He sighed.

What was wrong with him?

'Don't look so worried. Your virginity is safe for tonight, my little bride. I don't sleep well out in the open, especially not in unfamiliar territory.' That much was true at least.

'Oh, good! What a relief... I mean... Well, it's...probably for the best.' She swallowed, and then looked as if she were about to be sick with embarrassment.

It put a huge dent in his male pride, but he shrugged it off. Of course she would be nervous. He liked that she always spoke her mind. At least he knew how best to deal with her: gently. 'I think we will get along well. You and I.'

'Really?'

'Yes... If you learn to relax a little, I have no intention of hurting you. I know I can be...impatient at times.' She made a small huffing sound and he tried to smother his smile at her obvious disgruntlement. 'But I will be more patient in future...and in the bedchamber. We have a very tiring journey ahead and you'll need some time to recover once we reach Évreux. So...do not worry about *that*.' The sigh of relief she exhaled caused the dent in his pride to turn into a gaping chasm. He couldn't resist a playful jibe back. 'A day or two should suffice.'

She jerked a little at that but didn't question him, and for some reason he decided against saying anything further on the matter. Maybe she would be more comfortable with him in a couple of days? 'Tell me about Évreux,' he asked instead.

'Évreux? Have you ever been?'

'Yes, my men are there now. But I'd like to know a little more about it. How it was before...when you lived there.'

The change of subject seemed to please her and he was rewarded by one of her cheerful smiles. 'Oh, it's beautiful. The town has been there since the Romans.'

He didn't know what the 'Romans' were but he presumed it meant the town was old.

Her voice turned wistful as she continued. 'There's even some Roman walls around the town and along the river. They're very old, though, and a bit broken down in some places.'

'They're useless, then.' At her frown he softened his tone. 'Go on.'

'There's a fort on one side of the valley—that's where I grew up. The town sits at the bottom of the valley, by the river, and has always been very prosperous. There are orchards with delicious apples, and a forest skirts around the valley full of game. The majority of the land has been cleared for farms, and they always have a rich harvest. It will be harvest time shortly and you'll see how bountiful the land can be then—we have such a variety of produce. It might be different now, though. I haven't been there for a long time. I lived there as a child until my mother died...' She paused for a moment, her expression suddenly becoming sad. He had the overwhelming urge to comfort her but wasn't sure what to say or do, so he remained silent. 'After her death I moved to Paris to live at court, and then I went to the nunnery about a year ago to train as a novice.'

'How old are you?' he asked, curious.

'I've seen twenty winters...and you?'

'Twenty-five.'

'Really?' Her surprised gasp caused several of his warriors to look up. He scowled at them until they looked away. 'I'm sorry... I just presumed you were older.'

Great! She thought him an old man as well as a killer and a thief. 'I've always looked older. Due to my height... and general fierceness,' he joked. But she didn't laugh and that only made him feel worse.

She eased down into the blankets, turning slightly so that she could still look at him from her prone position. It suggested she was relaxing around him, which made him feel a little less awkward. Especially now her face was better illuminated by the fire, and he could read her expressions more clearly.

Looking at her was quickly becoming one of his favourite pastimes. The raven curls that pooled around her head were so black, it was as if they swallowed the light of the fire. Her round face, the only part of her visible in the darkness, was luminescent, as if she were a moon goddess. Her skin so pale it glowed with an inner light. He wanted to kiss her, to peel away her clothes so that he could see more of her pale, glowing skin. Wrap her limbs around him, and—

'When did you arrive in Francia?' she asked, smothering a yawn.

'You should rest,' he said, disturbed by his growing desire for her. He turned away to concentrate on the last bites of his meal.

She raised up onto her elbows and pleaded. 'Oh, *please* tell me… I like to talk a little before I sleep. Besides, I don't think I'll be able to sleep for a while yet. I'm not used to being so…out in the open.'

He doubted after her long and exhausting day that she would be unable to sleep. But she seemed insistent that he talk to her. And she'd said she needed to get to know him better, although there were some things about his past that even he couldn't face.

'I was born here.'

'Really?' It was the second time he'd made her gasp with shock. Again, he scowled at his warriors to mind their own business. Several were still listening to them, including Valda, who always took great delight in his general discomfort—as only a true friend could. Amée added hesitantly before sinking back down, 'I forget how long the Norse have…been here.'

'My mother was a shield maiden. She met my father at the second siege of Paris, and stayed with him for a couple of years after having me. I've never been to Viken— it was always my parents' homeland and never my own. After my parents parted ways, I stayed with my mother and her band of shield maidens until she died in battle.'

'I'm so sorry.' She raised up onto her elbows again, reached over and touched his forearm.

He looked down at it in surprise, unsure of what to say or do. When faced with an unpleasant situation he usually attacked. But he couldn't attack Amée for asking a few questions. In the end he decided on distraction. 'Did you meet Princess Gisla in Paris? Is that how you know her? She seemed to think highly of you.'

She eased back down into the blankets with a soft smile. 'Yes. We lived together in Paris. I was one of her companions as a child…and, well, she took a liking to me and insisted I stay by her side. She's a very kind soul.' Amée suddenly frowned and he tried to hide his smile. She was probably wondering why such a 'kind soul' had insisted she marry a Norseman.

'How do you know the Count?'

He blinked for a moment at the unfamiliar term. 'Rollo?'

'Yes.'

'I met him as a youth. At the time, I was fighting with a band of men who fought for Rollo when it suited them. But they always fled the battlefield when things turned for the worse or if there was little chance of silver. They lacked honour.' He moved on briskly, not wanting to dwell. 'I could see Rollo had a better plan for our future. So, I made a choice to fight for a man who valued loyalty and courage instead. Someone who wanted a better life for our people. I have been under his direct command ever since. Even when things turned sour at Chartres, I stayed by his side, and I've been richly rewarded because of it.'

'You are brave and loyal, then,' whispered Amée, a soft, sleepy smile on her lips. She looked drowsy now, her eyelids heavy. He wondered if her tiredness had caused her to confess her inner thoughts so freely.

His stomach churned at her admiration. She would not feel so kindly towards him after she saw the current state of her precious Évreux. 'Go to sleep. We've another long ride tomorrow.'

At the mention of riding, she gave a half-hearted laugh of disgust and buried down into her blanket. He watched her for some time, until he was reassured she was fast asleep.

When he eventually looked up, Valda caught his eye and shook a finger at him. She spoke in Norse. 'You are in trouble, my friend. I have heard you talk more to her in one night than I have heard you speak since you were born.'

It was true, he wasn't much of a talker. Valda knew that better than anyone.

They'd grown up together. She'd been one of the daughters of his mother's second. They'd learned to fight together—well, up until the time he'd chosen to follow his father—then they'd met up again when he'd fought under Rollo's command.

Maybe he shouldn't have said so much. It might reveal other things he had no wish to speak of. He would probably need to be more careful around Amée in future.

Jorund scowled at Valda's teasing and spat into the flames. 'What would you know, Old Spinster?'

It was a weak insult, as Valda could have her pick of any man. He wasn't quite sure why she hadn't chosen one—he suspected she liked her independence.

Valda laughed and lay down. 'True. What would I know, *Old Man*?'

Chapter Six

Amée wasn't sure what had woken her but the camp was silent and dark. An uneasy foreboding twisted in her stomach. As she began to rise a big hand pressed her shoulder back down into the blanket. Instinctively she did as she was told.

As expected, she could smell the crushed leaves and musty earth from the forest floor beneath her. But she was far warmer than she'd imagined she'd be after a night of sleeping outside.

'Don't move,' whispered a masculine voice, close to her ear.

It was Jorund and he was lying against her back, cradling her in a way that made her skin heat from the top of her head down to the tips of her toes. His breath fanned the curls at the side of her neck and she shivered against the unexpected touch.

It was like when he'd held her in his arms before, comforting in a strange way. Her head told her to be afraid, but her body revelled in the warmth and security of his touch.

Had he changed his mind about bedding her, and why did that create a disturbing swirl of excitement as well as

nerves in the pit of her stomach? It was as if she almost…
welcomed him. But that was madness!

His hand leisurely slid down her arm and rested on
the hilt of his sword in front of her. When had he put that
there? After she'd gone to sleep? When he'd presumably lain down behind her and cupped her body into the
curve of his?

Regardless, Jorund reaching for his weapon was a sure
sign all was not well.

The blood thundered in her ears as she realised they
were in imminent danger. Why else would he arm himself and ask her not to move?

Her eyes peered into the darkness of the clearing.
Nothing seemed amiss. There was light snoring from
some of the men and the fire had died down low to glowing embers. A couple of empty cauldrons and pans were
placed beside it ready for the morning meal.

All was well.

Then she noticed the shield maiden lying opposite
them. She had her eyes open, as did another man to the
side of her, and he was the one snoring.

They were all awake and they were waiting.

One of her hands lay close to a pan, so she reached
and wrapped her fingers slowly around the handle. It
wasn't much, but it was a weapon of sorts. She closed
her eyes and prayed that whatever was going to happen
did so quickly.

A twig snapped nearby, and then everything moved
with lightning speed. The arm around her tightened and
she was rolled at the same time as there was a whistling
sound followed by a thud. She looked towards the sound
and with a cry saw an arrow embedded in the blankets

where her head had once been. She had the pan though, and its heavy weight in her grip offered some reassurance.

Jorund shouted something and his warriors surged around them. Shields and weapons appeared from beneath blankets and furs as they converged together. Scattering embers from the fire as they swarmed around herself and Jorund, creating a wall of shields.

Jorund hunched low and dragged her down with him. He was still a giant of a man, however, and because of his size was still much larger than her even hunched.

'Stay here,' he said.

As if she would do anything else!

Jorund thrust his shield into the ground in front of her and reached behind him for the axe strapped to his back. Arrows whistled and struck the shields held above their heads.

'They're coming!' said the red-haired shield maiden, and Jorund nodded. With a deafening battle cry he leapt forward and out of the shield wall to face several armed men charging towards him. Two other warriors leapt with him, but that was all. In the blink of an eye the shields returned to encircle her in safety and he was blocked from her view.

Time slowed as she waited behind his shield and his warriors. The purgatory of waiting seemed like an endless eternity.

There were several screams of pain and the clashing of weapons against shields, and she gripped her iron pan until her knuckles grew numb. She felt so helpless here, but what else could she do?

She said a prayer for Jorund's safe return. Even though he'd threatened to lay waste to her nunnery, she couldn't help but admire his courage in facing their attackers.

Maybe laying waste to the nunnery had been an empty threat?

Certainly, her father had said much worse to her mother for a lot less. Should she judge him harshly for his threats, or for his actions?

During the attack his first thought had been to protect her. It already made him twice the man her father was. She doubted her father would give her his shield, or leap into battle to defend her. Maybe the weight of Jorund's 'boot' would be lighter than the weight of her father's after all?

If he lived...

As she waited, her own confused thoughts warred back and forth as the skirmish raged beyond the shield wall.

Eventually the horrible sounds cleared.

The group encircling her eased outwards and she was able to see the carnage with her own eyes.

She stumbled to her feet, walking out from the circle of safety with the pan still gripped in her aching fingers.

Dawn was breaking. A milky indigo light filtered through the shadows of the forest and into the clearing. To her relief she saw Jorund immediately, and to her surprise he was barely out of breath. Four men lay on the ground. She guessed they were Norse by their clothing, but she didn't recognise them as any of Jorund's men. Their clothing was dirty and torn, and one of them had a gaping hole in the sole of his boot, which oddly made her sad.

She looked up from the body and saw Jorund staring at her. He had a pained look on his face, as if he knew that she'd been thinking about the dead man and sympathised with her. He came to her side and raised his hand as if to touch her arm in consolation.

She gasped in horror. 'Are you wounded?' Blood ran down the length of his arm and dripped from his fingers.

The hand that had been about to touch her dropped back to his side.

'You're hurt?' came a feminine cry beside them, and Amée realised it was the red-haired shield maiden. She rushed to Jorund's side and gripped his arm as she inspected his body closely with an easy familiarity Amée found more than a little unsettling.

He grabbed the small flask of water at his side and poured its contents over his leathers and forearm to wash away the blood. 'I'm fine, Valda. It's not my blood,' he grumbled, pushing her aside with a light smile as if he were used to her worrying over him. Amée glanced away, feeling awkward, as if she were intruding somehow on their privacy.

It was then she noticed Luna tied to the tree with the other horses. The poor animal was dancing and jerking with frightened eyes. She dropped the pan and ran over to soothe the terrified animal.

'Oh, no! My poor darling. Don't be afraid. All is well. Shh...' She checked over Luna's body carefully in case any arrows had struck home. Thankfully, Luna was unhurt. It took a while, but after a few more kind words and loving pats she settled down.

A shadow fell over her. Jorund had followed and was now watching her with great interest.

'I presume you've never been in a skirmish before... Are you well enough to ride?' He gestured to the encampment. The bodies lay where they'd fallen, his warriors packing up around them as if they were nothing more than piles of fallen leaves.

Her heart swelled with pity. 'Should we not bury them?'

'They're raiders who wanted to kill us,' Jorund answered with a confused tilt of his head.

'But they were still people... They shouldn't be left like that.'

'They chose their fate.' At her flinch he sighed. 'If they have kin, they will come for them. If not, there is no dishonour in dying with your sword in your hand... It is our way.'

She thought for a moment and then nodded. She needed to be more open-minded about their differences.

'We can stay if you need more time to recover,' he said, although he didn't look pleased about the prospect. 'Not too long though...it might not be safe.'

She straightened her spine and began to untie Luna from the tree.

What did her discomfort matter when people's lives were in danger?

'I'll be fine—we should push on, especially if it's not safe.' Unable to deny her curiosity, she asked, 'Do you know *why* they attacked us?'

'To steal.'

'Even though you're Norse?'

'Why would that make any difference?'

'I suppose it wouldn't.'

They're not even loyal to their own people!

It was an unsettling thought.

After a pause he asked, 'Would you prefer to ride with me?'

'No!' She sucked in a sharp breath, and then let it out in a slow hiss. 'I mean, no thank you.' Luna skittered to the side nervously. 'Sorry, Luna.' Amée gave her an apple from her own supplies to show how sorry she truly was. Then she turned to Jorund with an overly bright smile.

'Honestly, I'm stronger than I look.' She didn't want him to think her ungrateful especially after he'd saved her life, but the idea of him holding her again made her stomach flutter in a way she found more than a little confusing, mainly because it wasn't from fear.

'You *named* it?'

She shifted self-consciously under the sapphire light of his eyes. 'Oh, does she already have a name?' she asked, cursing her own stupidity before she'd even finished speaking.

Of course 'it' didn't have a name. Did he look like the type of man to name a horse? Eat one? Possibly.

He patted Luna's neck in a sweetly tender gesture for such a brute of a man; even her horse looked small against him, like a gangly dog. 'Not that I know of. I bought her in Rouen with a handful of others. They're just work horses. I can get you a better one if you enjoy riding. A stallion or a gelding. One bred for hunting.'

She glanced at the huge beast Jorund rode. It would take a ladder for her to be able to climb it, and she doubted she had the strength to control it even if she could get on its back. 'I have no need of a stallion—'

A sudden frown wrinkled Jorund's heavy brow and he absently kicked the earth with his boot. 'Of course, you don't like riding. You're already sore from this journey. That was a stupid question.'

He turned to walk away, and Amée leapt forward, her hand reaching out for his arm to hold him back. 'I'd gladly ride Luna!' she cried.

He turned back, his eyes focused on the small hand that gripped him. She'd meant to grab his leather-clad upper arm, but he was so tall she'd grabbed his bare forearm instead. She was perilously close to his waist, and the memory of the last time she'd laid hands on his body rushed to the front of her mind.

A blush burned her cheeks as her hand dropped. Tilting her face as far as she could to see him better, she said, 'I haven't been riding in years. That's why I'm so…out of practice. But I do enjoy it. I've never had my own horse before—my father was…protective.'

He'd probably thought if he gave her a horse she'd never come back.

'And it would mean a great deal to me if Luna was mine… I mean, mine to ride. You are the Lord of Évreux. Everything belongs to you.' *Including me.* She brushed aside the depressing thought as quickly as it bloomed in her mind.

She bit her lip in embarrassment at her own pleading. But the idea of having her own horse was too tantalising to slip by.

Her own horse! Something of her own to love and care for.

The freedom—maybe not to run away, she wasn't a child any more—but the freedom to go and visit her people? Maybe some of her friends would still be there? Maybe even her mother's maid, Beatrice? She might have moved away from the town by now, but if she lived on one of the farms, she could ride out to visit her…

She waited, her breath held tight, her lip bruising from the pressure of her top teeth. His eyes fixed on her lips, his pupils wide and ringed with blue fire. His face was broad with high sharp cheekbones, a straight nose, heavy brow and firm but gently shaped lips. Not handsome, as such. Striking, definitely striking. However, it was his eyes that captured her. He had the eyes of a predator. She shivered under his gaze, and her heart raced.

When he spoke, his voice was deep and rough like the roots of an old oak. 'The mare belongs to you.'

'Thank you,' she whispered, surprised by the husky tone of her own voice.

'There is no reason to thank me.' He reached out to her, his large hand gently cupping her jaw with the same tenderness she'd seen from him moments before. Except his eyes were bright with heat rather than kindness. She stood breathless in his embrace, as his thumb lightly brushed along her bottom lip. Her skin tingled beneath as if she were kindling about to catch aflame, and she wondered if he would kiss her again.

Feeling as if she were on the edge of a cliff, unsure if she were brave enough to take the leap, she took a step back and his hand dropped. She used the excuse to look away and pat Luna's neck. 'Hear that, Luna? You're all mine.'

'Let me help you,' he said quietly, his hands sliding beneath her arms to wrap around her waist. His grip was firm but gentle as he efficiently lifted her up onto Luna. She tried not to gasp at the sudden touch or the way her bottom screamed in pain as it hit the saddle. In the madness she'd forgotten her aches and pains. But now that her frantic heart had settled down, she began to feel every needle and ache with excruciating clarity.

She gave him a light smile in thanks, which he returned before he strode away to his own horse. She'd never felt this way about a man before, equally excited and nervous in his presence.

It worried her.

They rode for hours. Jorund had decided against any more stops, better to ride hard and be in Évreux as fast as possible than risk any more attacks. His men were fine to do this, but he worried for Amée, although she'd not once complained. Even now she rode a few horses ahead of him, her dainty bounce in the saddle sometimes a little offbeat to the movement of her horse.

Valda directed her horse over to fall in line beside him at the back of their party.

'Your little bird has survived, then?' she said, with her usual grim amusement. Valda had a habit of finding life's events both disappointing and hilarious in equal measure.

He glanced at his friend and raised a golden eyebrow. 'Little bird?'

'Don't you think it suits her? She's so sweet. So little and soft. But also quick, when she needs to fly… You've been watching her all morning. Are you afraid she'll take flight again?'

'No.' He turned to her then. Proving to himself and to his friend that he could look away from Amée if he chose to. 'And she's your *lady* now, not a little bird.'

It was only meant to be a tease, but he saw Valda's eyes harden slightly before she looked away. 'I know.' After a pause she nodded towards Amée once again and said, 'You should warn her about Évreux.' This time he was unable to resist looking at his wife.

She looked tired, and the coarse wool of her hideously drab gown hung on slumped shoulders. The hem had lifted a little on the stirrups to reveal her battered boots beneath. Once they were home she would need new clothes, something that reflected her new position as his wife. Maybe something in red? The colour would look striking on her.

'Jorund?'

He turned back to Valda, embarrassed to have proven

her point about his 'enthralment.' Why did she bother him so much? Valda was right: he rarely spent time with women, other than Valda, who didn't count. Women were both beautiful and tiring... An odd thing for a hot-blooded man such as himself to admit, but it was true. He mostly avoided them if he could.

Strangely he found the softness and gentleness both incredibly attractive and terrifying. With his huge bulk and strength, he could crush a woman like Amée by merely rolling on top of her in the night. It didn't matter how strong her spirit was, brute strength was brute strength and he would always need to protect her from it.

'She will know soon enough,' he answered.

He was about to kick his horse forward but was stopped by the concern in Valda's voice.

'Can I give you some advice... As a friend?'

He frowned. 'Always. I may not follow it, but you are always welcome to give it.'

'Be honest and patient with her.'

He rolled his eyes with a snort. 'Thank you for that *revelation.*'

Did Valda think him stupid?

That in his lust he would force himself on Amée? The very idea was repugnant.

Valda's jaw tightened. She leaned closer in the saddle and spoke in a hushed tone. 'You need to be honest, Jorund. About your past, your...fears.' It was as if she'd stuck a hot blade in his back and twisted it. The shame burned red hot in the silence between them. He glared at her, feeling betrayed. They'd spoken of it only once before, and he'd made her swear never to speak of it again.

Valda reached across and touched his arm gently. He stared ahead unable to meet her eyes and then he saw

Amée further ahead glance back at them. As soon as his eyes locked with hers, she spun back around in her seat.

'It's never been my place to question you on it,' continued Valda, oblivious, and he shrugged off her touch, oddly worried that Amée might have read more into the touch than was actually there. Valda let go of his arm but refused to let go of her wretched point. 'She *needs* to know. She seems kind…she might even be able to help. If you talked about it—'

'You're right,' he retorted. 'It's not your place.'

Chapter Seven

Amée recognised when they entered the orchards of Évreux. The familiar apple trees, the path well-trodden. The light that filtered through the summer leaves was laden with bittersweet memory, and she swore that Évreux's air tasted sharper and cleaner than anywhere else in Francia.

As a child she'd adored playing amongst these trees. Picking as much fruit as she could carry. Running wild with the children from the town, and then trudging home in the twilight to make pies with her mother when she was feeling well enough.

Then she saw it. The tree that Amée saw in her darkest dreams.

It's just a tree...nothing to be scared of.

A familiar shiver ran down her spine, and her skin became cold and clammy. There was a sudden oppressiveness in the air as if a storm were approaching, but the warriors around her didn't look up from the path so she knew it was all in her mind.

As they climbed the hill, she leaned forward in her saddle and waited. Her heart filled with dread, her eyes searching. She couldn't relax, not until they passed it. It was the oldest apple tree in the orchard. The orchard's Mother Tree, some said, although Amée didn't believe it. There was nothing nurturing or sustaining about it. It was a scar upon an otherwise beautiful landscape. It had grown ugly and misshapen as if it had always known its fate was to bring misery.

Set slightly apart from the others at the highest point of the hill, it was as if the surrounding trees avoided it. As if they knew it was tarnished and deliberately kept their distance.

Amée drew Luna up alongside it and she found herself staring at one of the lower branches.

The branch.

She could just make out the clumsy old axe marks in its bark. The tree had healed over but the grooves were still visible if she looked closely.

They'd cut her mother down from that tree, and no matter how many years had passed she still saw her mother's feet dangling lifelessly from it.

'Why have you stopped?' asked a deep voice beside her.

She jerked in her saddle at the sudden intrusion in her thoughts, and gripped the reins far too tightly. Luna skittered and danced at the confusing instructions her legs and reins were giving. Concerned, Jorund reached across and soothed the frightened horse with a soft murmur and a gentle pat on its neck, even using Luna's name as he did so.

'I'm fine!' she gasped, realising belatedly that wasn't the question he'd asked her. 'Just getting my breath back.'

He frowned but nodded and pushed forward with a light kick of his heels. All the horses had stopped and the warriors were looking back at her quizzically. As she pushed Luna forward, the party began moving once more. She passed by the tree, her face aflame, and focused on the landscape in front of her.

Like an exquisite tapestry laid at her feet Évreux was spread out before her. All the land visible from this vantage point belonged to Jorund. The entire valley, with its villages and farms dotted across the landscape. As well as the market town with the Iton River threading through it like a ribbon of silver. The land rose up again after the town, with Évreux's fortress at the top, parallel to the ridge they stood on, and beyond it a forest that was also owned by the Lord of Évreux.

Amée sighed; it was a beautiful view. She could see why her mother had chosen it as her last.

But as they rode down and through Évreux she saw how much had changed since her childhood. The awful destruction of the last few years.

Rouen was Rollo's capital and he had used its advantageous location on the River Seine to travel up and down the subsidiary rivers to raid towns such as Évreux. His dominion over the land was written on the scorched Roman walls. Defences that had once protected its people a time long ago, encircling their town and holding it safe from invasion. But the Norse attacked from the rivers, and could sail straight into the heart of any town with incredible speed. It may as well have been built in sand for all the defence it must have given.

Many homes were gone, and the ones that remained were crumbling ruins. People peeked nervously from broken doors, or looked up from bleak, empty vegetable patches. They had the apples from the orchard but that wasn't enough to survive on. Violence and suffering were etched on their frightened, malnourished faces. They stared at the Norse with desolate expressions as they rode through their home without challenge.

Guilt and horror washed through Amée in equal measure.

She'd failed them.

Her people had been left behind and forgotten. No doubt her father had easily washed his hands of them— as he'd washed his hands of both mother and daughter all those years before.

A once bustling market town, Évreux was now reduced to a miserable wasteland where the abandoned scratched out a living in the muck of a once prosperous past.

She lowered her head in shame, unable to look them in the eye. She'd been a child when she'd left, but she should have shown more interest, asked her father what was happening to her home in their absence. A miserable lump of charcoal sat heavy in her stomach.

Of course, her words would have done nothing to help her people's plight.

She had no power then, as she had no power now.

Lord, how it burned!

The injustice, the resentment and the *anger* branded her soul like a burning sword plunged into her heart. Hatred and loathing swelled from the wound within her as she turned and stared at the huge warrior who rode beside her.

How could she have thought him any better?

His eyes locked with hers and widened, but he didn't say anything. Instead, he held out a skin of mead and urged her to drink with a gentle push. She took it, hoping to wash the taste of ash from her mouth. But as she raised it to her mouth, she tasted salty tears on her lips.

She washed it away with a sip of the honeyed, slightly stale mead. It was strong, and had a residual kick that made her suck in a sharp breath, but the warmth in her belly reminded her she was alive.

This time fear would not control her, and she would *not* fail them again.

Jorund spoke quietly. 'My men have already begun repairs. Firstly, we will rebuild the fort and the farms. Then the homes and defences of the town. Évreux will be reborn.'

'It was fine as it was before,' she said sharply. She had no idea where her courage had come from to question him. She suspected her rage was the reason behind it. Rage at Jorund, at her father and most bitterly at herself.

'It will be better.'

She glared at him, unable to temper the hot iron of her will. 'You could rebuild Évreux in solid gold and it *still* would not absolve you of your crimes!'

His jaw hardened and he looked away. 'I know.'

The heat of her anger diminished at his contrite, almost sad admission. She'd prepared herself for a battle and it appeared as if he agreed with her.

Deep ocean eyes looked back at her. 'You're right. I may not have done this—' he gestured with a sweep of his arm '—but I have done similar. Terrible things happen in war, and it is never just or right. Those days are drawing to an end. Not all of my people want treasure and destruction. There are those of us who came searching for more than wealth and glory. People who felt displaced by our motherland and were searching for a future, a home. Rollo was such a man. We wanted land, and we have found it here. If it had not been us, it would have been your rival tribes to the east, or some other who saw the weakness in your kings and took the opportunity to take what they could not receive at home. Your loss to us was inevitable. But this will be my home now, my land, my future, and I will care for it as such…with your help.'

Her eyes narrowed, surprised that he would mention her at all. Wasn't their tactic to steal without conscious thought of the victims they left behind? Had she not been stolen, and treated as a trinket to be bartered away? 'What can *I* do?' she asked bitterly. She was no better than his captive.

'You can do as my overlord, and your Princess, has requested.' He blinked at her derisive snort, but leaned forward and covered her hands as they held the reins with one of his own, his eyes never leaving hers. Clear and intense. Filled with heart and honesty. Once again, Amée felt as if she were on the edge of a cliff. One wrong step and she would fall. 'Let go of the past. Accept me as your husband and help me build a new land. One that is neither Norse nor Frank. But has its own proud identity.'

She swallowed hard, unsure of what to say. She did want to escape the past, more than anything. *Dare she trust him?*

'Mistress! Mistress!' An excited shout came from behind, drawing their attention away from each other. His hand left hers. They looked over their shoulders at a middle-aged woman in tattered serf clothing running towards them. Her weathered boots sticking and squelching as she struggled through the churned earth. Light reddish hair fell from her cap as she huffed and puffed towards them, her cheeks ruddy from the exertion.

'Beatrice?' Amée whispered, unsure if her mind were playing tricks on her. Then her heart kicked in her chest and she pulled on the reins to stop Luna from taking another step.

She winced as she tried to dismount.

'Don't move, I'll help you,' said Jorund, swinging out of his saddle with surprising speed for a man of his size. Once he was down, he immediately reached for her and plucked her off the horse with disturbing ease. It only reminded Amée of his absolute power over her.

Beatrice reached them at about the same time as Amée's feet sank into the mud. The old woman was out of breath and clutching her side as if winded. She eyed Jorund suspiciously and then dipped respectfully on shaky feet. 'My lady, if I'd known you were coming. They said he was marrying a Frankish lady... I prayed... I can't believe you're really here. I— We— Everyone... We're so happy to see you again, mistress!' There were tears of hope in her eyes. Beatrice was the voice of the people, had always been. It was Beatrice who'd helped manage things when her mother couldn't. If Beatrice could forgive her absence...could even take comfort in her return...

Amée lurched forward, wrapped her arms around Beatrice and clutched her tightly with all her strength.

Jorund stared at Amée in surprise. From what he'd known of the Frankish noblemen and women they were all proud—to the point of ridiculousness. They clung to the dynasty of their old 'Empire' like a babe to its mother's teat, with no acceptance or acknowledgement of the changing world around them. It was why they had been more willing to throw silver at their invaders than tackle them head on, as they should have done.

But Amée wasn't acting with arrogance or prideful conceit as she held the serf tightly. If anything, the woman called Beatrice appeared the most shocked by her lady's reaction. Her body stiffened for a moment before relaxing into the embrace. When Amée pulled away, with a bright smile and happy tears in her eyes, Beatrice returned it.

'It has been so long! How is your family? Your children? It seems so long ago that I was here… I'm so glad and relieved to see you! Have they married? Had children of their own? How are you?' The words rushed from her mouth in a flurry, barely catching her breath before she asked the next. Then she turned to Jorund, her earlier anger with him seemingly forgotten in the event of this joyous reunion. 'Beatrice was my mother's maid. She looked after me, especially when my mother was…unwell,' she explained, happy tears shining in her eyes. He suspected the woman had been more than a mere maid. She sounded like a second mother, especially if he read into the uncomfortable pause before she'd described her mother as 'unwell.' Had her mother been sickly? He knew little about her. Only that Amée's father was an ass.

'If you need a maid, mistress, my daughter or myself would be more than happy to come to the fort with you… If that's where you'll be living now? My husband died in the spring and we're currently living with my son's family.'

Amée turned to Jorund with a hopeful expression.

It took him a moment to realise what she was asking. 'You are the mistress of our household. All decisions about its running are yours to make.'

She gave him a bright smile. To Beatrice she said, 'I will need all the help I can get. You and your daughter are both welcome to join me at…the fort.' She glanced at him questioningly and he nodded, feeling a pang of guilt that he'd not informed them of their living arrangements until now. He'd presumed she would know.

Taking the opportunity to build a bridge between his men and the serfs of Évreux he said, 'We are rebuilding the fort and then the town. Any able-bodied men should come to the fort tomorrow to join with us.'

Beatrice nodded, although she gave him a cool look. 'We've heard, master. Your man Skarde *requested* as much while you were gone.' There was a bitterness in her tone that made him frown, and mentally he added speaking to Skarde about the serfs on his list of duties.

Amée shifted on her toes and gave an overly bright smile to both of them. 'I'm sure everyone who can help will help.' A look of mutual understanding passed between them—she would try to help him with the serfs... that was something at least. 'And please come as soon as you're able, Beatrice. I cannot wait to see Emma again.'

Beatrice looked away from him, warmth spreading across her face once more. 'She'll be as delighted as I am to rejoin you, mistress. We'll come straight away.'

They said their goodbyes and Amée turned back to her horse. She paused, staring at the saddle with a pained frown as if debating what to do.

'Would you like to walk up to the fort?' he asked.

She sighed. 'Yes, I don't think I can bear to get back on again.'

'Take the horses, Valda. We'll meet you there.' Valda did as he asked, and Jorund tried to ignore the quickly concealed horror on his wife's face.

'You don't have to walk with me... I'm sure I'll be perfectly safe walking up to the fort alone. It's not far and we're in your territory—'

'I want to,' he interrupted, and she closed her mouth with a quick nod.

They walked together in silence, although as they made their way through the outskirts of Évreux they were stopped on more than one occasion by a serf calling out good wishes to Amée. Each time she stopped and smiled, more often than not she remembered them by name and wished them well. No doubt Beatrice's bravery had caused others to come forward to greet their mistress.

'I thought you left here when you were still a child? How do you know these people so well?'

She blushed and avoided his eyes. 'As a child I went a bit...wild. I spent most of my time running in the woods with the local children.'

'Your parents didn't mind you mixing with the serfs?' Somehow, he couldn't imagine her pompous father allowing such a thing, but he liked the idea of a little dark-haired girl running wild in the forest.

She frowned up at him. 'You care about such things?'

He laughed. 'No, but I would have guessed your father did.'

Her shoulders dropped, and guilt twisted in his stomach. He'd not meant to upset her.

'Yes, he did. But most of the time he wasn't here to argue it. He lived at court mostly. My mother and I lived here...until she died.'

'I'm sorry.' That explained why she'd left Évreux, and also why she might have chosen holy orders as an adult. Anything to get away from her father by the sound of it. She was obviously nothing like him, and it must have been difficult losing both her freedom and her mother at the same time.

She nodded and looked away, the colour high in her cheeks and nose, as if she were trying not to cry.

He decided to change the subject. 'We have struggled to make headway with the local people. It will be good to have someone on our side.'

She didn't reply and that said a lot. His bad humour deepened. It deepened even further when she suddenly stopped walking. It took him a moment to notice why, but when he looked back, he saw despair on her face as she stared up at the fort ahead.

He sighed, seeing it with new eyes. There had been a high wooden wall around the fort at one time. That had been burned down. Limp rotten logs lay in charred heaps in a circular perimeter around the fort. It was vulnerable to attack and open to the elements. There was no gate, no ramparts, only ash.

The buildings of the fort had once consisted of four halls made out of stone. Built very much like Amée's nunnery and some of the larger abbeys he'd seen on his travels around Francia.

And yet, it was also completely different because it was obviously not a church, but a home. There were decorative arches and columns at regular intervals, a tiled roof and reddish stone displaying an array of shapes and patterns across its surface. But it was in too much disrepair, with cracks and scorch marks all over its walls. Most of the roofs were missing or partially collapsed. It would have looked impressively grand at one time. Now it looked broken and tired.

A three-tiered rotunda sat in the centre of the northern hall, flanked by two longer buildings either side. The opposite southern hall had collapsed, and only its gateway remained. An open courtyard sat within the central space. The gardens were divided by stone paths, over-run with rubble and grass. His men were camped in and around it in untidy groups.

Jorund was still in two minds as to whether to attempt to repair it or demolish it entirely and rebuild. He wasn't even sure if he could repair the southern hall, the design was so unfamiliar to him. What if he and his men replaced the stone wrongly and the arches collapsed on their heads?

He moved back to her side, unsure of what to say.

She sighed, not looking away from the southern hall as she spoke. 'It had been here for so long... I never imagined it would fall.'

'It might not be *completely* beyond repair...' he offered, although he cursed himself for offering even that. It was beyond any construction he'd ever seen before, and it wasn't like him to make false promises.

She gave a quick jerk of her head in acceptance and walked forward. He strolled beside her, shortening his pace as best he could. Fortunately for someone so small, she walked quickly.

'Who built it? I've not seen anything like it before.'

She didn't look at him as she answered. 'My great-grandfather. He built this after his pilgrimages to Rome and Constantinople. He wanted to create something as beautiful as he'd seen there. He'd seen many ancient ruins both in Rome and the Holy Land. Beautiful, majestic ruins, filled with history and shades of the past... This was inspired by those ancient people.'

'What happened to them—the ancient people?'

He wondered dryly if all their buildings had fallen on their heads.

She shrugged. 'They travelled the world, conquered and then they fell out of power. I guess…they're like us now.'

He'd never heard of these invaders until now. 'How do you know of them?'

'My mother told me, and, well…a holy life means a life of learning as well as faith. I learnt a lot at the nunnery as it was once an abbey and still has many scriptures and books, filled with ancient history. I always found it fascinating.'

He huffed at that; he always found the written word confusing and pointless. 'Why write down what you could just as easily say?'

'Because what you say cannot last.'

He shrugged. 'Nothing lasts. That's why we have oracles and sagas. To keep the past and traditions alive.'

'But the written word cannot be changed. It cannot be altered from one person to the next like stories can. It is there forever.'

'Until someone burns it.'

He immediately regretted his words as her face fell from bright enthusiasm to utter sadness in only a heartbeat.

'Yes,' she said softly, 'until then.'

What was wrong with him?

Why did he feel the need to repeatedly point out that her people had been conquered? He felt vile for being the cause of her distress, but he knew in his heart it was inevitable. The sooner she accepted him and his place as her husband, the better. He did not want her hoping for the return of the glory days of the past.

Except…part of him felt as if he didn't deserve this good fortune.

Her words from earlier were still lodged in his side,

like a broken arrow. Nothing could 'absolve' him of his crimes, she'd said, and she'd been right. No matter how much he wanted to rage against her words, he couldn't.

He felt no guilt about his time as a warrior under Rollo's command. He'd fought for a better life for him and his people, and he'd fought well. Decisive and brave in battle, he'd developed a reputation that most Norse warriors would be proud of.

However, there was a darker time before that when he'd been a youth. A hideous time of carnage and suffering. Watching helplessly as his father wielded slaughter and destruction like a sword wherever he went. Whatever feelings he'd once felt for his father had withered and died on the vine a long time ago.

Jorund preferred order and justice now, and hoped he would never become like his father. He would fight the darker side of himself for ever if he had to, like Thor wrestling with Elli, the goddess of old age. He could never win but he would put up a decent fight.

He might never deserve redemption, but it was right that he should at least search for it. And that had to be enough. Maybe his marriage would be the same? A constant battle to redeem the unredeemable.

Chapter Eight

Amée tried to shake off the horror of the fort's damage. There was nothing to be done, and what was the point in wallowing in the misery of what once was? Better to look to the future and try to build something she could be proud of. Years of watching her mother's stagnant misery had taught her that.

In fairness the fort had never been intended as a defensive building. It was only the curtain wall that had given it that grand title. The stone structures had been built in a time of prosperity, to display her family's knowledge, faith and progress. She had never been to Rome or Constantinople, but she'd seen sketches of her ancestor's travels. Sadly, in its current state it looked more like the ancient ruins that had originally inspired it.

Jorund's warriors were everywhere. Between the ruins they'd set up tents and campfires, as well as stables for the horses. There were far more people than could be housed comfortably. It looked more like a military encampment than a home.

As she and Jorund walked through the broken gate and into the large courtyard, many warriors called out greetings to him and he acknowledged them with a nod and a good-natured smile. Within the courtyard his men were busy on the timber for the new ramparts. Saws, chisels and hammers hard at work in a busy cacophony of rattles and bangs. Amée tried to not sigh at the once beautiful garden now bare and suffocated by a blanket of sawdust and rubble.

They headed towards the rotunda at the far side of the courtyard. The birds and bats had made their nests in the decorative arches. The evidence of their presence was splattered all over the tiled floor and frescoes. All the lower buildings had fire damage, and some of the roofs were completely caved in.

She wondered if anything inside had survived; she doubted it.

'Come, I'll show you to your room,' Jorund said, striding towards the spiral staircase. She followed, strangely distanced from herself as she climbed the steps of her childhood home. Wondering where he was taking her but wary of asking.

She couldn't help but admire his long legs and firm bottom as he pounded up the stairs ahead of her. He was so masculine and vibrant.

What was wrong with her?

Surely his size and power should terrify her…not *please* her.

It was probably just tiredness.

She trudged dutifully up the tower to the third floor. Determined to not let her fanciful thoughts get the better of her.

'I thought this chamber would suit you best,' said Jorund, opening the door to the lord's chamber and walking into the musty room laced with cobwebs. 'Once it's been aired,' he added with a frown, pulling a cloth from the window shutters and opening them wide. She focused on the air dancing with dust. She refused to look out of the window at the view beyond; her stomach heaved at the thought.

Then something he'd said filtered into her mind and pricked at her.

He'd said 'you.'

Would he not be sleeping in the same room as her?

Well, he'd said he would allow her time to recover from the journey.

She took her time absently walking around the room inspecting what little furniture remained.

'You will not be sharing this chamber with me, then… tonight?' she asked, trying her hardest to sound disinterested.

'No.' He looked out of the window and swayed deliberately from side to side, as if in great thought. 'There's no rush, and there's so much to do. I think it best we get to know each other first. Then, when you're ready…you can let me know.' He turned to face her then, his huge body blocking the light from the window and causing a nervous chill to rush over her skin. 'Don't you agree?'

'Yes.' She nodded and then cleared her throat noisily. 'That sounds prudent.'

'I know our marriage was somewhat…forced.'

'You threatened to destroy my nunnery,' she pointed out, and he had the grace to look embarrassed about it.

'Ah yes, I did say that… But I was eager to get back here. There's a lot to be done.'

She gasped and her eyes narrowed. 'You threatened to destroy a holy sanctuary because you were…impatient?' Strangely, it wasn't as shocking an admission as it should have been. She'd already begun to suspect he'd never really meant it at all.

He shrugged. 'I am sorry I threatened your friends. I didn't mean it.'

'I see.' She filled those two words with as much derision as she dared.

His nostrils flared and he stepped forward. 'Have I hurt you? Since I met you? Have I hurt anyone—'

'You killed those men in the woods.'

He scowled. 'They were raiders who would have murdered you while you slept. Have I hurt anyone that you cared for?'

She bit her lip again and shook her head. 'No.'

'That is because you are my wife and I have sworn to protect you. You are safe with me. Far safer than you were at that badly defended monastery of yours.'

'Nunnery,' she corrected, and he scowled. She really was testing the limits of her boundaries with him, and so far, she'd not reached them. A wicked part of her enjoyed needling him.

'I know I must seem a frightening prospect, but I am still just a man…like any other.'

He cleared his throat and swayed again from side to side, as if he were on a boat. It was an odd habit of his that she was beginning to associate with his times of indecision and uncertainty. She wondered why he did it, and then tried to remind herself that she didn't care.

But that was impossible—everything about him fascinated her. This wasn't the type of man her father would have willingly chosen for her. Lothair was cruel and cunning; he'd choose a man older and richer, someone to suit his interests alone. Not the type of man Évreux actually needed, a warrior, a protector, a leader.

Her stomach swirled at the thought. He was the strongest, most virile man she'd ever seen. A flush of pleasure and pride crept up her neck and she looked away, embarrassed by her traitorous body.

'You're not a *normal* man.' Her voice sounded nervously high as she fought her mortification.

Absently her gaze fell on the window, and her stomach flipped, the earlier pleasure she'd felt leaching from her bones until she shivered. Jorund had moved from the window and the awful view was getting the better of her, causing old wounds to bleed. Her mother's tree. Waiting and watching her.

She glanced back at him. For a moment raw pain flashed in his blue eyes and then he looked away.

'Yes. I am bigger than most. You can have as much time as you need. I will not force you,' he said.

Well, he'd be waiting until Judgement Day if that were the case, she told herself with new resolve. *Lord! How she hated this room!*

At least she'd seen Beatrice, and she had to take comfort from that. She had friends here. It was not as hopeless as she'd first imagined.

But…this room. Dare she tell him the truth as to why she would rather sleep anywhere other than here? But then she would have to admit to the horrors of her past. No, she couldn't face that.

She lowered her eyes, pretending to find the rotten bedding fascinating. 'This is my father's old room. My old chambers below are more…familiar. I'd happily stay there, or in my mother's old room?'

'No, the view and air are better up here. Lower down you only see the courtyard. Besides, Valda has the other one below.' He frowned and moved towards the middle of the room.

'Of course. You're right, this is the Lord of Évreux's chambers after all, and you will need to sleep here... eventually.'

'I prefer to sleep alone. But will join you occasionally...when you're ready.'

Amée wanted to cry, but closed her eyes tightly for a moment to stop the tears. Not only was she to suffer that awful view, but her husband and his mistress would be together on the level below. At least that was what she was beginning to suspect the red-haired shield maiden called Valda was. Her concern for him after the battle, the tender touch to his arm on the road... Why else would she be sleeping in the room beside his? Even her father hadn't settled his mistresses in his actual home.

Uncomfortable silence grew between Amée and Jorund. It closed in around them and threatened to take all the air from her lungs until she feared she would scream if only to make it end.

What did he expect from her?

He walked towards the bed and stood beside her. She swore she could feel the heat of his body against her skin, the weight of his impressive strength against her chest. Which was madness as he hadn't even touched her.

He was frowning darkly at the bed as if it offended him.

Or had the idea of bedding her put that frown on his face? He'd looked disappointed when he'd first seen her. She was the opposite in appearance to the strong, flame-haired Valda. Was that why he was happy to wait until she was ready? Or wait until his need for an heir prompted him to act? Did he see her as a duty? A chore? A burden?

She stared at her parents' bed miserably, longing to be anywhere but here.

'I hadn't realised how bad the bedding was,' he said gruffly, a flush of colour on his cheekbones. If she hadn't already known that he was the type of man who went charging into battle without a moment of hesitation, she might have thought him...embarrassed. Then his eyes sharpened, and her knees weakened under his intense gaze. 'I'll get all this taken away immediately. I'll have a new bed and bedding for you tonight, and more furniture by the end of the week.'

'If you wish,' she whispered, her own throat dry, a ghost of her normal voice.

'I have some duties to see to. You should explore... familiarise yourself with the new layout. We usually eat in the feasting hall at dusk. Uh...it's the longhouse that still has a roof on it. See you at *nattmal*...the evening meal.' Then he left, his strides long and purposeful, shutting the door behind him without a backwards glance.

She sighed. *Well, that was odd.*

Amée took a moment to steel herself with courage and then walked over to the high arched window. In the distance, across the valley, she could see her mother's tree staring back at her. She closed the shutter firmly with a bang and draped the cloth back over it.

She would need to find lots of candles, because she would never look out of that window *ever* again.

Shame burned Jorund's face as he made a hasty retreat down the spiral staircase of the tower. Thoughts of his repeated failings chased him with every step he took until he was out of breath on the bottom stair.

He was a thoughtless cur, and what made it worse was

that he should have known how the sight of her home would have affected her.

Valda had been right. Of course she'd been right. The damn woman was always right! Had he listened? No.

He leaned his head against the stone wall and closed his eyes, unable to face anyone at this moment.

Her face!

She wore her heart so openly he'd seen the exact moment her heart had started to break. And she blamed him—of course she blamed him.

It shouldn't hurt half as much as it did, but it did. He may not have raided Évreux personally, but he'd raided other towns, other villages. Some as acts of war—a necessary evil for the good of his people. But others had been when he was with his father, and it was those that plagued him at night.

He was not innocent. His soul was blackened by those deeds, because he'd allowed them to happen. It was only right that she should hate him for it. But that wasn't the only horror she'd seen. He'd taken her to the bones of her childhood home and he'd seen raw pain in her eyes.

Gone was the place built on knowledge and faith that she'd talked about so fondly. In its place was a broken wreck he wasn't even sure he could fix. He'd thought to comfort her by showing her to the best room. Offering her the best possible sleeping arrangements.

He'd only glanced at it when he'd last been here. He'd been impressed with the view but had not looked too closely at the grand furnishings. Shame washed through him in a cold wave as he realised what he'd offered his bride. A room filled with broken furniture, and rotten blankets. Not to mention the fact it was her *father's* bed! Hardly the most appealing bridal gift.

What had he expected? That she would see the devastation of her old home and thank him for offering her the best room in it? Be so thankful that she offered herself as a gift?

Ridiculous.

He scoffed at his own stupidity—no woman would see a huge ox like him and think herself lucky. If she never accepted him, then that would be a fitting punishment for his own stupidity.

Pushing himself from the wall he stepped out into the courtyard. The sun was low in the sky and there wasn't much time left before dusk. He quickly went to his carpenter and ordered a new bed to be made and fresh bedding to be sent to her chamber.

He didn't see Amée again until the evening meal. He'd worried he wouldn't notice her arrival, so he'd kept a close eye on the hall's doorway. As soon as he'd seen her he'd leapt to his feet, almost knocking over the table and causing several warriors to grab for their cups. Jorund didn't care—it would test their reflexes and he had a wife to appease.

Men shifted from his path as he moved. Those who were not quick enough were shoved to the side unceremoniously.

'Amée,' he said, surprised by the breathlessness of his own voice. She didn't seem to notice—she was staring at the huge number of warriors in her hall, her mouth slightly parted in bewilderment. He took her gently by the arm and steered her to the centre of the main table at the back of the big room. It wasn't the only table; there were several all scattered around and placed wherever there was space. The furniture was an odd mix of scraps they'd put together or new pieces they'd hastily made. Nothing looked right or functioned as it should, and there was so much that had been stored here that there was barely any room to breathe.

In short, it was a mess.

As they took their seat on the bench this fact was made even clearer by the creaking bow of the wood beneath his rump. She sat beside him carefully, bracing her hands on the table, as if afraid her tiny weight would be too much combined with his.

Jorund filled her trencher and wooden cup, then placed both in front of her. She gave an awkward smile with a murmur of thanks. A flare of irritation pricked at the back of his neck and with a roll of his head he cracked the tension in his bones.

'We are behind with the improvements,' he said sharply, glaring at Skarde in particular, who he'd left in charge.

Skarde looked up from his meal and answered him in Norse. 'The locals...' He paused as a passing serf placed a trencher of food beside him. He smiled warmly at her and she visibly flinched. Skarde gave him a pointed look. 'They've not been particularly obliging.'

'Maybe it's the way you ask them?' said Valda mildly from across the table, her eyes hard. He wasn't entirely sure what had happened between the two of them. But Valda had made her distrust of Skarde very clear. He supposed Skarde thought himself a potential second for Jorund, and that may cause tension between the pair. Not on Valda's part, he was sure—she knew her value to him, but perhaps Skarde didn't.

If Rollo hadn't asked Jorund to take Skarde under his wing he might have cut the man loose months ago.

Jorund stared at the departing serf thoughtfully. She weaved through the groups of men with barely concealed disgust. Then again... Maybe the fault did lie with the unwillingness of the people to serve them? And how could he change that?

'Be patient,' he said. 'Once they know they have our protection and that their land will prosper under our rule, they will be more willing to help us. Don't you think, Valda?'

Understanding passed between them, and Valda inclined her head with a smile. 'I agree.'

He happened to glance in Amée's direction and saw her watching their exchange with troubled eyes. 'Something wrong, Amée?'

Surprised by his question she blushed and lowered her eyes. 'I was only curious about what you were discussing.'

He realised then that they'd been speaking in Norse the entire time, as was everyone else in the hall. Guilt gnawed at his insides. How could he tell her that he'd been talking about her people and their lack of welcome? 'Nothing for you to worry about,' he replied, and she nodded, her eyes briefly straying back to Valda, who was laughing at something another shield maiden had said. 'But...' He raised his voice and it carried across the room like a roll of thunder. 'I have decided that we all must speak the language of the Franks. If we are to rule these people, we must have a common tongue.'

Chapter Nine

Amée ducked her head, mortified by her husband's declaration.

Great! Now all the warriors will definitely hate me!

She twisted her hands in her lap and avoided everyone's eyes.

Why did she have to open her silly mouth and point it out? They were Vikings—of course they wanted to speak Norse.

Yes, it was irritating that she couldn't understand what they were saying. Especially when Jorund seemed so 'intimate' with Valda. They'd passed knowing looks and smiles between each other all evening. Even now he was laughing at something she'd said.

Amée stopped listening as her mind churned.

Their behaviour only confirmed what Amée had already suspected. Valda was the real reason why Jorund was so happy to wait before consummating their marriage.

It should please her. After all, she had no desire for his affection or his touch. She could happily spend the rest of her days as a virgin. It was what she'd originally intended, and if they waited, the likelihood of her returning to her convent seemed more likely.

Why should she care if he already had a woman?

Except she could not shake the weight of the insult from her mind. Like a thorn it buried itself deeper into her skin with every passing moment. The callousness, the injustice and, frankly, *the rudeness*! Not just to her, but to Valda as well. He should never have agreed to marry her if his heart was already given to another.

Idiot! When has the heart ever mattered when land and power were at stake?

Men had the same desires regardless of religion, it seemed. She was the 'Lady Évreux'—she was a title, land and the bearer of heirs…nothing more. She would never be anything more. Wasn't that why she'd made the difficult decision to enter the nunnery in the first place? To become something else other than property, to build a life of her own choosing.

But even that had been a false hope. There were no choices but the ones her father had made for her. And now, those choices would be made by her husband. A man who also had no respect for her. Just like her father.

Battered and bruised, after the relentless journey and the sight of her ruined home, Amée couldn't stomach another minute in their company. She needed some time alone to digest her fate.

'I'm tired, I think I'll retire.' She pushed aside her trencher, her appetite gone. The movement as well as her words caught Jorund's attention and his bright eyes focused on her.

Such a pretty, vibrant blue.

She found herself drowning in them. The stuffy hall felt even more overheated and her throat dried under his watchful gaze.

She reached for her cup of milk. She'd have one last sip

to quench her sudden thirst before she left. To her mortification, she somehow managed to knock over the cup in her haste to take it. The white liquid spilled across the table in a foamy wash. The majority pouring into Jorund's lap.

Why on earth had she sat so close to him?

He jumped to his feet and she instinctively braced herself. Throwing up her hands to cover her face and head as best she could. Curving her body away to avoid a broken rib or a blow to the stomach.

To her surprise, nothing happened.

The room which had once been filled with friendly chatter fell into deathly silence. Amée heard nothing except the blood thundering in her ears and the slow drip of spilled milk upon the rushes.

She waited.

Still nothing happened.

Unable to wait a moment longer for the inevitable, she peeked out from behind her hands. Better to get it over with. Delay only made the eventual beating worse.

Jorund was looming over her, as she'd expected.

But he was *horrified*, not at the mess or the insult she'd caused.

No, his eyes were focused on her, as if he couldn't understand her reaction.

She lowered her hands carefully and straightened her spine. Maybe he wouldn't punish her in public…or at all? Dared she hope?

Everyone was staring at her as if she'd lost her wits.

Maybe she had? By instinctively showing her fear, she'd revealed so much. Her past tarnishing her present with its weakness and cruelty. She couldn't bear for him to know the abuse of her childhood, but she'd told him anyway without even opening her mouth.

Humiliation twisted hotly in her gut and she began to sweat, her chest so tight she feared she'd end up unable to catch her breath like the last time. She took several deep breaths and stared at her hands hoping that the roof would do as it threatened and cave in on all their heads.

She fought the instinct to run and hide, knowing that it would only make matters worse.

Strangely she remembered Jorund's breathing technique. The one he'd used to calm her down at the nunnery. She found herself doing the same again to keep the panic at bay. Forcing her body to take regular deep breaths in, then releasing them slowly and deliberately.

His wife was afraid of him.

He'd only stood so that he could avoid the wash of milk flowing across the table. Had thought nothing of the accident, and had been about to ask one of the serfs to fetch a cloth when he'd realised Amée was cringing away from him. Her hands held up high in defence, her body quivering in fear.

He glanced at his closest men; they were equally surprised and dismayed by Amée's reaction. Many of them had been with him and Rollo from the beginning, like Valda, and were forged under the same hammer. After a tense silence, some of them began awkward conversations amongst themselves, anything to avoid lingering on his wife's embarrassment.

He'd never appreciated them more.

Beatrice appeared at his side and began to mop hastily at the spilled milk. He waved her away, more concerned about Amée than his wet clothes. Slowly he sat down, careful not to make any sudden movements that might frighten her further.

'I will not hurt you,' he said softly.

She looked as she did the last time, when she'd run from him in the nunnery.

Pale, shaken and full of panic. At least she wasn't running this time. Some improvement—a poor improvement, but an improvement all the same. She was taking in long steady breaths. Good, that would help.

He kept his voice quiet and calm, hoping his words would filter through the storm in her head. 'You are my wife. I will never hit you... I do not abuse women. It would be wrong and an insult on my character. I would be a lesser man because of it. Do you understand?'

She nodded, although she could not meet his eyes. 'Can I go now?' she whispered. The words were dry and it sounded as if they hurt her throat.

He sighed and pushed his own trencher away. 'I'll see you to your room—'

'There's no need,' she said, her cheeks flushing like rosy apples.

'I *swear* I will not hurt you. I only wish to ensure you are safe and to check your new bed and furnishings are to your liking.'

She met his eyes and he noticed sparks of irritation flash behind her ebbing fear. 'They arrived before dusk. They're perfect, thank you.' Her words did not match her tone, and he wondered if she was still disappointed in the room.

He eased closer to her. 'It's dark, I should still come with you.'

To his surprise she crossed her arms over her chest and leaned away. Her courage was returning—that was a good sign. 'I can find my own way. I did live here for many years.' Jorund opened his mouth to point out that many things had changed since she was last here, but she interrupted him. 'Am I a prisoner now?'

'Of course not!' Is that how she viewed their marriage? The thought was appalling. Granted she'd not been happy about her change in circumstance, but surely she didn't see herself as a prisoner?

'Then I want to go to my room...' She leaned forward, the irritation blooming into furious resentment as she hissed, 'You said you were willing to wait!'

He reared back as if she'd slapped him. Was *that* what this was about? She thought he was following her for that reason? Had he not given her his word? It only raised more questions about his wife, and the worrying behaviour she expected from men. But this was not the time or the place to discuss her fears. 'I am,' he answered.

'Two winters?' she said with an elegant lift of her dark brows, as if she were mocking him.

Confused by the strange turn in conversation, he shrugged. He could cope with a little petulance from her if it made her feel more in control of her situation. 'I would hope it's not *that* long. But I will wait until you desire me...no matter how long that is.'

Amée flushed at the mention of 'desire'; surely he only meant her acceptance? Unless what she felt was... desire? It sent a shiver down her spine and she tried her best to focus on his answer.

The passage of time had no significance to Jorund. It was then Amée realised he appeared to be unaware of her father's contract and the condition of an heir before two winters had passed. Some of the heat went out of her bluster, but she raised her chin in defiance anyway. 'Well, then, let me go to my room...*alone*.'

He frowned darkly, but nodded his approval.

She left as quickly as she dared. Only glancing back when she reached the doorway. He still watched her, and she dismissed it as wounded pride.

Climbing the stairs, she wondered if he'd really meant everything that he'd said. About never hurting her. It should have comforted her, and it did, but it also confused her.

In her room she grabbed the pitiful sack of her possessions by the door. It had been delivered to her room at the same time as her bed and bedding. She emptied the contents out onto the new bed. A spare habit and veil, a Bible, a comb and the scroll.

A fire burned low in the hearth and she moved towards it. Lighting a few of the candles to see better by. Then she unfurled her father's contract and re-read it.

It was as she remembered. After two winters without an heir the land returned to her father. There was no mention of what would happen to her, or her marriage.

But surely without the land she would no longer be needed? The marriage could be annulled if it was never consummated, and Jorund may not wish to keep her anyway. Maybe she could return to the nunnery? Begin her life as she'd originally intended.

She sighed. There was too much uncertainty. Was she being naive in believing things could ever end well for her? She should not rely on the contract as her only hope. Still, the contract was between the King of Francia and her father. The seal had been unbroken when Jorund had handed it to the abbess, which suggested he'd never read it himself, which was odd. But if Jorund was unaware of its significance, then she would be the last person to reveal it to him.

Would he keep his word? Where would he sleep tonight? She shook her head—why should she care? Better that he should never see it, she decided.

She threw the scroll into the fire and watched it burn.

Chapter Ten

He was a child again.

Walking through one of those wretched villages of his past. In the smoke-filled sky crows circled and dipped ready to feast on the dead. The stench of blood and bitter death filled his nose and coated his tongue until it was hard to breathe.

Hard to think.

Bodies were all around him, none of them warriors. There was no honour in their deaths, only wild, senseless slaughter. He stumbled through the carnage, his bloodied sword dragging through the muck. He had no will to wield it any more, and it was heavy in his young hands. Deliberately he kept back during these kind of raids, only ever using it when he had to—to his father's disgust.

If his mother could have seen him now… She would have been ashamed.

He certainly was.

Something grabbed at his boot and Jorund's disjointed mind blazed with terror. Instinctively he struck down with his blade. Realising too late that it was a wounded man grasping at his boot and begging for mercy. For death or water, Jorund would never know. His sword had pierced his heart before the man could utter a word.

Screams were coming from one of the few huts not yet burning. Men were clogging up the doorway and the area outside of it. He walked towards it, squirming his way through the warriors as only a slim boy could. Suspecting what he would find, and not having the courage to do anything more than witness it. Tall for his age, he still had to stoop to enter the hovel.

Disappointed and saddened by the obvious poverty within, his guts churned with nausea. These people had far less than them—there was no glory in this cruelty, there was no wealth. These were poor peasants who barely had enough to feed themselves.

He blinked into the darkness and saw a naked woman screaming on a miserably thin pallet. Although at this point she sounded closer to a wild animal than a person.

His father raised himself from her and smiled at him. 'Want a turn, boy?'

Even now, amongst the twisting images that disappeared and reappeared like smoke, he knew it was only a dream and that something was different about the memory. Jorund looked down at the frightened woman's face. It wasn't the peasant woman's face any more. It was someone else's.

It was Amée.

Reality shifted, and he was no longer a young boy, but a man. He charged forward instead of back. Hands grabbed him and held him tight, and he fought them as his mind screamed back to consciousness.

Jorund awoke shaking and covered in sweat, his blanket ripped in half down the middle. His hands gripped the cloth with bone-white knuckles. Gasping, he struggled to clear the memory of the ash-soaked air from his lungs. As if he could block the memories that haunted him from within. He pressed the heels of his hands into his eyes until they ached.

'*Enough,*' he whispered to himself. He sucked in a deep breath, held it as best he could, then forced it out in one long sigh. Then another and another. He repeated the process until his heart began to ease, and the fear subsided.

Had he screamed? Sometimes he did.

But Valda would have come in and woken him if he'd become too loud, and she hadn't.

He refused to talk about it with her, but he appreciated that she would always wake him when he'd had a particularly bad night. He'd made her promise to never get too close, to wake him with a thrown blanket or a sharp clap of her hands, which she thought ridiculous, but he didn't trust himself when he was lost in his nightmares.

In the silence he waited until his blood cooled and his breath returned to normal.

No, he couldn't have been vocal this time.

He used the torn blanket to wipe the sweat from his body and then tossed it in the corner. He grabbed one of the rich furs from the bottom of the pallet to cover himself and lay back down.

It was strange that Amée's face had been in his dream tonight. But then he supposed it was from spending so much time with her.

The worst dreams were always of that time with his father. But sometimes he would dream of his mother's death—when he'd been too slow to reach her on the battlefield. Other times it would be of the friends he'd lost along the way. All the other boys who'd been too young to carry a sword and had not lived long enough to learn how to wield it.

The only certainty with his dreams was that he would have a bad one at least once a week. Usually more if he'd slept badly the night before, and maybe his father's recent death had something to do with it too, had made the nightmares more frequent and vivid.

Imagine if he'd been in bed with Amée during one of his nightmares? Not that he would ever risk sleeping beside a woman, and especially not Amée. What if he lashed out and hurt her in his sleep? Ripped her apart with his bare hands. She was so tiny… His stomach curdled at the thought.

If she did accept him in her bed, their intimacy would have to end there. If she'd been afraid of him earlier, imagine the terror she would feel if he started screaming like a madman in the middle of the night!

He could never sleep beside her. He'd always known that, but part of him longed to be closer to her. To have her body wrapped in his arms, as she'd been when they'd camped out on their journey here.

Impossible—tonight had proven it. They would always be separate, for her safety as well as his pride.

Chapter Eleven

'Is this all?' Amée asked as she stared at the food on offer—or more aptly the *lack of* food on offer. The pantry and cellar were bare. Aside from the baskets of apples—the only food readily available in Évreux—there were only a couple of barrels of mead, a few gnarled vegetables and a haunch of salted pork.

It was utterly hopeless!

She had an army to feed, as well as a giant. This wouldn't last more than one meal.

Beatrice nodded gravely. 'This is the last of what your husband brought with him from Rouen.' She bit her lip and then asked hesitantly, 'Mistress, may I speak to you plainly?'

'Of course.'

A look passed between Beatrice and Emma. Mother and daughter both deeply worried. Amée reached out to give Beatrice's arm a reassuring squeeze. 'Please, you can tell me anything.'

'Your father hasn't been back since you left—'

'I'm so sorry,' interrupted Amée, releasing Beatrice's arm. Who was she to offer comfort when her family had forsaken the people of Évreux?

'Why would you? You were still a child when you left. And then we heard you were going to take holy orders?' Beatrice looked pointedly at her habit and veil. She'd taken to wearing the veil again, anything to tame her unruly curls into some kind of order.

'Yes, but…my father changed his mind.'

Beatrice's mouth pinched but she didn't say anything. 'I see. Well, the fort was raided not long after you left and has been pretty much abandoned ever since. They killed many of our men, stole livestock, grain, even our tools and weapons for hunting. We gave up trying to protect the land. They come and take whatever food we have. There's the harvest to come, but it will be a poor harvest as many of the farms were burned and the grains taken. We've hidden a few supplies…for the winter. But most of the food has already been handed to Rollo's army… to maintain the peace. We can give you our winter supplies, but they won't last long, and when winter comes…' She shrugged sadly, and Amée's chest tightened with guilt and sorrow.

'Thank you, but you have given enough already. It'd be wrong to take any more from you. Besides, we have Jorund's protection now, and with proper management the land will prosper.' She tried to sound positive, but even as she spoke, she knew she had no reason to trust or hope for a better future for anyone, not even herself.

Emma saw through her words. 'Until another band of warriors comes to raid—' she said bitterly.

Beatrice elbowed her in the ribs, and Emma scowled darkly at her mother, but said nothing more. To Amée, Beatrice said, 'Although…if there is any danger of an attack from another warlord…I suggest you run and hide.'

Emma nodded in agreement. 'We've hidden in the orchard in the past. Waited it out in the trees until they've gone. If the worst happens, run.' She was a younger version of Beatrice but with more fire in her hair and temperament. Amée adored them both.

It broke her heart to hear that her people had had to live in such constant fear.

What horrors had they faced in her family's absence? She stepped forward and hushed her voice. 'Did you do that when Jorund first came? Was anyone hurt?'

'We tried to hide, but he must have heard of our tactic because he split his men and rode in from both sides of the valley.' Beatrice patted her arm gently. 'No one was hurt. He told us we owed our fealty to him. No one dared argue with him. Then he left and returned with you. So, he *must* be the new lord.'

'Yes, he is. But in truth, this is his land first. His marriage to me is a mere formality, nothing more.'

Beatrice and Emma looked saddened by her words. 'That's what we feared,' said Beatrice with a resigned sigh.

'But that does not mean I am unable to help—'

'Be careful when you speak with him, mistress,' Emma said, her expression pinched. Amée noticed that Emma was no longer the giggling mischievous girl who'd climbed trees with her as a child. There was a hardness to her mouth that had never been there before. She was still the kind, passionate person she remembered, but there was a deep sadness in her eyes that suggested she expected only disappointment in life. 'Skarde, your husband's man, has already demanded we supply everything we have to the fort. He's threatened…repercussions if we refuse.'

The bitter lump in Amée's belly began to burn. Her

land, her people, they needed her, and she would not fail them as her father had. 'There will be *no* repercussions.'

Mother and daughter exchanged another look. It was obvious that although they hoped Amée was right, they were resigned to the possibility that she might not be able to prevent any punishment.

Determined not to disappoint the only two people in Évreux who actually cared for her, Amée resolved to find Jorund and force him to rescind his demands on her people. 'I will go and speak with my husband. I will not stand idly by while my people are threatened and terrorised!'

She strode to the doorway, glancing back with a final thought before she left. 'Maybe you can search the gardens while I'm gone? There might be some roots left, and putting those back in order should be our first priority. If not for now at least for spring. I'm sure we'll be able to make this stretch for a stew tonight. The winter supplies will remain safe. I will find another way.'

It appeared that what God could not provide, her optimism would have to make up for.

Her optimism and her husband, that is. She would force Jorund to see sense!

'You want to repair it? Are you sure?' asked Valda as she frowned at the collapsed southern hall. 'But... We could reuse the stone to patch the others.'

Jorund chewed the inside of his cheek for a moment before answering. 'Possibly... We can use some of the stone from the old town walls for the others. The new outer buildings can be timber. Let's leave the southern hall for now, focus on the ones we can repair first.'

Valda raised an eyebrow. 'I see, and pleasing your new wife has nothing to do with it?'

He turned to Valda with a scowl, and she held up her hands in mock surrender.

'I'll try my best to find a stonemason, but Skarde is right. The serfs aren't the most hospitable to us.'

'Be patient with them.'

A small smile teased Valda's mouth. 'I am the most patient woman who has ever walked the realm of men. But I cannot change people's hearts. That is beyond even the will of the gods.'

'You have become very thoughtful of late, Valda. Brooding does not suit you.'

Valda barked with laughter. 'I am insulted that *you* of all people would call *me* brooding.'

Jorund had no response to that. It was true, he wasn't the most jovial of men. He would have pressed his friend further if a small dark figure hadn't been heading towards him in a flurry of drab skirts.

It was Amée charging towards them, eating up the space between them with surprising speed. Her practical boots thudding over the stone path with purpose, and—if the firm set of her jaw was any indication—anger.

A prickle of awareness ran down his spine as her eyes fixed on them and then narrowed. Her speed, already considerable, seemed to pick up. She arrived with a bad-tempered flush on her cheeks and her breathing laboured. He found her emotional state oddly arousing and worrying in equal measure.

'Is something wrong, wife?'

A cold, polite smile spread across her face as she tilted it up to see him better. The summer light hit the glow of her face and illuminated her beauty to dazzling effect.

'I'm glad you asked, *husband*. Your men have eaten

every morsel of food in my kitchens and tonight you will be treated to the miserabilist of stews because of it!'

Was that all she was concerned about?

He relaxed. 'Skarde mentioned the supplies were low. They will be replenished soon.'

Her nostrils flared and her fists clenched at her sides. He had the uneasy feeling that he'd only made matters worse by reassuring her, which was madness.

'By forcing our people to give up the few supplies they have left for the winter? By *stealing* it from the mouths of hungry *children*? I shall remind you, *my lord*, that the land is both our responsibility and our privilege. As its guardian you cannot take without *consequence*!' Her words started off reasonable but grew in temper with every word until her final word was a shout of outrage. It rang around the courtyard and several of his men turned to look. He didn't care about the embarrassment—

Well, he did. No one had stripped the flesh off his bones quite like that since he was a child.

He might have killed a man for talking to him like that. But when Amée did it, it only filled him with shame that he'd failed her in some way. Determined to rectify the situation he searched the courtyard for one face in particular.

'Are you even *listening* to me?' Amée hissed, her voice raw with insult and despair. He didn't answer her. He'd finally caught sight of the man he wanted.

'Skarde! Come here,' he called, his voice deliberately calm in contrast to his wife's, to save what little dignity he had remaining. Years of command carried his voice easily across the courtyard. He would sort this mess out quickly and as painlessly as possible.

Skarde walked forward, his swagger confident. Obviously glad he didn't have a wife to please.

'What are the plans to replenish our stores?'

Skarde shrugged before he spoke to Jorund in Norse. 'The serfs are due to provide their remaining stores tomorrow.'

Before Jorund could reprimand him, Amée was quick to intervene. 'I will *not* be treated as a stranger in my own home! You were ordered to speak in the Frankish tongue last night by your lord! Do you dare to defy him?'

Skarde repeated his words in her native tongue, his eyes hard like stone. Amée didn't flinch. If anything it added fuel to her fury.

'Or there will be *repercussions*, correct?' she said. Once more she turned on Jorund. 'And what repercussions will those be? You said yourself these people have been raided *repeatedly*. They have nothing left to give!'

Skarde's mouth twisted in disgust. 'They have secret stores that they have deliberately been keeping from us. We found one cache a few days ago, before you returned. They should not be hoarding supplies from their master!'

'Those stores are to feed them and their children throughout winter. The serfs have always been allowed to keep back food for themselves and their families. Otherwise, no one would be left alive to work the land in the spring!' Amée snarled, her eyes burning with sparks of gold. Despite her barely reaching Skarde's shoulder she was brave enough to tackle him head on and Jorund couldn't help but admire her for it. She was sometimes so nervous and frightened around him. But it appeared there was one thing that made her brave despite herself. Her concern for others. It was an admirable trait. Maybe she was right and she was stronger than she looked.

'Did you tell them we are expecting more supplies by the end of the week?' asked Jorund wearily.

Skarde shook his head before grumbling, 'They are no better than slaves. I do not explain the decisions of free men to slaves.'

Jorund rolled his eyes.

This whole conflict could have been easily avoided.

He shouldn't have taken Valda with him. She would have handled the serf's situation far better than Skarde. He'd been misguided in allowing him so much responsibility. Favoured by Rollo or not, he was quickly losing patience with the man.

Jorund explained to Skarde the situation as if he were an idiot. 'They are not slaves. They are tied to the land but they are not owned by us. They deserve to know their children will not starve if they open their stores.'

'I will speak with them again,' said Skarde, finally having the wisdom to lower his eyes.

'No!' barked Jorund, allowing some of his own irritation to steel the command in his tone. 'You have done enough damage. Valda will deal with it. Leave us.'

Skarde walked away with a little less confidence in his step.

'*You* should speak with them,' Amée said firmly. 'They are frightened and need reassurance from their master.'

'I will not fail them,' he growled. In time they would learn not to question him, and trust in his capability to protect them.

Amée cleared her throat. 'Then…I should speak with the serfs, not Valda. I am the Lady of Évreux…am I not?'

Jorund cursed himself for forgetting her position. Of course she should be the one to deal with the serfs. He was so used to relying on only himself and his second that he'd completely forgotten Amée's role as his wife.

'If you wish,' he replied, too embarrassed by his own stupidity to admit his fault.

'Are there *truly* more supplies coming?' she asked with narrowed eyes.

He stared incredulously at her. 'You doubt my word?'

All she seemed to do was doubt him!

Her resilient chin tilted upwards once again, and it was almost a relief to see the fire still burned within. He deserved it.

'At least tell me how much? I will need to know what to ration,' she replied with barely concealed frustration.

He told her what supplies were due to arrive and felt a glow of pride as her shoulders relaxed a little, and the lines on her brow smoothed away at his long list of supplies.

'Then there will be plenty to feed our people throughout the winter,' she said.

He could always rely on his far-reaching memory and foresight to get him out of any awkward situations. 'Yes, I suspected there would be little left in Évreux after all of the raiding. I made provision. Although perhaps I should have brought more with me, or encouraged more hunting in my absence. I swear, anything taken from the serfs will be replenished. The harvest is almost ready—yes, it will be small, but it will be enough to last the winter when my other supplies arrive.' In truth, he'd used most of the silver and treasure he'd accumulated over the years to provide for his new people. Only fitting considering how tarnished much of his treasure was by the blood of this land. He shook the distasteful thought from his mind and explained further. 'But the boats needed to be loaded and they're slow moving. They were going to take a long time to reach Évreux. I thought it best to secure the land and our marriage first. The rest of my army guards it with their lives—it will arrive without issue.'

'You have *more* warriors coming?' gasped Amée, her eyes wide.

He nodded. 'Yes... Although most of them are ready to give up their sword and shield for the plough and a...' He hesitated, unsure whether he should continue.

'And?' Her head tilted, and he wished she didn't wear a veil so that he could see the midnight curls fall freely around her face.

'A wife... I have many men who wish to settle in this land, many without wives.'

She bristled at that, taking a step back. 'I hope you have not promised them...' A flush rushed up her neck. 'Serfs are not cattle to be bartered and bred.'

'I know that.' He sighed, feeling as if he were tripping over rocks whenever he spoke with her. 'I will need your help.'

Her eyes widened, and he took a step towards her, reaching out and taking her small hand in his own. Its size against his own only reminded him of their differences, but he couldn't let her go. 'We need to encourage the mixing of blood between our people. Our land is divided. If we do not work together it will fail. Others will see our weakness and invade.'

'As you did.' Her tone was sour but there was also acceptance there.

He took hope from that.

'Yes. We saw the petty in-fighting, your weak King and the pressure of the tribes from the west and we took advantage of it.' *This* he was not ashamed of. *This* was life. Brutal and ruthless. 'My people are strong. We will not bend or surrender easily. Not when we have fought so hard to win. But we cannot do it alone. It is why Rollo and Princess Gisla are keen to forge alliances. Ours will not be the last marriage to bridge the gap between our people. Rollo dreams of a kingdom independent from both the Norse and King Charles. To do that, all of Northmannia must be his in both heart and mind. A man is more loyal when his wife and children's safety are at stake, and a land is more prosperous when the people work together to build it. Maybe you could speak with the women? Ask them to at least consider my men as potential mates.'

'What do the women gain by this? It's certainly not freedom,' she grumbled.

Was that what she thought she'd given up by marrying him? Her freedom?

He wanted to deny it, to tell her that she was free to do whatever she wished. That as his wife she ruled his household, but he did not rule her. That wasn't completely true though, was it? She was the Lady of Évreux. She had a responsibility to her people and that duty was intertwined with her vows to him.

What could he offer her?

'Protection,' he said, and she gave a sad smile as if he'd disappointed her in some way, even though she nodded as she replied.

'True, protection is important, especially in these uncertain times.'

'And...' he added as he brushed his thumb over the soft warmth of her hand and wished desperately he could offer her more. Her eyes flickered to her hand and then back up to his eyes in silent question.

What could he offer? Happiness? No one could promise that.

The air grew hot and heavy between them. Her lips parted ever so slightly, and he longed to lean down and kiss her. To offer her pleasure at least. *Damn it!* She was so innocent he was afraid he would only frighten her.

'And?' she whispered, her voice so light and fragile it was almost snatched away by the summer breeze. His skin prickled with a shiver of cold despite the sunshine.

'Devotion,' he said, his voice husky. She would have his sword and protection always.

What else could a woman want?

'Oh,' she gasped, and with a nod of her head she took a step back, the distance between them an empty chasm. 'I'll speak with them. But tell your warriors that my women also deserve loyalty and respect.'

Her words were harsh, as if she were criticising him for some earlier insult. Then she clasped her hands together in front of her. Her thumb lightly stroking over the skin he'd touched moments before. She noticed the focus of his gaze and with a blush she hurried away, her drab skirts swishing around her legs as she strode back towards the hall.

Later that afternoon Jorund watched in awe as the serfs arrived with carts of food for the fort. He was not under the illusion that they did so willingly. The serfs watched with anxious eyes as they handed over the meagre remains of their stores. It was a credit to Amée that they'd obeyed so quickly and without complaint. He doubted they believed his word, but the trust in his wife was clear: if she believed in him, they would too, despite their fears.

* * *

He spent the following days working continuously to prove Amée's trust in him was justified. When he wasn't working on the improvements to the fort, he was out with his hunters in the forest ensuring there was plenty of fresh meat for both the fort and the town. The serfs had no tools or weapons to hunt with, the raiders having stolen them. Until he'd had enough weapons fashioned for them, he and his men would have to hunt instead.

Amée spent her time reordering the household. The furniture in the hall was better arranged now. The gardens were looking tidier and more organised too.

He'd not noticed any improvement in the hospitality and manners of the serfs. He suspected they were waiting to see if he made good on his promise regarding further supplies.

He imagined that was another reason his wife was so distant with him. She rarely spoke with him at meals and avoided him most of the time. No doubt, she was also waiting to see if her trust in him was well placed.

He was relieved when three days later the boats arrived, overflowing with food, livestock and his remaining warriors.

Chapter Twelve

Amée's growing worry from the past week disappeared in one long exhale of relief as she watched Jorund's boats row into town. Emma came running and stood beside her at the fort gates to watch. They exchanged a grin and then hugged each other with a squeal of joy.

He'd not failed her.

Fragile hope bloomed in her heart. Jorund had kept his word.

When Emma pulled away, tears glistened in her eyes. 'Forgive me, mistress.'

'What is there to forgive?'

'God forgive me, but I...I doubted... I didn't dare believe...' Emma's voice cracked and she shook her head.

Amée took her hand and squeezed it.

How many times had the sight of dragon ships cutting through the waters of the River Iton struck terror into the hearts of her people? Today the sun was bright and heavy with the perfume of wild flowers. These boats brought hope and prosperity, but that had not always been the case, and Emma knew that far better than her.

'There is nothing to forgive. Thank God they came in time.'

She supposed she should thank her *lord husband* as well as the Almighty.

He'd not lied to her. Maybe Jorund would never be a faithful husband—as his relationship with Valda proved. Wasn't that the way with all men though? It had been for her father. At least Jorund hadn't beaten or lied to her. Not yet.

The sound of horses behind them caused Emma to part from her and step aside. It was Jorund, followed by Valda and a few other warriors.

Jorund stopped his horse beside them. 'There you are. I've been looking for you. The supplies have arrived.'

She raised a hand to shield the bright morning light from her eyes. 'As I can see, my lord.'

A petty part of her refused to thank him. After all, it *was* his responsibility to ensure the survival of his people. And besides, it was obvious where she'd been. She'd been working on the gardens with the rest of the serfs when the horn had signalled the approaching boats. It was only the warriors that had not been concerned by it. They'd seen the familiar green shields marked with a bear hung along the boats' sides and had immediately relaxed. While her people had hurried to see if it signalled famine or deliverance.

He shifted in his saddle and cleared his throat gruffly. 'Yes, well…are you coming? I thought you could distribute the goods amongst the people. You know the families best.'

So, he hadn't handed all of her duties over to Valda after all?

She tried to brush off the bitter voice that plagued her whenever she thought of Valda's *place* in her home.

'Yes! I'll just get—' She turned to the stables and stopped speaking. Luna was already saddled and waiting. Jorund jumped down, and walked with her towards Luna. Part of her was grateful that he knew she needed help. Another part of her hated how pathetic it made her look, especially in front of his *woman*, whose horse was much taller than Luna.

She'd wager Valda *never* needed help mounting her horse.

Hands wrapped around her ribcage and lifted her effortlessly up onto Luna. Then he was gone and Valda was handing her the reins with a smile. Amée returned it, reminding herself that she had no *real* reason to be unkind to her.

The boats were already being unloaded when they arrived at the town's river dock. Many families had gathered to watch, their eyes brimming with desperate hope. She was certain many had questioned her trust in Jorund. She'd had to swear on her Bible that the supplies were coming. Even then, she'd seen the fear in their eyes when they'd handed over the last of their food.

The warriors dismounted and began to tie up their horses to a trough in the square nearest the boats. She slipped down from Luna and gave her an affectionate pat. She'd visited her every day since their arrival, but she was probably due a long ride soon. Cantering around the fort wasn't enough exercise for her, even if she'd been allowing her time to recover from their long journey.

'I'll tie her up,' said Valda, and Amée was once more surprised by her friendliness.

Did Norse women feel no jealousy?

Did she not care that her lover was married to another?

Of course, *Amée* didn't care. She didn't want Jorund as her husband.

But did Valda?

'Thank you.' Amée handed her the reins and then made her way to the boats. People smiled with relief at the sight of her, and she felt the weight of their trust bear down on her with every step.

Jorund joined her, and he slowed his stride to match hers. He was always so considerate in her presence and it confused her. Shouldn't she loathe him? Avoid him, as she'd done for the past few days? Rejecting his attentions at every opportunity, and yet, on this lovely, hopeful day she couldn't help the thrill of excitement that shot down her spine at his closeness.

'The people look pleased,' he said mildly.

She bristled, irritated by her wayward thoughts. 'They're no longer facing a winter of starvation. Of course they're pleased.'

He stopped and turned her by the elbow to face him. 'I would *never* have let them starve.' Fierce sincerity etched his features and she knew he meant every word. She tried to stifle her growing admiration of him, as it could only lead to heartbreak. She nodded dumbly and shrugged out of his grip, taking a hasty step backwards.

'I still think you should have reassured them personally,' she grumbled, hating how petulant she sounded, even as she made her hasty retreat.

Irritation sparked in his eyes at her sudden movement and he looked away with a curse. 'I told you I would never hurt you,' he muttered under his breath.

'You surprised me—that's all, and… I'm sorry,' she said quietly, genuinely feeling bad about her rudeness. He'd been true to his word. She should be grateful, not snide.

What was wrong with her?

They began to walk again, tension thick and heavy in the air between them.

'I will leave you in charge of the distribution. Return their winter supplies and arrange whatever is left to be stored at the fort. There are grains and seeds for sowing next year's crops too. I trust you'll know what to do with those. There are some bolts of fabric as well, for clothing, and you're welcome to make use of it. I realise you have little from the nunnery…to wear.' He glanced at the habit and veil, then cleared his throat. 'I need to greet the helmsman, Arne, but then I'll go hunting.'

She didn't much care for dressmaking, but she supposed she should create a better wardrobe for herself. She added it mentally to the very bottom of her list of chores.

Jorund greeted the helmsman with a brotherly slap and spoke with him for a time, and then he left with a small nod of goodbye for her.

True to his word, the distribution was her sole duty. The show of confidence should have gratified her, but the victory soured in the pit of her stomach as she watched him ride off with several warriors including Valda.

She shook it off. She had responsibilities and duties. She did not care if Jorund slept with a hundred women, as long as he left her alone.

Amée turned to the eager faces of her people and took a deep breath.

It took her most of the morning but eventually she'd completed the allocation of the supplies. They'd returned the serfs' personal winter supplies, as well as bulked up some of the more pitiful stores, ensuring everyone had enough to see them through the cold season. There were some families whose farms were farther out, and she'd ensured carts were sent to fill their stores as well.

There were still plenty of animals, vegetables, grain and seeds left over. She sent those up to the fort with strict instructions that Beatrice and Emma were in charge of arranging them in the stores. The warriors had made a terrible mess of storage before she'd arrived and she wouldn't allow them to do it again.

Then she decided to visit the blacksmith because she had a long list of items she needed mending or repairing back at the fort. On a whim she gave him her wedding ring and asked for it to be resized. She'd worn it around her neck every day, but that felt odder with every passing day and she didn't bother to wear her crucifix again afterwards, as the cord had frayed from the weight of her ring.

Next, she met with some key families. Spoke with them about their troubles and what they needed. By early afternoon she was done, and she decided to let Luna have some much-needed exercise. She rode towards the outskirts of the town, furthest away from the fort. Jorund had said she wasn't a prisoner, so she decided to take full advantage. Run a little wild as she'd done in her youth. She suspected she needed to clear her head, if her earlier snapping at Jorund was anything to go by.

She urged Luna into a full gallop and raced up the hill towards the far side of the orchard. Deliberately avoiding the sight of that hateful tree, but she thought Luna might appreciate an apple or two. After never having her own horse she was glad of Luna and the freedom she gave her.

Her heart raced to the pounding rhythm of Luna's hooves as they climbed the hill. Vitality rushed through her veins like a waterfall, and she felt glad to be alive.

It had been a pleasure to hand out the supplies and meet with old friends.

For the first time in years she was needed and useful. Not a burden or an asset to barter away, but a woman with a purpose. Her heart almost burst with happiness.

The wind rushed over her, pulling at her veil, and with a laugh she tugged it off and stuffed it into the pocket of her habit with her wooden cross. She really did need to change her clothing, but there was always something more pressing to spend her energy on. And besides, maybe she would need these clothes again, if the marriage was annulled. That thought did not comfort her as she thought it would and she felt some of her confidence drain away.

She would miss Évreux.

As she slowed, she noticed a couple of children in the trees. Doing exactly what she'd done many years before. Climbing trees and picking apples. She smiled at them and waved. They were hesitant at first but then waved back with wide smiles. A little boy dropped down from his branch and approached.

'Does your horse like apples, mistress?' The boy was painfully thin and his clothes looked as if they'd been repaired one too many times, the knees covered by threadbare patches.

'I think Luna likes apples very much.' She smiled brightly, determined to know his name by the time she left so that she could add him to her list of struggling families. If, of course, they weren't already on her list— she'd tried her best to check on everyone's condition. Maybe he was from one of the outer farms?

The boy carefully took an apple from the sack at his waist and walked forward with it held up high. Luna sniffed it eagerly. But then her ears pricked and her eyes darted to the side.

A thunder of hooves made the boy jump in fright and he dropped the apple as Jorund and his men rode into the clearing.

'Halt!' shouted Jorund, and his men stopped. The boy stopped too. He'd been about to flee with the rest of the children who'd bolted into the canopy at Jorund's arrival. Now he stood still, his body quivering in terror.

'What are you doing out here alone?' Jorund thundered at her, and a little shiver of fear snaked down her own spine.

'I thought I'd ride to the orchard and back. This young man was going to feed Luna an apple.' She looked towards the shaking boy and spoke softly, 'Weren't you, sweetheart?'

The boy fumbled in his bag, trying to grab another apple.

'The one on the floor is fine for Luna—she likes the bruised ones best. You eat the good ones.'

The boy dipped and picked up the dropped apple and offered it to Luna. The whole time he kept glancing nervously at the group of warriors. Her heart ached for him, but she refused to have her people live in fear a moment longer. Especially the children—she needed to show them that they had her protection and love. That as long as she was with them, she would ensure their safety.

For two winters. She stiffened at the thought. *Could she leave them then?*

Jorund jumped down from his horse and walked over, his voice a little softer now. He stared at her, his eyes bright with concern. 'Please don't go out without an escort in future. We were attacked on the road less than a week ago. I worry about your safety, *Amée*.' Her heart leapt but not with fear. It was the way he'd said her name, gently but with a bite of something else beneath. Something hot and wild that set her heart aflame.

'I'm sorry, I'd not thought to tell anyone.' Truthfully, she'd forgotten her position. As a novice she'd had no value, no reason to inform people of her plans. Her only restraint had been the need to complete her chores in a timely fashion, which she always failed to do.

'May I g-g-go, mistress?' whispered the boy beside her, and her heart broke. They still saw Jorund and his warriors as a threat, even with her there.

'Who's your family?' asked Jorund, and the poor boy looked as if he were about to cry.

'So I may thank them for your kind service,' she added, with a reproachful glare at Jorund. Which he chose to ignore.

'Odo is my father. Our farm is east of the orchard. Mistress, y-y-you used to say we could take some of the apples… We don't have many.' Fear washed off the boy in waves, despite the reassuring smile she tried to give him.

Jorund answered before she opened her mouth to speak. His tone casual, oblivious to the boy's distress. 'You may continue to do so. Valda, fetch a couple of rabbits for the boy's family.'

Valda hopped down from her mount, grabbed two fat rabbits from several hung at the back of her saddle and handed them to the boy, who took them with wide grateful eyes.

'Also…tell your family,' Jorund said. 'They are welcome to feast with us tomorrow night.' He looked at Amée. 'I thought we should hold a feast for all of Évreux. To thank them for their loyalty and hospitality to my warriors. What do you think, my lady?'

'I think that a fine idea,' she said, stunned and delighted by his suggestion. If he'd wanted to ingratiate himself with the local people a feast was a fine way of going about it.

'Thank you, master,' said the boy as he bobbed on wobbling feet and then ran off towards the east. She grinned as she heard him shout excitedly to his friends. They peeped out from their hiding places as he held up his two rabbits proudly and crowed about the feast.

For the second time that day, Jorund had surpassed her expectations. He'd shown kindness and patience when dealing with the boy. He'd made good on his promise to her people regarding their winter supplies. She was beginning to think she'd stumbled on a fairly decent man.

Ridiculous. It was his duty!

She looked towards the hunting party. 'I take it the hunt was successful.'

Besides the rabbits there were also three wild boars, as well as three deer strung up and carried on poles by men on foot.

He nodded, appearing distracted as he lightly stroked Luna. His hand sliding down the mare's neck and flank, brushing down the side of Amée's dress as he did so. His bronze arm ring with serpents entwined glinted in the soft dappled light. She couldn't feel much through the thick wool, but the intimacy and gentleness of the touch caused her stomach to flip.

'Shall we go home?' he asked quietly, and dumbly she nodded.

Jorund rode beside Amée at the head of the hunting party. He'd seen her riding up to the orchard at a full gallop and had feared for a moment she was being chased.

To his relief she'd only been racing for the enjoyment of it, and not out of necessity. Still, he'd be having words with the men he'd left in charge of the boats. She should not have been left to ride out alone.

'What are you thinking?' asked Amée beside him. He glanced over at her in surprise. There was no need for her to worry about his concerns.

'Nothing.'

'Really? You were frowning… I thought something might have been troubling you. I hope you're not too angry about me leaving without an escort. I promise not to do it again.'

She sounded so defeated.

Am I a prisoner? She'd asked him that and he'd said no; she must think he'd lied to her.

'You are allowed to come and go as you please. But the area is still not entirely secure. It might be best for you to have an escort when leaving the fort. I…' He paused, wondering if she would consider his next suggestion an insult. The Frankish women were so very different from the Norse. But he'd seen how she'd cowered the other night. How nervous she was of his wrath even now. He hated it. 'I wonder if you would like some training?'

'Training?'

'In weapons and single combat. I could teach you.'

She surprised him with a shout of laughter. '*What?* I mean… Well, I don't think I'd be very good at it. Besides, I thought you said you would keep me safe? Surely I don't need any more than you for my protection?' The look she gave him was a mixture of teasing amusement and trust. Unexpectedly his chest swelled with male pride at the apparent change in her view of him from conqueror to protector.

'And I will… But you might feel more confident when I'm not with you if you knew some techniques to protect yourself. You would no longer feel…vulnerable.'

She swallowed and looked at the ground, biting her lip as if she were struggling with two conflicting thoughts. 'But I could never do what you do. I'm not strong enough or big enough. What's the point of even trying?'

'Skill with a sword is more about your reach and speed than your strength. Besides, I was thinking more hand-to-hand skills or defence with a dagger. Just some simple techniques so that you could break free from an attacker and run to safety if you needed to.'

Amée choked back the laugh she'd tried and failed to hide. 'That's a fine thing for you to say. You're a mountain!'

Her amusement made him smile. He wished she laughed more, particularly with him. It brightened her whole face, especially when her curls flowed freely around her as they did now. She looked like a spirit of the forest, and earlier, if they'd been alone, he might have given in to his urge to pull her off her horse and kiss her. He'd had to satisfy himself with the briefest touch of her skirts. The rough wool against his calloused fingers had been enough to remind him that one day she might welcome him to her bed, if only he remained *patient*.

He focused his mind away from her skirts and back to their conversation. 'I have known shield maidens half my size who are as deadly in battle as I, or any other man. In some cases, better… Like Valda.' She frowned at that and he wondered for a moment if she disapproved of his female second. The Franks didn't believe that women should fight. Compelled to defend his friend's position, he added, 'Her strengths are that she is fast and flexible. Practising against her has improved my stamina and reflexes tenfold.' He noticed a flush bloom on Amée's neck as he spoke.

'Your stamina... Indeed,' she muttered, avoiding his eyes.

Was he missing something? He hoped she would realise he thought women just as capable and as intelligent as any man. It also helped that such training would mean they could spend more time together. He'd barely spoken to her in the last three days, so desperate he'd been to prove himself worthy of her trust that he'd focused solely on the repairs and feeding of the fort. 'Yes... And I learned how to fight from one of the greatest warriors who ever lived.'

That caught her interest. Curiosity sparkled in the amber flecks of her dark eyes as she turned in her saddle to face him. 'Your father?'

He stiffened. He'd learned nothing from that snake. Except how *not* to live.

Amée wasn't to know that though, and he softened his expression when he caught the alarm in her eyes. 'No. My mother, the greatest shield maiden who ever lived. She was fearless. When she died in battle I was lost.' He took a deep breath and filled his heart with the pride he'd always felt when he thought of her. He'd made mistakes, and lost his way, but he was sure she'd be proud of the man he was now.

'How old were you when she died?'

'I'd seen thirteen winters.'

Amée nodded sadly, concern shining in her eyes. 'I'm so sorry. I lost my mother around that age. A little younger, maybe. Afterwards I was sent to live at court with Princess Gisla. She was like a big sister to me and helped me through the grief... Who looked after you?'

She knew how he'd felt, knew that he'd searched for comfort too, except he'd chosen the wrong person to lean on. He found himself telling her the truth, something he'd not confessed to anyone else. 'Her shield maidens wanted me to stay with them. I see now that I should have. Instead, I joined with my father. Later I realised... he lacked honour. Thankfully, Rollo saw something in me, and he allowed me to join him and leave my father's war band for good.'

'I'm sorry,' she said gently, raw sympathy etched on her face. She'd read more into what he'd said than he'd thought he'd revealed. With a sigh she closed her eyes and lifted her face up to the sun, allowing the light to bathe her face. 'Sometimes fathers can be a great disappointment.' She turned to him and opened her eyes, and they seared him like a brand. 'But we are not our parents, no matter how much their actions shape us.'

He nodded, unable to speak. A knot had formed in his throat and his eyes burned with caged emotion. Her words were oddly comforting despite cutting so deeply into his heart and causing it to bleed. For someone so sweet, she understood suffering. He suspected her father was the one to make her afraid of angry men, and it made him want to rip the coward in two for betraying his child like that.

Amée looked ahead and after a moment said quietly, 'I will think about it—you teaching me to fight. But I am not Valda and I fear you will be wasting your time.'

He wanted to tell her that she could never waste his time. But his throat hurt from holding in the pain of his past and he found he could not speak another word the entire ride home.

She'd weakened him, as surely as if she'd cut him

down with an axe. He could not speak of the past with
Amée. It hurt too much, and some things were better
left buried.

He would not shame himself by opening up to her
again.

Not about that time at least.

The hall seemed less overwhelming tonight, although
it still looked a disorganised mess. But for some reason
Amée didn't feel quite so intimidated any more. Maybe
it was because Jorund seemed less frightening now that
she knew him a little better. Either way, her ease seemed
to be rubbing off on the rest of her people.

There was even some good-natured talking between
the warriors and the serfs. Amée hadn't gone so far as
to encourage relationships—she'd felt hypocritical doing
that considering she doubted her own marriage would
last long. But she had reassured them that no harm would
come to them under Jorund's protection.

She turned to look at Jorund beside her. He was watching Valda arm wrestle one of his warriors. He bellowed
with laughter when Valda won. She grinned and then
poured her drink over her opponent's head in triumph.
The man didn't seem bothered by the soaking and in
fact laughed heartily in response, flicking the mead at
her with his fingers.

Amée couldn't help but smile—the Norse had a
strange sense of humour, but she rather liked it. There
were no hidden agendas or politics when they spoke with
each other, or at least none that she'd noticed. Although
she felt a twinge of jealousy that it was Valda once again
who had her husband's attention…because it was *rude*,

she reassured herself. He shouldn't have a mistress under her nose like this.

For some reason she decided to start a conversation with him. Maybe it was because he'd been so open with her in the woods earlier that day.

She'd spent a good part of her time afterwards thinking about her husband's past. He'd lost his mother at a similar age to her, and when he'd spoken of his father... she wasn't sure, but she could have sworn she'd seen far more pain behind his eyes than he'd revealed in his words. Something else too: shame.

Well, she knew all about that.

With a deep breath she grasped for the most obvious thing to discuss without appearing to pry. 'Your name, Jötunnson. Is it your father's name or a nickname?' She'd heard some of the Norse favoured nicknames over family names.

Jorund turned to her, a look of surprise on his face. To be fair, she'd rarely spoken to him during the evening meals, and tended to leave quickly for bed as soon as she'd eaten.

'I refuse to take my father's name...' He paused. 'So, I took my mother's and twisted it slightly to fit a male,' he said with a warm smile she felt all the way to her toes. 'My mother was called Angrboda.'

At her blank look he added. 'Sorry, I should explain. Angrboda was one of the god Loki's wives. She was a Jötunn—a giantess. But...you should know... I am not from a noble Norse family.'

'Oh, I thought it was because—' she blushed '—because, you know, you're rather tall.' Amée prayed he didn't think her observation rude.

He laughed. 'Ah yes, because of my height and general fierceness. I'm sure that helped too.'

He'd said something similar beside the campfire when she'd been shocked by how young he was. She cringed now, realising how insulting that might have seemed to him. 'I'm so sorry. I have a habit of speaking without thinking, especially when I'm tired. It's got me into a lot of trouble over the years.'

His face sobered and he leaned a little closer towards her. 'It will never get you into trouble with me. I like a woman who speaks her mind.'

The chatter of the hall seemed to dim and all she could do was stare back into the vibrant blue of his eyes, unsure of what else to say.

Thankfully, he spoke first, his voice quiet and gentle as if he were patiently reeling her in like a fish on his hook. 'And you're right to say that. My mother's family were all very tall. It was why she was named after a giantess. My mother told me stories about her great-grandmother—she was seduced by a frost giant. She had to climb an oak tree to kiss him… Don't worry, you will never have to climb a tree to kiss me.'

The air was sucked from her lungs and spun in the air around her, making her hot and dizzy. Would he kiss her again? Or was he inviting her to kiss him? She felt herself falling ever so slightly forward, and she had to grip the table to steady herself.

She gave a light nervous laugh and then asked, 'Tell me more about your gods and giants. They sound…fascinating.'

He smiled indulgently and nodded. 'I will tell you anything and everything you wish to hear.'

He told her about his gods, myths and legends. It

mostly sounded fantastical, but there were times when she saw an odd similarity between his world and hers. Like the prophecy of a final reckoning which reminded her of the second coming of Christ. Except in Norse tradition, it would lead to a final battle between the gods rather than a judgement of souls. There were similarities also in phrasing, as with the god Odin being known as the 'all-father,' an omnipotent being who could see into the future and know all things at all times.

It made him and his people seem less strange to her somehow. More human.

They talked well into the evening. Eventually she noticed the hall was beginning to empty and it was long past time she should head to her bed.

'I should go.' She felt a little unsteady from the mead as she finally rose from her seat.

'Let me help you,' Jorund said with a lazy smile as he stood to his feet and took her by the elbow. This time she didn't argue as he led her to her chamber.

Outside her door she turned and bent her head back to look up at him. The action made her a little light-headed and she swayed on the balls of her feet. 'Goodnight... Jorund,' she said, and she wondered if he would try to kiss her again.

'Goodnight, Amée,' he said softly, then he turned away and walked back down the stairs to his chamber below.

Amée released the breath she'd been holding and her misty breath swirled in the torchlight. She was strangely disappointed that he'd not tried to kiss her.

Chapter Thirteen

The next day a dusty messenger arrived from Rouen.

'Greetings, my lord. I have a message from Count Robert of Northmannia,' the Frankish youth said, thrusting the scroll of parchment towards Jorund. He waited patiently, with a hard straight back, for Jorund to take it. Amée thought him a sweet-looking young man, if a little over-enthusiastic in his role as messenger. She would wager her morning meal that it was a new position and that his parents were very proud of him indeed.

Jorund frowned, and spoke between bites of his apple. 'From Rollo, then?'

'Uh… Yes…' said the messenger. He swallowed nervously, glancing in confusion at the rest of the men in the hall. They ate their morning meals uninterested in his presence, oblivious of his important news from their overlord. 'Except… He is to be called Count Robert… of Northmannia.' His words lost a bit of their power and conviction at Jorund's now scowling countenance. Amée thought the boy very naive to have corrected him like that, but thankfully Jorund ignored the insult.

'What does it say?' asked Jorund as he bit into the apple with a sharp snap that sounded like the breaking of a bone. Amée glanced at her husband and smothered a smile. Was he deliberately frightening the boy? And yet there was no anger in his expression, only mild boredom. He was probably distracted. He had much to do today. The hall roof needed to be completely repaired to allow for the feast later. The repairs were making slow progress, but she'd been delighted that the fort was looking more like its old self every day.

However, when Jorund caught her eye, he winked at her, and then behaved as if nothing had happened. Amée stifled a surprised giggle. She'd heard about that Norse custom last night. It was a nod to their god Odin, who'd given up an eye for 'secret knowledge,' and it was a playful gesture.

She'd loved listening to Jorund talk about the Norse religion and customs. Including the meaning behind a 'wink.' She felt comfortable around him now, as if by understanding his outlook on the world she subsequently knew him a little better too. Sometimes he could appear silent and fierce, but he was actually only being thoughtful. Considering his options carefully before taking any action. There was also a playful, dark humour to him as well. He took great pleasure in laughing at those who were proud and disdainful of others. She suspected it was because he'd had humble beginnings himself.

Despite the busy day ahead of him, it appeared Jorund was taking the time to tease this unsuspecting youth. Her husband had the strange Norse sense of humour, which she found she rather liked. It spoke to the devil within her that longed to do something wicked but was always too afraid of consequences to dare.

Saying that, today she also had a lot to do. Due to the feast, she had an almost never-ending list of chores to

Lucy Morris   141

complete, and she was eager to begin. If the messenger hadn't arrived, she might have left already to check on the work in the kitchen. As it was, they were both watching a youth fumble the delivery of a simple message.

He still held out the scroll and was now beginning to sweat. 'I don't know... I haven't read it, I swear.'

Jorund sighed wearily. 'But he must have told you.'

The boy blinked. 'Ah... Yes, he's... He's coming to visit.'

'When?' Jorund asked as he threw aside his apple core and ripped apart some bread. His hands were so large they shredded the loaf of bread with ease. The messenger stared at those deadly hands with a pale face.

Jorund continued to ignore the offered scroll, and the poor boy was trembling. 'Ah...before the next full moon?'

Unable to watch any longer, Amée reached forward and took the parchment from his hands. 'Thank you. Please warm yourself by the fire while we consider our response.' She looked at Jorund as the relieved messenger stumbled away. 'That was unkind,' she said softly.

'True, but he'll not be such an ass next time.' Jorund looked up from his bread with a smile, and she rolled her eyes, placing the scroll at his side. He nudged it back to her. 'Read it if you wish.'

'But it is addressed to you.'

'And I can't read it.' He shrugged.

'Oh, I see.' She tried not to appear shocked. Many people were unable to read, and he was a Norse warrior. He hadn't been born into nobility like she had. Besides, the Norse wrote in runes, and letters had no meaning to them. Still, she would hate to never know the joy of reading and writing. She had thoroughly enjoyed that aspect of monastic orders, especially the beautiful illuminations in the ancient texts. She added searching for her family's old books and documents to her list of chores.

The seal broke with a soft crack beneath her thumb and she unfurled the scroll to read it, recognising the handwriting of Princess Gisla immediately. 'It says Count Robert and Princess Gisla will be visiting us on a tour of their new realm. They are due to reach us before the next full moon. They hope to stay with us for a few days before moving on.'

Jorund huffed an acknowledgement and drained his cup. He looked as if he were about to leave and her nerves twisted until she was unable to hold back any longer. 'I'm sorry!' She couldn't let him go without saying it.

He'd just started to get to his feet when she'd blurted out her apology and he eased back onto the bench with a frown. 'What for?'

'For presuming you could read. You probably know runes better…'

He laughed dryly. 'It wouldn't matter if it were written in runes either. I still couldn't read it. Rollo knows that, so he always tells a messenger the words as well.' He frowned at the youth by the fire. 'Although this messenger was decidedly poor.'

She followed his gaze with a light smile. 'I think you intimidated him. Jorund Jötunnson.'

He rolled his eyes at that and she couldn't help the low laugh that escaped her lips. He smiled, his features softening as he watched her. For all Jorund's dark frowns and loud bluster, he still had not lashed out at her. No matter how much she teased or needled him.

It gave her the confidence to speak. 'Would you like to learn? All the nobles are taught in Francia, and there are many documents sent from court regarding taxes, so it's an important skill. If you'd like… I could teach you?' It wasn't until she'd spoken the words that she realised how much she wished he would say yes. She loved teaching. It was one of the things she'd miss most from her holy life, that and the peaceful gardens. But the idea of teaching Jorund?

A daydream of them huddled together, a single candle burning between them. His golden head lifted to hers with a warm expression of gratitude and admiration. Another wink…

He tilted his head and stared at her with an unwavering gaze.

Had she done something? Sighed wistfully? *Oh, sweet heavenly father!* She hoped not.

His next words were carefully considered. 'We will pay no taxes to your court. I deal directly with Rollo as all his chiefs will.'

She felt the press of her father's boot upon her neck as she remembered the contract. Jorund was wrong if he thought the Frankish nobility would give up this land so easily. Fleetingly she realised that her father must have known Jorund couldn't read. He tended to learn all he could about his enemies.

Jorund leaned closer towards her. 'But…if you let me teach you to defend yourself, I will allow you to teach me to read. How about that?'

'I fear you will be the better student,' she replied with a shy smile.

'We can begin tonight.'

'We have the feast tonight,' she reminded him.

'I'm sure we can sneak away to your chamber at some point.'

His words made a fire light within her belly. She nodded as the glowing ember of excitement started to blaze. She liked the idea of spending time alone with him, which was odd in itself.

With a regretful sigh he rose. 'However, I must begin work if we're to be ready in time. The roof in particular needs a lot of work.'

She nodded quickly. 'As must I... Oh, I will need to pay the blacksmith—' Before she'd finished speaking, he dropped a purse on the table in front of her.

'Buy whatever you need. Inside is also the key to the silver chest in my room. As my wife its contents are yours to manage.'

'Oh, I didn't mean that!' she cried, horrified that he might think she was demanding such a thing.

'It's Norse custom,' he said firmly, before adding with a shrug, 'And I would feel more comfortable leaving it in your hands anyway.'

'Oh, well—thank you.' She stared at the purse as he walked away. She'd never been allowed such independence before. She picked it up and gently opened it. Inside there was more than enough silver to pay the blacksmith as well as a thick iron key.

He'd handed her his fortune as if it were a burden he was glad to shed. She stared after his retreating broad shoulders and wondered why he trusted her so readily when she'd done nothing to warrant it.

In two winters, the marriage would most likely end and she would return to the nunnery. Which was what she wanted, wasn't it? She only needed to continue to re-sist him...and even if—for some reason—she couldn't, the likelihood that she was as unlucky as her mother in pregnancy was high, and then Jorund would probably set her aside anyway.

Two winters and this would all be over.

Every day she wondered a little more if that's what she really wanted.

Jorund stared at his hall with proud satisfaction. It heaved with bodies and laughter. Amée had managed to space the benches and tables at diagonals. Everyone could move around with ease, while also having plenty of room to sit and eat. It also meant that the groups of warriors and locals were forced to mix. Serfs and farmers sat elbow to elbow with his warriors. He'd even seen some of the younger women laughing and joking with a few of them and it was like a beacon of hope for the future.

Music played from a few lyres and drums that the townspeople had brought with them. The tables were decorated with wild flowers that perfumed the air sweetly and glowed with life in the torchlight. The mead and food flowed from the kitchen in a constant stream of steaming platters, and everyone was in high spirits.

This was what he'd fought so long and hard for.

This was what his mother had wanted for him.

He only wished she'd lived long enough to see it.

He looked up at the fresh, hastily completed roof of his hall and lifted the cup towards the ceiling. '*Skol, Modir,*' he whispered, before taking a sip.

As he lowered his cup, he realised Amée had turned slightly in her seat and was watching him. She raised her cup mimicking his salute to the ceiling before taking a sip herself. Then she gave him a bright smile and the dark clouds cleared from his mind as if they'd never been there.

A flash of scarlet on her hand caught his eye. 'You had it resized.'

Lowering the cup to the table, she brushed her fingers over the jewelled ring self-consciously. 'Yes, I know you said you would arrange it. But I was passing the blacksmith anyway—'

'I'm glad,' he interrupted, taking her hand in his own. 'I'm glad you're wearing my ring.' It felt like another step towards her acceptance of him, and it was an unexpected and perfect addition to his first feast as the Lord of Évreux.

He raised her hand to his lips. He moved slowly, deliberately, as if he were stalking the most precious and flighty of prey. One wrong move and she could bolt away, and all his hard work would be lost. Gently he kissed the back of her hand.

Wide-eyed she watched him, her eyes never leaving his, and when she bit tenderly into her bottom lip, a surge of victory rushed through his veins, as sweet and heady as any honeyed mead. He'd longed for a family of his own ever since his mother's death.

Maybe with Amée he could build the life of his dreams? A life of peace and companionship, children of his own... Love. He smiled at the fanciful turn of his thoughts.

Tonight was the best night of his life and it wasn't even over yet.

'Shall we go to your bedchamber...for the lessons?' Unable to resist teasing her, he tried not to smile at the alarm and blush on her face.

'Are you sure? Won't...' Her blush deepened as she looked past his shoulder at something. However, he wouldn't have cared if the roof had caved in; he wouldn't risk looking away from his wife for anything. It could potentially break the connection between them he'd fought so hard to forge. Her eyes came back to his, and they looked troubled as she whispered, 'Won't Valda mind?'

'*Valda?* Why should I care what she thinks?' he repeated, a little confused as to why his wife cared what Valda thought about them slipping away. Maybe she worried about their absence from the feast? 'Besides, she's more than capable of handling any problems that might arise.'

He brushed his thumb over her hand once more. A gentle reminder of his touch. Her eyes dropped to the sensation, and she gave a small nod of agreement. As they rose and quietly left the boisterous hall, he'd never felt more triumphant.

Jorund held her hand until they reached Amée's bedchamber. Only releasing her hand so that he could light the fire and some candles. She had a lot of candles, and she hoped he wouldn't think her odd, or ask about them. Next, he moved the table closer to the fire and pushed two chairs side by side in front of it.

While he prepared the room, she went and picked up the little box she'd earlier filled with supplies for this exact purpose. Although she wasn't entirely sure if the evening was going to turn out as she'd planned.

What did he want from her *really*? And what…more worryingly…did she want?

She was still recovering from the intense moment they'd shared in the feasting hall. Had it all been in her mind? She'd been touched by the tender gesture he'd made in memory of his mother—if she'd guessed the meaning of his words correctly, he'd been toasting her.

It was sweet.

But when he'd taken her hand, it had been anything but

sweet. The way he'd spoken had almost seemed *sugges-tive*, as if they were sneaking away to do something sin-ful…like kiss? She'd spent far too many hours as it was daydreaming about their last kiss. Memorising the touch of his lips, the slide of his tongue, the grip of his arms. A wicked part of her hoped he would kiss her again… But wouldn't that encourage more?

And hadn't she encouraged him enough? He'd noticed the ring—she still wasn't entirely sure why she'd had it resized. She'd told herself the ring was a gesture of col-laboration. One that she owed him after all his kind ges-tures and patience with her. It genuinely seemed as if all he wanted in life was peace and prosperity. How could she argue with that?

And yet he'd cast aside Valda without a moment's hesitation. She'd seen the hurt look in the other woman's eyes when he'd kissed her hand, and she'd hated being the cause of it. Even if she was morally right as his wife to accept his affection.

Or was she?

She'd still not confessed about the two-year contract, and even her willingness to teach him to read was tar-nished by her guilt at having kept that information from him.

Jorund sat at the table and waited for her to join him. She placed the box down and sat beside him. Their sides brushing against each other as she did so. Had he delib-erately placed them so closely together? It felt as if he were trying to seduce her, but she'd never been seduced so she couldn't be entirely sure.

She fidgeted and cleared her throat noisily before speaking. 'I thought I could teach you the common tongue first.' The mention of tongues made images flash before her eyes and she squirmed a little in her seat. 'The missive from Rollo was written in it, and it's a language you already speak fluently.'

He shifted beside her. His big body so warm she was already hot and flustered, and yet she couldn't move away. She tried to focus on the teaching methods she'd learned during her time at the nunnery. She'd carefully planned how to teach him, but now her meticulous plans were fluttering away like feathers in the wind.

She still couldn't believe he'd agreed to be taught, especially by her. Her father—in fact, most men—would have been insulted that a woman would even dare to think she knew more than a man. But the fact that Jorund had been raised by a strong shield maiden had given her the confidence to at least offer.

'They are both my mother tongue.' He shrugged, dismissing his skill lightly.

'Later I can teach you Latin if you wish, as it's the language mainly used at court and in books.'

He didn't even try to hide his groan. 'Urgh, not the dead language that priest spouted at our wedding?'

'Afraid so. It can be quite helpful…' she said, although her voice lacked conviction. The mention of their wedding reminded her of him kissing her and she absently fanned the spreading heat at her neck.

'You have a lot of candles in here… Maybe we should open the window? Let some air in. It's a mild night, and the stars may give us some more light to see by.'

'No, it's cloudy—there'll be no light,' she said dismissively, hoping he wouldn't insist any further. 'And stop avoiding the inevitable. You said I could teach you.'

'Yes, and in exchange I'll teach you how to defend yourself,' he said, and although his face lacked a smile, she swore she saw a glint of mischief in his eyes. It made her insides melt like the candles that surrounded them.

She coughed, trying to focus. How had he made teaching her how to defend herself sound so...carnal? 'Well, let's first start by looking at the different letters and the sounds they make.'

They didn't work for long. Amée knew from experience that learning something new, especially when you were older, took time and perseverance. She was pleased that not only was Jorund willing to learn, but he seemed to enjoy the challenge too. She only had some charcoal and old linen as writing tools at the moment, but she was determined to root around the fort tomorrow to find something better.

Maybe even the old books might be tucked away somewhere? She'd ask Beatrice. Perhaps not everything had been lost in the raids?

'Now, it's your turn,' Jorund said.

Her mind flickered like a candle as he rose from his seat, her body so aware of him it reacted at his slightest movement. He pushed the table and chairs to the side of the room, clearing space for them. Strangely she felt as if the room was shrinking rather than opening up. She could think of nothing more than that he would soon be touching her.

She shook her head to clear her mind.

It was training, that was all!

He might not even wish to bed her! Had she considered that? She might have completely misunderstood his behaviour from earlier.

'Where do we begin?'

'Firstly, let's try some techniques for getting out of a hold.' His hand struck like a viper and grabbed her by the wrist in the blink of an eye. Instinctively she shrank backwards, curling inwardly with shock and fear.

He moved his other hand to gently caress her wrist and still her movement. 'I'm sorry. I shouldn't have frightened you like that.' She peeked up at him warily and he released his hold with a curse. He ran his hand through the short blond hairs on the side of his head with a frown.

She took a step towards him and straightened her spine. 'I'm fine. How should I get out of that hold?'

A smile tugged at the corners of his mouth, suggesting something devilish. 'You make your attacker drop their hold.'

'But how?'

'You cause them pain. A fast attack is the best form of defence.'

She frowned. *Was he mocking her?* 'I'm not exactly a strong warrior who could hurt a man like you, am I?'

'There are a few places you can hurt a man like me *very* easily. A quick hard kick or knee to the groin is the best option. Although a man might expect that. While a stamp on the foot can surprise your opponent long enough for you to add the knee.' He demonstrated the movement on an invisible attacker. 'Now you try.'

She did, and to his credit he didn't laugh at her weak attempt, or the way she rocked from lack of balance.

He rested his hands on his hips and swayed from side to side gently. 'Find your balance.' She stared at his narrow hips for a little longer than would be considered appropriate. Blushing, she grasped without thinking for something, anything, to say. 'You do that a lot... When you're thinking or uncertain... Sway from side to side.'

He blinked with surprise and then smiled. 'I suppose I do. It's to check my balance. As a boy I grew up fast, and sometimes I struggled to keep up with the changes in my body. Clumsiness can get you killed, so I developed checking my balance regularly as a habit to help me in battle.'

'You must have fought when you were very young,' she said quietly, her voice full of concern.

How terrible to be so young in battle that your body is not even fully grown?

Jorund ignored her comment and demonstrated the movement again. 'Harder jabbing. Down with the heel. Then up with the knee. You may want to grab hold of your attacker's arms to increase your power and aim.'

Amée took hold of his arms. 'Like this?' She looked up at him with wide, trusting eyes.

He'd thought about her ever since he'd left that morning. He'd pushed himself harder, worked tirelessly to fix the roof and give back at least part of the home she'd once loved.

And she did love Évreux. Loved the people, and the land of her home. She loved with such an open and giving heart he felt compelled to please her.

She gave kindness and joy wherever she went, and she was loved in return.

What had he ever done but bring misery and suffering to Francia?

How could he win their loyalty, when people such as him had hurt them so terribly in the past?

Amée was his only hope for bridging a peace between his warriors and the serfs of Évreux. For them to even consider him as their lord and protector, they would need a mother figure, someone they believed in. Princess Gisla was wise to suggest the match, and he was grateful to her for it.

Now with Amée holding his arms and looking up into his eyes, he felt as if he'd won a war. She trusted him; she'd told her people to trust in him and he'd not failed her. They were building a home together, a relationship—if her acceptance of him in her bedchamber was any indicator.

Maybe she would trust him enough to allow him to kiss her tonight? Not on the hand, but on the lips? He wanted that; he wanted to seduce her, to see the passionate warmth in her eyes come ablaze at his touch.

He leaned down and stared at her pink lips. He couldn't resist, brushing his against hers in question. They were warm and soft, and they parted on a light gasp, her fingers gripping his forearms more tightly. Her eyes closed and her lips parted a little further. He pressed closer, his mouth covering hers so that they shared the same hot breath. She moaned as his tongue slid against hers and her eyes opened mid-kiss, her pupils wide with surprise, and what he hoped desperately was desire.

In all his years of raiding, he'd seen no gold or treasure brighter than the flecks of amber in Amée's dark eyes. His hands curved around her hips and squeezed the lush curve of her bottom. She jerked in surprise at his shameless touch.

The bang to his foot was firmer than he would have expected. It crunched his toes and made him rear away instinctively. Then her knee connected with his groin, and he saw only the lightning flash of blinding pain.

He crumpled in front of her, clutching desperately to protect himself from further injury as he wheezed and grunted in pain.

So much for seduction.

'I'm so sorry!' she gasped, falling to her knees in front

of him. 'I'm so, so, so sorry! I thought it was a test! I… I… I thought you would move!'

'So…did…I…' He grunted, slowly clawing back the ability to think and breathe without wincing. 'You did well… I think…that's all for tonight.'

It was probably for the best. Had he forgotten? She was a virgin and he was a giant!

Slow steps, patience. He could wait. It would be worth it in the long run.

She would be worth it.

'Goodnight, Amée,' he said with a reassuring smile as he shuffled away with as much dignity as he could muster.

'Goodnight, Jorund.'

As he opened the door, he turned back to her. She looked so embarrassed. He couldn't leave without offering some form of reassurance. 'You did well tonight. You are an intelligent and formidable woman, Amée. I'm proud to call you wife.' He gave her a broad smile and a wink that caused her rosy blush to deepen to bright scarlet. He took heart that amongst the blushes there was also a smile of pleasure teasing at the corner of her lips.

It was enough.

Today had still been the greatest day of his life.

For the first time in a long time, he welcomed tomorrow.

Chapter Fourteen

'**O**h! I'm sorry! I didn't mean to disturb you!' gasped a mortified Amée as she stared at her half-naked husband.

She was surprised to see him in his bedchamber at this late hour of the morning. Although she conceded that she, too, had been getting up later these past few days. Their evening lessons, which had started on the night of the feast, had been running for almost a week now. Each night they burned more candles than the night before.

Both the reading and the self-defence lessons were exhilarating, and they seemed to talk more too. About their plans and concerns regarding the town and fort. An easy friendship had begun to develop between them and she had to admit she was flattered he no longer spent quite as much time with Valda. Leaving her in the hall each night to spend his evenings alone with his wife.

Maybe he went to Valda after their meetings? A wicked part of her hoped not, and even dared to imagine he might put Valda aside altogether.

He'd not kissed her again since that first lesson, although there'd certainly been moments when she'd thought he might. There'd even been a couple of times when she'd longed to press her own lips against his and end the unbearable waiting.

She'd had another sleepless night in which she'd tossed and turned fruitlessly, imagining how he would react if she did kiss him, so she'd decided to throw her restless energy at something more substantial. To search the last possible hiding places of the fort for anything that might have survived the raids. There was only one place left to look and that was in Jorund's bedchamber.

'Did you need me?' Jorund asked.

Naked from the waist up, he stood by the open window, shaving. Amée's mouth dried at the sight of him, and she wet her lips. She should leave, but her feet turned to rock and she couldn't move...only watch.

He held a viciously sharp blade to his throat and was using it with slow precise strokes. The sides of his head were freshly shaved too, the skin smooth, where it had once been rough with stubble. A soapy bowl of water was on the table in front of him. A polished plate leaned against the wall. He only glanced at it occasionally, suggesting he was well practised in the art of shaving without one.

'I...' Amée wasn't sure what to say, she was so distracted by the view. It was not often that she could stare at him without him noticing. Usually those blue hawk-like eyes of his took note of everything she did.

She walked forward fascinated. What would he do if she joined him by the window and stroked her fingers up his bare chest...like she wanted to do? Would he kiss her again? Wrap his strong arms around her, pull her close, brush his lips over hers once more? In that tantalising and intoxicating way of his?

Her cheeks grew hot at the thought. Later she would blame her behaviour on her lack of sleep.

It had only been a few hours since he'd left her room, but in the light of day, with his torso bare, he looked magnificent, and all her longing rushed forward in a wave. The muscles and breadth of his chest made her heart quicken and her blood sing with awareness. He was beautiful, breathtaking…and hers. All hers, if only she reached out and—

'Is something wrong, Amée?' he asked, glancing at her. His eyes widened in surprise at how closely she stood beside him. He lowered the blade and placed it on the table. His eyes searching her face for answers she couldn't give.

'This used to be my room,' she blurted out, her mind completely empty of anything better to say.

'It's a good room,' he said carefully, as if he were trying to judge the weight of her words. 'Smaller…because it's divided into two separate rooms. It's better that you are upstairs in the larger room.'

She glanced longingly at the view. She couldn't see the tree from this level. 'I suppose. My mother used to sleep in the other room.'

'I see.'

'Have you always shaved your beard?' she asked curiously as a mad thought raced across her mind. She'd wondered fleetingly if he did it for her.

'Yes,' he replied, turning back to wipe away the last of the soap with a nearby towel.

She nodded, dampening down her ridiculous disappointment, and chastising herself for daring to presume such a thing.

Amée allowed her mind to wander, and as she watched

the linen towel smooth over his skin, she wished she could be that cloth. A vision of herself rubbing up against him like a cat filled her mind and she shook her head to dislodge it.

What was wrong with her?

Most Norsemen seemed to favour some form of facial hair; it was what set them apart. Unable to restrain her curiosity she asked, 'Why?'

'Because I would look like my father if I didn't.' His answer was simple and honest, but discouraged any further questions. She took the information and squirrelled it away with all the other little details she'd discovered about him.

It seemed as if her curiosity only increased with every new piece of knowledge she'd learned about him.

What would he do if she kissed him? If she jumped up, wrapped her arms around his neck and pressed her mouth against his. Would he be shocked? Pleased? Her heart began to race as she imagined his tongue sliding intimately against hers.

'Is there something you wanted from here?' he asked, and she blushed furiously, realising she'd been daydreaming again.

How many times had she been scolded for it at the nunnery? Except, this time, she'd been doing something far more sinful. Daydreaming about kissing him, and about him kissing her back. Not because they were married and he needed an heir. But because he wanted to. Because he wanted her.

'I was wondering about my hiding place,' she said, before she had to admit the real reason for her continued presence. She should have left immediately and returned when he was gone for the day. But then she'd have missed the sight of him shaving, and that would have been a terrible pity.

'Hiding place?' He frowned.

She blinked, realising that she might have to tread more carefully in future. Some men didn't like to discover they'd missed something so obvious. 'Yes… Beatrice said the old steward might have hidden some things here…during the raids. I'm hoping something still remains. Although it's been ransacked several times, so there may be nothing.'

The large shelves were still in their place in the corner, although they were no longer filled with the trinkets of her youth. It would be easy for her to move them as they were so bare. She walked over and pushed. The shelves slid along the floor marking out their lack of use by creating tiny riverbanks of dust on the stone floor. A candle of hope lit within her heart. Maybe some things had been saved?

The short narrow opening was revealed. She turned to get a torch, but instead bumped into a wall of muscle.

Jorund's solid golden chest.

Oh, Lord! Had her lips kissed the light bronze of his chest hair? Mortally embarrassed she stumbled back a couple of steps.

He seemed unaffected by the blunder, reaching out to steady her by the arm, while distractedly he looked into the dark space beyond. 'A secret room?'

'More of a cupboard, really. My great-grandfather liked to include tricks in his designs. He designed some of the palaces and abbeys built for the Carolingian kings… but that was a long time ago.' It made her sad to think of her country's demise. He let her go and she missed the warmth of his fingers keenly.

'I see.' Although by the turned-down shape of his mouth, she suspected he didn't approve of her great-grandfather's mischievous nature.

'And you hid there as a child?' he continued, peeking into the darkness and cobwebs.

She looked away, trying to keep her tone light. 'Children like such things. Their own secret adventures.' She tried not to think of what she'd actually been hiding from.

Angry words and fists.

She glanced up and he gave a slow nod of acceptance. 'I'll light a torch.'

'Thank you.'

It wasn't long until Jorund was back, handing her a torch. Entering the darkness, she was delighted to see three large chests placed against the back wall of the small space. She turned away, moving the torch along the old stone until she saw the iron holder. She slotted the torch in place and moved back to the chests now that her hands were free.

'Now, let's see what remains? Shall we?'

She knelt and lifted the lid on the first chest. Inside it were her mother's gowns carefully wrapped in waxed linen. 'Could you help me bring these out?' she asked tentatively. 'If...you're not needed on any other business, that is.'

'I'm not,' he answered simply. Bending down into an awkward hunch, he squeezed into the narrow space with a grunt. He grabbed the chest and dragged it out with one light tug of his arm.

She lifted the lid on the next chest and squealed. 'Just as I hoped!' Her fingers fluttered over the delicate contents for a moment before she closed the lid quickly. She didn't want the damp air to damage what was inside any more than it had already.

Jorund returned. 'Would you like me to bring that one out too?'

'Please!' She smiled, leaning out of the way so that he could drag it out and into the light. 'Maybe you could bring them all out? There's only one more.' She peeked inside the last chest. There was some silverware thrown in as if in a hurry.

She sent up a little prayer to the steward who'd died during the first raids. It had been kind of him to save what he could. It was a consideration her father did not deserve. Then again, maybe the steward had been afraid of what would have happened if he'd not at least attempted to protect his lord's possessions.

She knew from experience that didn't bear thinking about.

She walked out of the alcove so that Jorund could grab the last chest.

She was surprised to see that he'd not opened any of them as yet. The Norse were known for their love of treasure, and she'd just revealed three chests of extravagant wealth. Except Jorund wasn't a *normal* Viking. He'd handed her the key to his own silver chest days ago. She'd opened it once, gasped at its impressive contents and had quickly closed it again.

Deciding the best course of action was to be as open and honest as Jorund had been about his own wealth, she opened the last chest first. The one filled with silverware. He looked at it with mild interest.

Then she opened the chest of her mother's gowns and jewellery.

'You should wear them,' he said. She tried not to take

offence. After all, she was still wearing her old novice habits and veils every day. She'd started making a few gowns, but preferred working in the gardens or talking with Jorund in the evenings rather than sewing. But he was right, she should really be dressing better as the Lady of Évreux. It just hadn't seemed like a priority. It would be nice to wear a few of her mother's gowns. It would remind her of the happier days with her...when she'd been more herself.

Finally, with trembling fingers, she reached for the chest she valued the most highly. As she lifted the lid Jorund stepped forward, his body so close to hers that she could feel its warmth and smell the soapy musk of his skin.

The contents looked surprisingly intact. Many of the scrolls were carefully wrapped in waxed linen and there were herbs inside to repel insects. They'd probably been packed away long before the raids, when she'd left for court.

Jorund's shadow covered the chest. She heard him huff with disappointment when he saw the contents.

As if he'd insulted one of her closest friends, Amée turned on him with a disapproving scowl. Had none of her lessons got through to him about the importance of such precious texts? 'Don't look at them like that! These are the books and scrolls of my family! They are beautiful and precious...some were illuminated by the Byzantine scholars in Persia. There are manuscripts from the Holy Land which hold history and faith in every page. They were made by people whose names are long forgotten in memory, but look, these still remain! There may even be the designs of this building from my great-grandfather's time. With them we can repair the southern hall to its full glory.' She jabbed a finger into his bare chest, shocked at her own breathlessness but unable to stop herself. 'They may not seem like much to you, but they are worth more than gold or silver. We must protect and cherish them. They have more value to me than your hoard of treasure. They are meaningful, and beautiful, and most of all *important*!'

He stared down at her, his expression blank, and she realised then how desperately she wanted him to understand. To value the same things she valued. To want the same things in life that she wanted. *To want her...*

Her chest was heaving with the effort to remain calm and her fists were clenched so tightly at her sides she was afraid she would burst at the slightest provocation. 'I... I...feel *passionately* about them.'

He continued to stare at her, his blue eyes as bright as the sapphires that winked from the silverware. Then to her utter surprise he swooped down to kiss her. He grabbed her by the waist and dragged her up against his body, crushing her against him.

Her heart hammered against her ribs and she found herself clinging to him and tugging him closer. The urgency to feel his heart beating against hers was almost unbearable. Her arms wrapped around his neck, dragging him towards her as she'd imagined so many times over the last few days. Her lips pressed back against his, already open and ready for his invading tongue.

She moaned as his body silently obeyed everything she'd craved.

His hands moved to cup her bottom as he pressed her hard against the wall, hitching one of her legs up and onto his hip. Instinctively she wrapped her other leg around him, desperate to ease the sudden ache between her thighs. He groaned and pushed his hips against her core. Something hard rubbed against her and she cried out at the sensation.

His free hand roamed over her body, cupping her face as their tongues entwined, pulling off her veil and throwing it to the floor. Then one of his hands stroked up from her waist and gently squeezed her breast. His lips were hot and fierce against her mouth. As if he wanted to consume her entirely. Take her body, mind and breath all at once.

She gladly abandoned herself to him. The embers that had glowed over the last few days between them burst into an inferno of flames that devoured her whole.

'Do you want me?' he gasped, between kisses.

He was fumbling with something at the back of her neck and belatedly she realised it was the ties of her habit.

'It's…a…difficult…knot,' she managed to gasp between the press of his mouth and the panting of her own breath.

With a curse he growled, 'No more of these ugly things!' And he grabbed hold of the rough habit and coarse linen shift beneath it. Then with one savage rip he split the material in two, straight down the front of her chest.

He groaned as her breasts were revealed and bowed his head to taste them. The sensation of her tight nipple in his hot mouth caused a jolt of astonishment to shudder through her veins. Unable to control her thoughts or actions, her head rocked back in a blissful gasp of abandon.

Cool air kissed her thighs as he dragged up her skirts and squeezed the feverish flesh of her hips beneath his rough fingers. The contrasting touch of his silky mouth and his calloused hands was too much for her and she bowed under him, wanting more of both.

A shout from the stairwell interrupted them. 'Jorund! Surely you're not still abed?'

Jorund looked down at Amée's shredded clothing in horror as if he were waking from a dream. He paled and, within the next gasping breath, dropped his hands from her body and ran to the door.

Amée grabbed the wall to steady herself as she was cast away from his arms. Light-headed she stumbled a little. Dragging in desperate breaths as she frantically tried to cover herself with what remained of her habit.

Jorund was almost at the door as Valda climbed the last stair, but it was clear by the surprise on her face that she'd seen both Amée and Jorund, as well as their mutual state of undress.

'I'll be there shortly!' he barked, his voice echoing off the stone walls as he slammed the door shut in her face.

He braced both arms against the closed door and dipped his head, his shoulders moving with the labour of his breath. Shame and humiliation suffocated her as she tried to tug the bodice of her tattered habit back together. He'd been caught with her and he obviously regretted it.

She watched him with growing anxiety, and when he finally twisted away from the door, he refused to look at her.

'I am *so* sorry,' he muttered as he grabbed his tunic and boots. He tugged them on quickly, his lips thin and his jaw clenched.

He was angry.

Was he angry at her—because he'd been caught by his lover with his wife?

It made sense in a strange sort of way. And Amée felt utterly wretched because of it.

He left the room, quickly banging the door behind him as he went.

Amée stood there for several minutes wondering what she'd done to deserve such passion and such censure. Wasn't he the one who had started it? She'd merely been doing her duty by accepting him.

But that wasn't true, was it? She'd wanted to kiss him too.

More.

Cold dread washed through her, causing a sob to escape her lips. She'd wanted him *more*, just as her mother had always wanted and loved her father *more*.

What had she done?

Chapter Fifteen

Amée looked up from the vegetable patch she'd been weeding to take in the ever-changing view of the fort.

It looked more secure now. A wooden curtain wall had been erected around the old stone villa, and included a large heavy gate at its entrance. The doors were currently open, allowing free movement, as they'd used to when she'd been a child. But these defences looked far stronger, taller and more substantial. A palisade was built high up around the curtain wall allowing Jorund's guards to walk along it and look out for miles. The tower of her room was slightly higher. She should have felt imprisoned now that the defences were complete, but she didn't.

It gave her peace of mind. No raider would see Évreux as an easy target any more. Her people no longer had to fear constant attack. The fort was so much bigger than it was previously, and it offered the town greater protection and shelter.

Simply put, Jorund's rule had improved Évreux.

The villa had always been a slowly crumbling relic of a time of majesty and wealth long gone. Now it felt as if new life were being breathed back into the stone. The imposing wooden additions adding a golden warmth and security that had previously been missing.

She spotted Jorund on the roof of one of the new half-built halls. The sun beat down on his bare back as he sawed through a log. His muscles moved with the rhythm of his saw and she found herself admiring him.

He was a huge bear of a man. Even the Norseman beside him looked like a green youth in comparison. And yet, he moved with precision and grace, as he leaned down precariously to exchange the saw for a hammer with another man on the level below. She let out a long sigh as she watched his abdomen crunch and flex with the movement. The sight did strange things to her insides, making her feel warm and languid, as well as causing a low ache within her.

She wet her lips, remembering his kisses. The first two had been so tender and gentle, with only the smallest bite of passion beneath. The last one had been…overwhelming. She'd surrendered to it. Would have allowed him to do… She still wasn't certain what…

Key in a lock.

Well, whatever it was, it could lead to children, of that she was certain, and she didn't want that. It would have ended all of her hopes to return to the nunnery. And she wanted to return to the nunnery. To forget Jorund and Valda. To leave the mad passion he incited within her, and live peacefully once again.

Didn't she? Of course, she did! She couldn't live with the heel of a boot against her neck. But would life as Jorund's wife really be so bad?

With a sigh she looked down at her mud-covered hands.

She wasn't sure what she wanted any more.

That kiss in his chamber! It had been…*astonishing.*

Passionate kisses that had caused her body to bow and mould against his. All thought had disappeared on the summer breeze, leaving only heady heat and lust in its wake. She'd wanted him. Wanted him so badly that she would have allowed him to do *anything* to her.

That alone was terrifying to accept. Her desperation, her own lust, had been so all consuming she'd not even minded when he'd torn her clothing… No, she'd *welcomed* it.

She'd not wanted him to stop, had instead mourned the loss of his big body pressed against hers as soon as he'd run for the door. How *humiliating* that had been! Even more humiliating was the ache she'd felt long after he'd left, as if her body still yearned for him.

As the days of her marriage passed by, her belief that she could return to her old life seemed more and more ridiculous. The roles and duties as the Lady Évreux came easily to her. Far easier than the role of a devout novice had. She was always busy and surrounded by friends. She didn't miss the constant prayers, or the draughty dormitory.

Maybe the abbess had been right. That there was another path in life meant for her.

Rather than rejecting her marriage and waiting for it to end, maybe she should accept it? And quickly, especially if she did struggle to conceive children like her mother. Further indecision might actually ruin her future chance for happiness…or contentment at least.

But…could she accept Valda's place in her home?

Possibly… She hoped she was stronger than her mother. At least Jorund's infidelity had been clear from the start. She was braced against it, she reasoned. It could not hurt her in the same way, because she would not let it.

She peeked up in the direction of her husband and was surprised to see he was looking straight at her. He gave her a hesitant wave and she returned it.

Immediately she felt foolish and stupid for drawing attention to herself. Staring at her husband was becoming an embarrassing habit. Maybe her sudden thirst and stomach ache were due to lack of sustenance? It was not even midday, but she decided to go to the kitchen for some bread or fruit to keep her going until the evening meal.

She got up and dusted her hands off on her apron, then headed towards the feasting hall. Deliberately she avoided looking at Jorund as she walked.

As she entered the hall, she heard a bang and a clatter from the kitchen. As if something big had been knocked over. Amée hurried her step, presuming that Emma or Beatrice had dropped something by mistake and would welcome her help to clear up the mess.

As she walked in she was distracted by the sight of a stone pestle and mortar rolling towards her. Presumably it had been knocked off the table, scattering herbs everywhere as it fell. It must have made the noise because it had come halfway to the door by the time she entered.

Then another movement caught Amée's eye at the back of the room. Curiosity quickly turned to horror when she saw that Emma was being held down by a man on one of the tables.

The man was one of Jorund's warriors—Skarde, she thought his name was. One of his grubby hands covered Emma's mouth, while the other was fumbling under her skirts. Emma was struggling but he was a big man. Obviously using all of his weight and brute strength to pin her down tight, as he roughly tried to force himself on her.

'Get off her!' shouted Amée.

He looked up and stilled, then snorted with amusement. 'I'm doing as your lord and husband commands! I suggest you leave unless you wish to join in?' To Amée's outrage he didn't release Emma, and she heard a pitiful whimper from beneath his hand.

Jorund had commanded this?

Fire raced down her spine. She was the mistress of Évreux.

She would not allow it!

She would *never* allow it!

'I said get off her!' Amée grabbed the mortar bowl from the floor and threw it at the warrior. It sailed through the air in a perfect arc, and clipped Skarde on the forehead with a dull thud. He immediately slumped to the floor clutching his bleeding forehead with a cry of pain.

Emma took the opportunity to leap off the table and ran weeping into Amée's arms.

'What's happening here! Skarde?' shouted Jorund as he and Valda raced into the room.

'You said to mix with them. Breed with them!' howled Skarde, still clutching his head. Jorund took in the scene with wide eyes. Then understanding dawned across his face and he paled.

'You *did* encourage your men in this?' She felt outraged and betrayed. 'After everything?'

'I did not say to rape them, only to encourage relationships between you,' Jorund answered, and her blood boiled. He turned to Valda. 'Gather the men.'

Valda was staring at the weeping Emma with raw concern, but at Jorund's command she nodded and hurried away.

Jorund turned to Amée with intense eyes. 'I will make this right!'

Amée gathered the weeping Emma closer, and glared at her husband. 'If you don't, I will!' Of course, she wasn't certain how she would enforce such a bold statement, but she was determined that she would.

Valda gathered all the men in the fort. Jorund had thrown on his tunic and strapped his sword to his hip. A ruthless leader ready to take command. Amée wasn't sure if that was a good or a bad thing.

They walked down in procession to the centre of Évreux. Amée hated how Jorund had insisted Emma accompany them, especially after her ordeal. At least her attacker was being led by a rope around his wrists. That suggested some form of retribution.

When they reached the centre of town, it looked as if the whole of Évreux had come out to join them.

'Everybody's staring,' whispered Emma, and tears shone in her frightened eyes. She wrapped her arms around herself, as if to protect against any uncharitable thoughts.

Amée knew how this event could tarnish Emma's reputation and she put an arm around her in comfort, drawing her close. 'Everyone should see his shame and know your courage. I will make certain of it.'

Emma raised her bruised face a little higher at her words, and she couldn't have been prouder of her friend.

Their procession halted in the main square. Jorund didn't bother with standing on the old dais as her father would have done. He was head and shoulders above everyone anyway. His eyes swept the faces of his warriors with the fierce power of command, and a shiver ran down her spine.

'Let me be clear. You are my warriors and these are my people. Their protection is your duty and my responsibility. If I hear of any man, woman or child harmed by a warrior under my command the retribution will be swift and final. All crimes will be punished with either banishment or death, regardless of who commits them. I have encouraged my warriors to form marriage alliances with the people of Évreux and I encourage the women of Évreux to consider such matches. But—' he barked the word, his deep voice carrying across the crowd with ease '—I condemn force of any kind. Understood? We are building a new land. A home to a new and independent people. Free from corrupt Frankish control and petty raids. This land is called *Northmannia*.' He looked at Emma. 'You are all Northmen now and live under my protection.' He looked at his warriors, who were all glaring at Skarde in disgust. 'Rules of honour and justice apply here, and I will enforce them.'

Jorund waited a few moments for his words to sink in. The townsfolk glanced around at each other and muttered behind their hands. Amée could see a slow acceptance rippling through the crowd. Their eyes darted between that of the beaten Emma and the tied warrior either side of him.

'In this case,' he continued, 'the warrior mistook my orders. Thankfully, the maiden's virtue was not harmed.' Amée tried to stifle her gasp of indignation. She glared at her husband.

Surely that didn't excuse Skarde's actions?

Jorund's eyes pleaded with Amée to give him time before she clawed out his heart. She sucked in an angry breath through gritted teeth but she waited for him to finish.

He turned to face the prisoner. 'He *must* be punished for attacking one of my people. Skarde Ulfsson, you are banished from my land. If you are seen within my borders, you will be captured and hanged. Is that understood?'

'I should never have joined you!' Skarde spat on the floor, the ropes only taking a savage twist of his wrists to undo. They fell to the floor and he began to walk away. 'This is an army of nursemaids and cowards! I leave you willingly—'

Jorund's long legs covered the short distance between them in two strides. He grabbed Skarde by the arm and spun him back around to face him. Towering over Skarde, he growled, 'I am not done with you yet!' And with one savage punch he threw the man clean off his feet and into the mud. Jorund nodded to Valda, who responded with a wicked smile.

'Two lines of ten,' she shouted.

Amée hurried to his side. 'What are you going to do?' she asked quietly, turning her back to the crowd.

His voice was hard and sharp when he replied, 'I will punish him. Skarde deserves no mercy. *This* is how I deal with betrayal.' The men had formed two lines, and Jorund lowered his voice as he spoke to her. 'If you cannot stomach it, I will understand if you wish to return to the fort.'

He thought her weak.

She shook her head and turned back to watch. 'I will stay.'

Skarde staggered to his feet, but he was already at the beginning of the path between the two lines of warriors. The first man struck out with his foot and kicked him down. The man opposite waited for him to rise and then slammed him down with a balled fist. Skarde made slow, brutal progress through the line of warriors, each one hitting him at least once as he passed. Always they waited for him to recover and try to rise before they landed yet another blow. In the end he had to crawl to the end of the path, his face a bloody mask barely recognisable anymore. A scatter of teeth sank into the mud in his wake.

The punishment was brutal, but an unchristian part of her welcomed it. He'd hurt her friend, had tried to rape her. A man like Skarde had no place amongst decent people. He deserved everything he received, and Jorund was right to show everyone that his actions were not acceptable in their land.

Her mind was set.

No longer did she wish to return to the nunnery. It was not the right place for her. She had a duty to her land, her people and…to her husband.

The trust between them was growing, and today he'd proven himself a worthy Lord of Évreux. Far greater than the previous man.

He was not without fault—there was, of course, Valda. But—and this shocked her to the bone—she might be willing to accept him in spite of it.

If he ruled her people well, and remained honourable in all other matters, then he was a good lord for Évreux, and she should support him.

Évreux deserved peace. Would they get that in two winters' time when her father demanded his land back?

No.

Which left Amée with a decision that really wasn't a decision after all.

She could not trust him with her heart, but that was something she'd never be foolish enough to give away.

However, she did need to accept Jorund as her husband, and the sooner the better, because who knew how long, if at all, it would take for her to conceive a child. She must act quickly—there would be no peace for Évreux otherwise.

Chapter Sixteen

'They still fear us,' grumbled Jorund. He nodded towards a father who quickly ushered in his two daughters as his hunting party rode past on their return to the fort. They'd had another successful day. But despite all they'd done to rebuild a prosperous community, the locals still looked at them with fear and suspicion.

Who could blame them?

One of their women had been attacked only a couple of days ago.

Valda glanced at the family in question and nodded. 'Even after Skarde's punishment, it will take time for them to accept us. You knew that.'

'I had hoped it would not take this long.'

Valda laughed. 'It's only been a few weeks since your marriage. It's merely the dawn of your rule here. Within a year you will have won these people's fealty, and this time of uncertainty will be forgotten.'

'I wish I had your confidence in me.'

Valda raised a bronze eyebrow. 'As do I.'

With a dismissive snort he scrutinised the fort as they entered. The outer walls were strong and complete. The southern hall of the old inner fort was still a pile of rubble. Unfortunately, the time for a decision regarding it was at hand. As they passed through the gateway, and through its ruins, he exhaled a heavy breath. It would upset Amée to see it cleared but he couldn't see any other way.

Hurting her was becoming a habit of his.

He'd been avoiding her since the day of Skarde's punishment, claiming to be too tired for their evening lessons. He'd then spent two long days visiting the local farms, and today he'd been hunting since dawn.

All lies, anything to avoid facing his wife.

The truth being that he was too humiliated by his own behaviour.

Who was he to mete out punishment to Skarde when he'd acted no better?

He'd behaved like a beast of the field on the very same day Skarde had attacked Emma. Almost taking his wife without care or patience. Consumed by lust, and without thought to his innocent wife's comfort or feelings. Shame curled around his chest like a serpent.

She'd looked so vulnerable afterwards, her drab nun clothes torn around her breasts and her skirts a rumpled mess. It reminded him of some of the horrors he'd seen and disgust boiled deep in his belly. Was he no better than his father?

He spat on the ground, revulsion coating his tongue.

If she'd considered him nothing better than a barbaric heathen before, then the public punishment would have only confirmed it. Amée was gentle and kind; she believed in Christian love and charity. There was no way she'd approve of his brutal vengeance, even to a man such as Skarde.

And yet it had to be done, for the good of his land.

Skarde had to be punished, and severely. Skarde was the son of Rollo's oldest friend, and he'd asked Jorund to instruct him, smooth out his rough edges. But even Rollo would understand Skarde's punishment. An army could not function without order.

It was a clear message to his people: he would not tolerate injustice or disorder of any kind. If only he'd seen the corruption in the man sooner. He should have recognised it, especially after those bitter years with his father. But he'd been too distracted by his growing feelings for his wife.

He should have listened to Amée before. She'd told him that he needed to speak directly with their people, offer reassurance and clear instruction. But he'd not listened. He'd thought his honour and actions were enough. He'd not been clear to the serfs what he expected from them and his warriors. Now, because of one man's lack of honour, his reputation was tarnished. That was his fault, no one else's.

He only wished someone would beat him senseless for his own awful behaviour. Maybe he could ask Valda to do it? She'd seen what he'd done. He'd tried his best to give Amée back her dignity after his ravishment, but it had been too late. He glanced at Valda. She'd certainly seemed more distant since that day.

No, he couldn't face talking to anyone about how he'd debased himself. It was far too humiliating, even if he did deserve it.

Dismounting from his horse, he handed the reins to a waiting serf. Thankfully, the labour from the town had increased since Amée's arrival and the running of the fort was growing smoother by the day.

He checked the courtyard for Amée as they walked

through, and then looked up at the rotunda. As usual her shutters were closed. The woman had a strange obsession with drafts, and kept the windows closed no matter the weather.

'Why do you do that?' asked Valda mildly. 'Look for her but then avoid her? I mean, you obviously want her.'

Jorund's spine straightened with hot pride. 'She's my wife.' He wasn't sure what he meant by that answer. His friend looked at him with narrowed eyes.

'I know. And… You told me once that she was merely a stepping stone to your dominion over the land. But I have seen you staring at her. It is as if there is no other sun or moon in the sky when she is near.'

Jorund rolled his eyes. 'You think yourself a Skald now? Your poetry is as bad as your aim with a bow.'

Valda thumped him in the side with a jab of her elbow. It was a light, good-natured blow. 'If you care for her, then you should spend more time with her. Not less.'

'And what makes you such an expert on relationships? I presumed you had sworn off all men for ever.'

Valda abruptly stopped walking and turned to him with a brittle smile. He worried for a moment that he'd pushed too hard. It was not like him to interfere in Valda's private life…much less to mock it. 'Not *all* men, and not for ever,' she said. 'But at this moment, I am content to be your second and your friend. And as your *friend*, I am compelled to give you advice. I know your nights have become worse of late.'

Jorund felt the vein jump in his jaw as he clenched his teeth tight. Why would she speak of that? 'It will pass,' he said. *It always did*, he reassured himself. Like a tide it had its highs and its lows. He only needed to wait it out.

She took a step closer to him and lowered her voice.

'I've had to wake you every night for the past three nights.'

'I'm sorry to have disturbed you,' he snarled, beginning to walk away. Valda grabbed him and pulled him closer, her eyes hard with purpose and frustration.

'Stupid ox! Do you think I care about that? You call her name—did you know that? You shout it out!'

He shook his head and lowered his eyes. He'd dreamt of Amée; he knew that. But he hadn't realised he'd called out her name.

'You care for her, and for some reason you're worrying about her. Talk to her, it will help. I swear it.' He snorted, and Valda grabbed his arms and shook them with a vicious jerk. 'I know you, Jorund. I know you better than yourself. *Tell her the truth!*'

'I would appreciate your opinion on something…husband.' Amée stood in the doorway to the hall, and she was staring at them with wide eyes, a cup in her hands.

Valda was the first to move, stepping away from him with a quick hop to the side. 'I'll tend to the kills.' She gave Amée a polite bow before heading in the opposite direction.

'I thought you might like a drink after your hunt,' she said, thrusting it towards him. 'Would you follow me inside?'

Familiar guilt gnawed at his bones, and he took the cup with an awkward smile. Briskly she spun on her heel and entered the hall. He followed feeling no better than a dog with its tail between its legs.

She was wearing one of her mother's gowns. It was a beautiful red russet that complemented her dark colouring and poured over her curves seductively. He drained the mead in one thirsty swallow, forcing his eyes to move away from the luscious dips and swells of her body.

Why had he ripped her nun clothes?

It appeared he'd made his daily torment far, far worse.

To distract himself, he looked around the hall. Amée had been busy again; there were more comforts and furnishings dotted around. Each day his new home improved, and that was not solely down to his or his men's efforts. Amée had worked hard in such a short amount of time. The silverware was out, the table and benches looked cleaner and brighter. No doubt Amée had spent one of her days oiling them. The image of her bent over the table, scrubbing at it, rose the fire once more in his veins and he cursed himself for being so easily led by his desire of her.

She stood at the lord's table, took the cup from his numb fingers and poured him another drink. 'The hunt went well?' she asked, passing it back.

With a nervous smile she gestured to some papers laid out on the table, a couple of candles lit beside them.

I feel...passionately about them.

He still wasn't sure why her words had caused such a violent reaction in him that day. Maybe it was because he had lost such wonder in his own life? Treasure held no interest for him, nor battle, or conquest, or glory. He'd seen so much death and wickedness that he knew such things were hollow victories. But Amée had *loved* those crumbling, yellow pieces of parchment that had smelt of mould and dust. She'd *loved* something that to anyone else might have appeared ugly and useless.

True love, with a full and passionate heart.

And *Loki take him!* He'd wanted her to feel that way about him. And like a thief he'd tried to take it, force it from her, confusing desire with something far deeper. Something far more unattainable.

With a heavy heart he watched her pick up a large parchment gently as if it were a babe.

'These are the designs of the original villa,' she said, her fingers tender as she held the parchment up to the light.

He peered at the intricate drawings. They were strangely charming, and filled with tiny words he could barely see let alone understand. He glanced at her and saw the excitement brightening in her dark eyes as she looked at it. She'd never been more beautiful.

'Much of the original stone might be unusable…'

Why did he have to ruin all her enjoyment with his big stupid mouth?

Luckily, Amée seemed prepared for his negativity. 'Yes. But I also have some ideas…if you don't mind considering them?' She bit her lip, uncertain. Did she think he would not listen to her? She was obviously knowledgeable and skilled in this area. Why would he not?

'Go on.'

She smiled, her full mouth spreading wide across her face, dazzling him with the pearls of her teeth. 'Here are some plans I made.'

She spread out an animal skin that was covered in similar markings and drawings. An impressive plan of a new southern hall was laid out before him, as if he were an eagle wheeling in the sky above it. 'We will need more stone. But with these arches we may not need as much, and they reflect some of the decorative aspects of the original… And, what with the new stables and outer buildings for the men, we might not need as much room anyway. The fort could return to its original use as a family villa.'

'Impressive.' He nodded thoughtfully, although he couldn't shake the word 'family' from his mind. It resonated within him and whispered of a blissful future.

A blush crept up her neck as she beamed with pride at his words. 'Do you think you could ask your men to repair the southern hall using these designs?'

'No.'

Her disappointment was immediate. Her shoulders slumped and she bent her head slightly as if she had a sore neck. Why did he always tease her like this? He immediately regretted it and felt like a monster.

Impulsively he reached for her and took her hand in his. 'Because I could not explain it to them. But I think you could.'

'You grant me permission?' she gasped.

'It is your home too. Speak with Valda, she'll help you.' He looked down at their clasped hands. His were covered in purple bruises around the knuckles from where he'd punched Skarde, hers were pale and unblemished. She stiffened and he dropped her hand.

'I'll put these away and speak with her later.'

Had the sight of his bruised fist disgusted her?

Damn! Why must he always find an excuse to touch her?

He stepped away from her, giving her room—which she immediately took. Then she turned and gathered up the scrolls and parchments quickly.

He nodded, desperately wanting to make her stay while knowing he had no right to hold her back.

He shouldn't have touched her.

She went to leave and then seemed to think better of it. Spinning back to him with a deep breath, the piles of parchments nearly overflowing in her arms, she said, 'I meant to say…thank you… For what you did for Emma.'

A muscle cracked in his neck as his spine straightened.

It was sweet of her to thank him, but he didn't deserve it. Not when he'd sunk so low in his own impatience for her. When he'd been moments away from violating her innocence against the wall of his bedchamber!

The mead soured in his stomach.

The responsibility of his people and Amée's safety weighed heavily on his shoulders. He'd never had to care for anyone but himself in the past and that had suited him. Now he felt weakened by the presence of his wife; she was so small and fragile. Skarde could have easily overpowered her as he'd overpowered Emma. No matter how many hours he spent training her to defend herself, she would still be vulnerable in the presence of a seasoned warrior.

His desire for her had not dulled, but he feared he had sullied their relationship with the events of the last few days.

He'd apologised and had hoped she would have forgiven him quickly; at least her passion had matched his. It wasn't *exactly* as bad as what Skarde had done to Emma, but it still made him feel hideous. Like Skarde, he'd been consumed by lust.

Jorund felt as if he'd swallowed a boulder ever since the ugly incident. Skarde had never been one of his loyal men. And yet, he'd stupidly given him trust and responsibility when he'd deserved none. Hoping to shape the spoiled and proud warrior into a better man and into the leader that Rollo had hoped for.

To think that worm had pushed back his people's growing confidence in him made his muscles burn to chase him down and strangle the life from his wretched body. Banishment was too good for him. Death was too good for him.

It was a mistake he would not make again. Jorund would personally check the character and reputation of all the remaining men unfamiliar to him. Something he should have done before he allowed a man like Skarde to live with his people…his wife!

Thank Odin, he'd followed her. He'd been cheered by her returned wave. He'd hoped that he could apologise more thoroughly. Shame and anger at himself had caused him to leave before apologising properly, and she deserved better than that.

When he'd heard her shout, he'd felt as if the dark serpent Jörmungandr had plunged its head in his chest and swallowed his heart whole.

What did strong defences matter when there was a beast within its walls?

He'd failed her and his people by allowing such a toad to live amongst them, albeit it had been on Rollo's orders.

Amée was staring at him. Still waiting for a response. He cleared his throat and shrugged. 'It was my duty to punish Skarde.'

'Yes, but…you handled it well.' She smiled, as if he'd somehow done her a great service in the utter neglect of her safety.

His jaw and neck ached with tension. He ran his fingers over the smooth skin of his freshly shaved head. It reminded him of that morning, of the feel of her flesh under his rough hands, the bud of her nipple under his hot tongue. As if burned, he dropped his hands from his head. 'I failed. Don't praise me for it.'

'If there is one thing certain in this life, it's that there will always be some bad people,' she said softly, her gentle eyes full of kindness and reassurance as she reached a hand up to touch his arm. 'You can no more control their actions than control the changing of the seasons. You are a good man and the people have seen that they can trust you to keep the peace. That is all the people want.'

He tensed at her description of him. He wasn't good. He was a wild animal ruled by lust and rage. He shrugged off her touch. 'I have been a disappointment as a husband too.'

Her eyes widened at his admission of guilt and she opened her mouth to say something, but they were interrupted by a shout from the doorway. It was Emma with Beatrice. They came rushing in from the garden, out of breath and their basket overflowing with herbs. 'They're here! The Count and the Princess! They've just sailed into Évreux... There's so many boats!'

Chapter Seventeen

Amée didn't have time to ponder Jorund's words. She already knew what he meant by his description of himself as a 'bad husband.' He was confessing to his affair with Valda, something she would rather avoid discussing all together.

Besides, they had important visitors coming to stay, and she'd not missed the anxious looks exchanged between Beatrice and Emma. The idea of the arrival of an army, especially a Norse army, disturbed them. She could only imagine the worry it caused the rest of her people. She had to show them she wasn't afraid, and that they in turn had nothing to fear.

'Then we must prepare to welcome them!' said Amée brightly as she put the parchments back down on the table and brushed the dust off her hands. 'Emma, please tidy these away in my chamber. Beatrice, please prepare some refreshments for when the Count and Princess arrive. Warm drinks and honey cakes—Gisla always liked those.'

Jorund's warhorse was already saddled and being led towards them as they headed outside. He mounted it in one easy movement.

'Should I not come with you on Luna to welcome them?' she asked.

'There's not enough time.' He leaned down, his arms open, his expression hesitant. 'Ride with me?'

Butterflies fluttered in her stomach and she nodded, stepping into his arms so that he could lift her up. Large warm hands wrapped around her waist and her feet dangled weightless for a moment, before she was placed sideways on the saddle in front of him. He shifted backwards so she could have a more comfortable seat. But it still felt a little precarious and instinctively she grabbed the dark wool of his tunic for balance.

Sky-blue eyes struck the earth of her own, and she felt as if lightning had passed between them. Her fingers flexed against the wool. She watched the knot of his throat swallow, and her eyes drifted down past it to the 'v' of skin just visible beneath his tunic.

What would he do if she clenched the wool and dragged him down to kiss her? If she ripped it in two, as he'd ripped her habit? Would he welcome it? As she'd welcomed his kiss? She wet her dry lips with her tongue, lost in the tantalising dream.

'Ready?' he asked gruffly, and she thought for a moment he was asking if she were ready to kiss him.

'Yes,' she whispered, her eyes softly trailing back up his strong neck to his soft mouth.

With a flick of the reins and click of his tongue he urged his stallion forward. Amée bit her lip to stifle her yelp as the horse began to move. The beast obeyed with frighteningly quick reflexes, rushing forward into a fierce gallop that had her grasping Jorund even tighter in panic. He shifted the reins to one hand and gathered her close with his free arm. Finding comfort in the wall of strength and heat behind her, she rested her back against his chest and relaxed knowing that he would not let her fall.

The air rushed against her face. Thankfully, she'd braided her hair tightly that morning rather than wear a veil, but she suspected a few of her curls would still escape. At that moment she didn't care—they could have ridden through a hailstorm and she doubted she would have minded. She rather liked being held by Jorund, his clean rich scent bathing her as he held her close. It almost felt as if she were cherished, and although she knew it to be only a fantasy, she leaned into the embrace. Glad of the excuse to feel his body close to hers, if only for a moment.

That time in his bedchamber had awakened something within her and it yearned for him more urgently with every passing day. She wanted him to kiss her again, to lose himself with her and with his passion.

The town and people flew past as they galloped towards the royal fleet. Rollo and Gisla had arrived with nearly twenty boats. Many of them had docked outside of the town, and she could see camps being built along the riverbank. Stretching out from the town and into the countryside.

Rollo and Gisla had not come empty-handed. Hundreds of men, women and horses arrived with heavily laden carts of supplies. At least they would not have to feed their entire army. It also opened up the possibility of trade with the townsfolk, which was encouraging. This could be a prosperous visit for all involved.

Jorund slowed his horse a little and she saw some of their people smile as they passed. No doubt they saw them as a true husband and wife, together in body and spirit. She tentatively reached with her other hand to hold tight to Jorund's waist rather than the saddle. He stiffened a little with surprise but then gathered her even more tightly to him. It felt so good that she could have sworn her insides turned to honey. Amée knew it would end shortly, so she allowed herself to imagine that he rode with her not out of necessity but because he couldn't bear to part from her. That he longed for her touch as much as she did.

But the daydream was short-lived.

They were already approaching the Count's magnificent longship at the dock. It was beautifully carved with red sails and a golden lion at its head. An enormous stallion that could have been the twin of Jorund's warhorse was being led down a ramp followed by a handsome grey gelding.

At the bottom of the ramp stood Count Rollo and Princess Gisla, beautifully dressed—the summer light striking the gold and silver of their Byzantine silks in such a way that they appeared to shimmer and glow with an inner light.

'Rollo, it is good to see you, old friend!' called out Jorund as they approached, and Amée gasped in shock at the over-familiarity of his words and tone.

Thankfully, the Count seemed equally familiar. 'My boy!' he shouted, clapping his hands together with a booming smack.

Jorund slipped down from his horse, carefully so as not to unseat her. Then he reached up to help her down. Without him it suddenly seemed very high, and she gratefully dropped into his embrace with a little less dignity than she'd intended. Her body bumping hard against his before he set her on her feet. She muttered a quick apology as he sucked in a sharp breath.

He took her arm and led her towards the Count and

Princess. It was wonderful to see Gisla again and Amée couldn't help but smile broadly at her. Gisla smiled warmly back, although, as always, the Princess was far more elegant in her response.

'It is good to see you, and to meet your wife. Greetings, Lady Évreux,' said Rollo.

Rollo was a large man, almost as tall as Jorund, with a thick dark beard and hair styled in a slightly longer version of the Frankish crop. It reached to his broad shoulders and was streaked with grey. He was much older than Jorund but still formidable, with broad shoulders and slim hips. At his neck hung a golden cross, but when he reached out to take her hand to kiss it, she noticed he also wore a Norse arm ring similar to Jorund's.

'Count, you are most welcome.' She inclined her head, and then smiled at the Princess, lowering her head once more. 'Princess Gisla, I hope you are well?'

Princess Gisla's green eyes sparkled. 'I am so glad to see you, Amée.'

Princess Gisla was all beauty and grace. Some of the court ladies had turned their jealousy into spite and cruelty when faced with such perfection. Amée had sworn never to behave so badly, even if she did feel a little drab sometimes in her presence.

Like now, Amée thought with a smile. The Princess stepped forward and kissed both of her cheeks. She wore a dress that looked like liquid gold, and a purple mantle trimmed with silver fur. A gold circlet crowned her head and held a veil in place, the silk so delicate Amée could see her golden braids shining beneath.

'Come show me your new home!' barked Rollo, swinging onto his stallion with ease.

They rode back to the fort with only the Count's immediate guard and retinue following. Even that was substantial. The trail of warriors and supplies flowed through Évreux like a river of wealth and power. Her people watched anxiously as they passed, lowering their eyes in respect and awe.

It was a good thing for her people to see. This was not a barbarian warlord whose rule would flicker and fade in the passage of time.

A new dynasty had been born.

'So, tell me. How's married life—do you like the giant I picked for you?' whispered Gisla as she nibbled on a honey cake. She raised a golden eyebrow in far too knowing a manner, and Amée felt exposed.

She risked a glance at her husband and found him deep in conversation with Rollo on the other side of the fire. Beatrice had placed their refreshments on a small table surrounded by fur-covered chairs. It created a cosy atmosphere, especially as it had begun to rain on their way back to the fort and they'd only just managed to get inside before the downpour.

Taking advantage of Jorund's distraction, Amée allowed herself a rare moment to admire him. 'He's a good man.' The words seemed hollow and meaningless as a description, but as they were not truly man and wife, she feared anything else would reveal too much. 'He's a good Lord of Évreux. Honourable, brave and—'

'Handsome?' teased Gisla.

Amée couldn't help but laugh. It was as if they were young girls again, sneaking into each other's rooms with honey cakes and chattering well into the night about court intrigue and distant lands.

The memory soured as quickly as it had arrived. 'Why

did you do it? Arrange this match? I was all set to take my holy orders.'

Gisla's face softened with sympathy and a touch of guilt. 'Many reasons. But you must believe I only wanted the best for you.'

Amée spoke in a barely audible whisper. 'I didn't want marriage.'

'I know.' Gisla gathered her hands in her own, her pretty face fierce with sincerity. 'But, Amée, you are *too* good to rot away in a nunnery for the rest of your life! Rollo needs loyalty more than anything now. And I trust you—more than anyone else at my father's insidious court. You deserve to be here—you *deserve* to be Lady Évreux.' She took a deep breath and Amée braced herself for the bad news she could sense on the horizon. 'There are rumours that your father's new marriage is not going well. It was only a matter of time before he dragged you back and sold you to one of his *supporters*. I could not allow that. I spoke with Rollo and he…well…he can be very persuasive with my father at times. Believe me, I arranged this *for* you.'

Tears burned at the back of Amée's eyes and she nodded, squeezing Gisla's hand tight. Her friend had not betrayed her in arranging this marriage. She'd been thinking of protecting her in the only way she could.

The revelation regarding her father did not surprise Amée. As his only heir he would have been a fool to give her away to the church so readily. He probably just wanted her away from him until he needed her again. Maybe that was another reason why her holy orders hadn't been officially granted—it probably had nothing to do with her doubts. Her place at the nunnery was merely a holding cell until she was required to show her face again. 'I understand.'

How *stupid* she'd been to think she'd escaped his power. He'd only been pacifying her, keeping her within reach in case his first plan failed.

Now, her freedom was dependent on her conceiving a child. Something she had no hope of managing within two years if she didn't at least consummate her marriage with Jorund. She'd decided to accept him after Skarde's punishment, but Jorund had spent the days since away from her. Busy hunting or visiting farms with Valda. He'd even stopped their lessons—claiming exhaustion.

How would she ever entice him away to conceive a child? Especially as she wasn't even sure what *it* involved!

Gisla sighed, obviously misreading the worry on Amée's face. 'Give it time. When I was first married to Rollo, I loathed him. I thought he could never make me happy. But over time I have come to love and respect my Viking. I'm sure you will too. Rollo promised me that he would only offer my ladies the best of his men, and he swears Jorund is the very best. Believe me, you'll soon be glad you left that drab life in a nunnery behind.'

'Thank goodness I'm not trapped in a dusty, crumbling ruin,' laughed Amée dryly, looking pointedly at a leak that had sprung from the ceiling a few feet away. A bucket had been placed under it to gather the water and soon Beatrice would need to change it.

'I passed through Évreux after marrying Rollo...' Gisla's face sobered with memory. 'It was a pitiful sight. Be proud. The rebuild and improvements you've managed in such a short amount of time are impressive. And it's yours. Don't forget that. This is *your* home, as it was your mother's before… No one can take it from you. Not even your father.'

A jolt of pride stiffened Amée's spine. 'You're right. Thank you, Gisla. You've been so kind to me.'

If Amée wanted to keep her land, which she did, then she needed to become pregnant. At least after that passionate morning in his room she was no longer quite so nervous of that aspect of their union. But she had to stop Jorund's avoidance of her so he could bed her… She just wasn't sure how.

Gisla smiled, drawing Amée's wayward thoughts back to the present. 'There is nothing to thank. You have always been good to me. You never sneered behind my back and called me a bastard like the others. You have always been a loyal friend, and if anyone deserves to be happy, it's you.'

Amée waited less than a heartbeat before asking. 'What do you know of Valda?'

Gisla frowned for a moment before a flicker of recognition crossed her face. 'Is that Jorund's shield maiden second?'

Amée nodded, glancing guiltily at Jorund, relieved that he still seemed fully focused on his conversation with Rollo.

'I believe she has two sisters. All shield maidens like herself…I think. And from a long line of shield maidens loyal to Rollo—'

'But Jorund *and* Valda?' Amée asked pointedly.

Gisla frowned. 'Are they lovers?'

Amée shrugged helplessly. 'I don't know for certain… but… Yes, I think they are.'

Gisla tilted her head thoughtfully. 'Rollo never mentioned it.' She visibly brightened, as if brushing away

Amée's worry was easy, and only required a few words of comfort. 'Mistresses are nothing to worry over, they're forgotten quickly. Wives are who really matter. Poppa, Rollo's mistress, has become a dear friend to me. Maybe Valda will become the same to you?'

All the court had heard about Rollo's 'first wife' before Gisla. He'd married Poppa, the Countess of Bayeux, in the Norse tradition before marrying Gisla—obviously not in a Christian ceremony. Poppa had given Rollo two sons, who he'd already claimed as his heirs. Gisla's marriage had been a political match, its purpose being to lend sovereignty to Rollo's rule and nothing more.

She prayed Jorund didn't expect the same from her.

'I don't know if I could accept it. My mother… It *destroyed* her.'

She didn't need to say any more; Gisla knew and understood. 'That's understandable. But don't throw your potential happiness away because of what you fear will hurt you. I've found honesty has always helped in these matters.'

The idea of talking to Jorund or Valda openly about their relationship made Amée feel sick to her stomach. 'You're probably right,' she answered with a tight smile that hurt her jaw.

Gisla reached for a honey cake and bit into it with relish, before easing back into her chair with a sigh. 'I really should stop eating these, but they are delicious.'

Amée smiled and picked up her silver chalice. She drank deeply. There was a lot to think about.

Jorund's kisses overwhelmed her. In his arms she felt alive, as if until now she'd been living her whole life missing one of her senses. Suddenly the world was brighter, louder, more filled with possibility and flavour than it had ever been before.

But the idea of him kissing Valda with equal passion made her miserable. It wasn't as if she could demand he stop. It didn't appear that men were ever loyal...even if they loved you, like Rollo loved Gisla. If beautiful Gisla had to share her husband with another, what hope did Amée have of seducing Jorund away from Valda?

And what if her father claimed back the land after two winters? She'd been stupid to think he would allow her to return to the nunnery. No, she would be married off again. Bargained away. Évreux and all their hard work would be given away as a prize to the highest bidder.

She would have to *insist* that Jorund bed her...tonight. Even if she had to explicitly demand it. Her future depended on it.

Her eyes drifted to the crack in the ceiling and the steady drip of rain from above. A single cruel thought filtered through her resolve.

My mother couldn't accept it and it drove her mad.

Determined to banish the nasty thought from her mind, she gathered all her inner strength and reminded herself: *I am not my mother!*

Chapter Eighteen

Jorund had noticed Amée looking at him more often than usual since the arrival of Rollo and his wife. She'd spent most of the afternoon deep in conversation with her friend and he'd struggled to focus on Rollo's conversations. Had they been talking about him? Is that why she glanced thoughtfully over at him from time to time? Had she told Gisla about how he'd behaved like a rutting beast? He squirmed at the thought.

The arrival of Rollo and Gisla prompted a feast that evening. There would be a feast every evening until they left. Thanks to their preparations there was plenty of food on offer, although the weather had dampened the celebrations a little as the hall overflowed with far too many people.

The Count and his retinue would sleep in the newly finished western hall. Amée had seemed keen to offer them the rotunda, but the western hall had more room for their personal serfs, and was in better condition than the tower. Most of the halls had been rebuilt and repaired, and the once 'better' buildings now needed further attention—as the leak in his feasting hall had proven. He'd rushed those repairs and would need to fix the roof again because of it. However, it was only a minor issue.

As Rollo had brought enough furnishings with them to fill a palace, it seemed the better option was to give them an empty space to do with as they wished. He suspected they would have a more comfortable night than any Amée had had since arriving.

He shrugged off the guilt.

Rebuilding would take time.

'I'm off to bed,' announced Rollo, causing Jorund to look away from his wife for the countless time that evening.

'Oh? But it's still early…'

'Take your wife to bed. That's obviously what you've wanted to do since this feast began. Consider my early night tonight as a belated wedding gift.' Rollo laughed as he rose from his seat. Gisla stood as well and took her husband's arm with a serene smile.

He watched them go with a pang of guilt. There was no reason for them to leave early. He was not taking his wife to bed tonight…or any night soon, and that was his fault. But male pride kept him from admitting it to his friend.

'Jorund, can I ask you something?' Amée whispered, her voice uncertain.

He turned to face her, surprised by her closeness. 'Go ahead.' She'd been sat beside Gisla, but had moved to his side after they'd left. It made sense for her to fill the gap, but he found himself oddly touched that she'd gladly joined him.

'Rollo has another wife…other than the Princess. Is that normal? For men to have more than one wife…in the Norse tradition?' Her face was filled with intense purpose, as if she were waiting for him to explain it in more depth.

Did she want him to take another wife?

He hoped not. He was struggling to please his first, let alone a second. One woman was more than enough to disappoint with his presence. 'Some men do... Normally kings or jarls. But it's not common. Why do you ask?'

She stared at him hard as if she were expecting something else, but he couldn't imagine what. Eventually, she answered with a firm tilt of her jaw. 'I would not appreciate a rival to my title as Lady Évreux or a rival heir to our children's inheritance. The people... They'd find it insulting...and hard to accept. But I suppose it's not up to me, is it?' She asked the question with narrowed eyes.

He smiled, relieved he could reassure her in this part of his nature at least. 'I will have no other wife, and there will be no rival to your title or any embarrassment. And no child other than ours will ever inherit. I swear it.'

Her eyes closed for a moment and she took a deep breath. When she opened them again, she bristled as if she were a cat shaking off the rain. 'Thank you.'

She didn't need to thank him. In time she would realise that although he was consumed by desire for her, it was not—and would never be—directed at another. Poor Amée, she didn't even understand what she'd accepted from him.

Hoping this uncomfortable conversation would draw to a close, he looked away.

She laid her hand on his forearm and like a moth to a flame his eyes followed. Tracing up her milky pale hand, up her arm to her delicate collarbone, and finally to her pretty face.

'There's something else I need to say to you...privately.

May we go to my chamber—once you're finished here?' She bit her lip as she waited for his answer. There was uncertainty in her eyes, but also warmth and…hope.

She *wanted* to be alone with him.

Air rushed into his lungs as he thrust aside his trencher. 'I'm done. Let's go.'

Her willingness to spend time with him again was a treasure like no other. He'd thought it might have taken weeks to regain her trust.

That she might be happy to resume their lessons so quickly after his lustful behaviour was a relief. Not because he particularly wanted to learn to read, but because he'd missed her. He'd given her time in case she needed to adjust after his behaviour. If she wished only to begin them again, and nothing more, he would gladly do it. He doubted he could deny her anything, especially not being alone with her. He wasn't sure if it helped ease or increase the suffering of his lust for her; either way he couldn't resist her.

They rose from their chairs and walked to her room. Her bedchamber was prepared for the night. The shutters closed and covered as usual, the fire lit. It hurt to see the little table empty. There was no charcoal or animal skins laid out.

There wouldn't be any lessons, then. She *really* did want to discuss something with him. The stores, perhaps? The ongoing feasts for Rollo? Whatever it was he hoped it would be a long discussion. Ideally something dull rather than unpleasant.

'What is it?' he asked, and he busied himself lighting a few candles.

She took a seat and placed her hands in her lap purposefully, as if preparing herself for an important discussion.

'Will you sit?' she asked eventually, gesturing at the remaining chair opposite her.

Not something dull, then. A pity.

He sat down, a little deflated.

She fidgeted in her chair as a blush crept up her neck. 'I thought I should tell you that I accept you—as my husband.' She finished her words with a firm nod, as if she were reassuring herself about her decision.

What on earth was she talking about?

Then it hit him square in the chest.

Sex.

Had the Princess spoken to her? Insisted they consummate the marriage for the good of the land? He sank back against his chair with an even heavier heart—if that were possible.

'No.' He sighed. 'That's not enough.'

'What?' She blinked rapidly, as if there was smoke in her eyes. 'I don't understand. You said that when I was ready to accept you, I should let you know. Well, I'm ready to accept you.' The heat in her cheeks brightened with a touch of anger. 'You can't *reject* me! I'm your wife—I might not be… But…in your room you almost…' He shifted awkwardly and the chair creaked loudly. He knew all too well what he'd *almost* done. She took a deep breath as if to steady herself. '*Surely* you want an heir?'

'Of course I want an heir. But I haven't changed my mind. I don't want your *acceptance*. I want you to want me.' He knew exactly what he needed and it wasn't his wife feeling duty-bound to lay with him. The idea made him sick to his stomach. 'I want you to feel the same way I do. I want your desire. Not your duty. I meant what I said: I will wait.'

She stared at him, her mouth forming a small 'o' of

surprise. Then she leaned towards him, her voice the tiniest whisper. 'You *desire* me?'

'Yes, completely,' he answered, his throat rough. The confession torn from him by his own pitiful hope. Her eyes locked with his, the amber flecks appearing to spark in the firelight.

She didn't say anything and he stood up to leave, unable to bear the tension a moment longer.

'I want you too,' she gasped before he had time to walk away.

They were the sweetest words he had ever heard, but he didn't quite believe them. 'If the Princess has pressured you to—'

'No.' Amée quickly shook her head. 'I have some misgivings…I can't deny that. We're very different… And our ideas on marriage obviously differ, that much is clear. But we suit one another in a strange way and, well, I *do* desire you. So…I think we should consummate our marriage—the sooner the better, really.' A shadow of worry flickered in her eyes at the last statement, but just as quickly it was gone and replaced with a shy smile.

It was the most blunt and savage invitation to bed he'd ever received.

She wanted him—but not completely. Love and family were not a reason for marriage in her world. She'd not been brought up in the dirt like him. Hoping for love in his future like others might dream of treasure. She thought well of him, and she knew that he would be a good husband, and that he had honour. She wanted a peaceful life—she'd always said that—and he'd proven that he could offer her that. The heat between them? He'd merely awakened her passionate heart and, as such, would be the lucky man to reap the reward.

He should leave.

But he wasn't *that* good a man.

She had said the only thing he'd ever wanted from her—for her to say that she wanted him too, despite all that he was, and that she was willing to overlook their differences.

Longing gnawed at his bones but he refused to move.

'I'm...nervous,' she said, her neck bent almost backwards trying to look up at him from her seat. 'I don't know where to begin...'

He was reminded of the first time they'd been together in this room, when she'd said with a whipping crack of disgust: *You're not a normal man!*

'I know I am not the size of a *normal* man. But...' He'd been about to promise that he wouldn't hurt her. But if she were a virgin, could he truly swear that? 'I'm still just a man... I'll show you.'

In his mind, she should at least know what she was agreeing to.

He unstrapped his weapons and laid them on the table. He undressed quickly and methodically, not daring to look at her until he was completely naked before her.

Only when he was done did he dare look. Her eyes were huge in her small face and they were staring openly at his groin. Colour bathed her face and neck as if she'd been thrown into a hot bath.

His manhood had risen to the occasion. Her eyes flashed up to his face in alarm and he tried not to laugh. He'd presumed she was innocent but now he wondered if she even understood...

Odin's teeth! He didn't have to explain it, did he?

'You understand about sex, yes? Between a husband and a wife?'

'Yes, I understand.' She moistened her lips and what little blood he had left in his head rushed with dizzying speed to his groin. 'I lived at court for a while,' she said, as if that explained things.

Maybe it did.

'You've had a lover before?'

She rushed to her feet, her shock flashing with lightning speed into outrage. 'Of course not!'

He raised his arms in surrender. 'I meant no disrespect.'

She cleared her throat loudly and looked up at the ceiling. 'I know about the key and the lock…but not much more.'

Key and the lock?

He stared at her in confusion.

Did she want to be restrained?

That couldn't be right.

The significance of the imagery slowly dawned on him. 'Oh, I see.'

So, she knew the theory of sex, but not the practice. She believed it was as simple as sticking a key into a lock. He supposed he could see the reasoning, although he hoped she would enjoy it more than that.

She looked at his body. Then she must have realised where she was looking and with a gasp her eyes darted back to the ceiling above his head.

'Do you still want me?' he asked, his muscles tense, half afraid she would reject him.

Heavens above! Why did he keep asking her that?

Amée stared at the cobwebbed ceiling, not far from her husband's head, and tried her best not to faint with embarrassment. She'd never seen a naked man before, and she'd certainly never had a full conversation while in the same room as one.

Their eyes met and it felt as if hours had crawled past before she remembered to answer. She nodded.

Jorund had no shame! None!

But neither did she...

God forgive her, she *enjoyed* looking at him.

More than once her eyes had strayed to below his waist out of curiosity, and it did strange warm and achy things to her insides when she did. She knew about sex...theoretically. She'd heard enough whispers at court to understand the basics. Still, she'd never imagined how the sight of him would affect her.

His huge golden chest rose and fell with a steady beat. Marked by scars and the blue ink that marked him out as Norse, he was built for war. His arms were bigger than her thighs and sometimes they flexed and did strange things to her heart when she looked at them. His legs were long and planted firmly, dusted with dark blond hair like on his chest and tapered to his narrow hips. He was perfectly in proportion despite his enormous size.

She wanted him more than anything.

Strangely, the fear she felt when she looked at Jorund's sheer bulk and strength only added to the liquid warmth of desire that ran through her veins. It made her want to sigh with pleasure and stare at him for ever.

It hadn't been until he'd almost left that she'd realised how much she did want him.

In fact, she wanted him as much, if not more, than he wanted her. Which was terrifying in itself. When he'd said he desired her 'completely,' the needy and desperate part of her soul had almost burst with joy.

Would he forsake all others for her? Would he put aside Valda?

Probably not, and that hurt, but she did want him and what was the point in lying about it?

His voice brought her back to the present. 'It can some-times hurt a little…the first time. But I will do all that I can to ease it,' he said, his blue eyes pained.

'I've heard that.'

Whispers at court—about certain ladies who 'shame-fully failed to bleed' on their wedding night. It had always seemed such an uncharitable thing to criticise a woman for. So, she'd always been quick to leave such conver-sations. Maybe if she'd stayed, she'd be less in the dark about what was about to happen.

Jorund stepped forward, his body heat flowing from him in waves, rivalling the fire that crackled beside her. 'Your turn.'

'My turn?'

'To take off your clothes.'

'Oh.' Her knees weakened, and she hesitated, as if she'd forgotten how to undress.

'Let me help.' He removed her veil, which she had to admit did very little to contain her unruly curls most days, tonight included. He threw the veil on her chair and she untied the girdle of her gown and placed it care-fully on top.

Jorund gestured for her to turn around and she did as he asked, moving her hair over her shoulder so that he could reach the laces at the back of her neck. Her gown consisted of one of her mother's heavily draped and em-broidered tunics with a tighter fitted shift beneath.

He made quick work of the ties. She gasped with a shiver of excitement as he kissed the base of her neck with a gentle brush of his lips. Both tunics slid down to land at her feet. She took a moment to carefully place the precious garments on the table.

When she turned back to Jorund she was only wearing her shift and boots. It reminded her of when they'd first met—it felt like a distant memory, so much had happened since. She wondered if Jorund was remembering the same thing as there was a soft smile on his face as he looked at her.

She bent to take off her boots, but Jorund dropped to his knees first. 'Let me do it.'

He lifted each foot and slipped off her boots one by one. Then he lifted the hem of her shift up to her knees, offering it to her with clear blue eyes.

Her nipples tightened, sensitive against the linen fabric, as she loosened the ties further on her sleeves and neck. Then she reached down and took the hem from his warm fingers.

She swept the fabric up and over her head. Dropping it on the chair behind her.

Amée sucked in a nervous breath. Jorund was eye level with her navel...as well as the private parts of her no man had ever seen before. Her thighs clenched together as liquid heat pooled between her legs.

She took a step away, the backs of her legs bumping into the chair behind.

When he looked up, his eyes caught the firelight and glowed with a blue fire intensity that made her heart skip erratically in her chest. His hair looked golden as one hand swept around her calf and nudged her back towards him. 'You do not need to run, my sweetling.'

His voice was as smooth and as intoxicating as the wine at court.

She took a step forward, enthralled by the romantic gesture of his endearment. No man had ever called her 'sweetling,' especially not a giant of a man like Jorund, who knelt at her feet as if she were an empress.

'I am a lucky man.' His hand trailed up the inside of her calf. He pressed his lips to her knee and goosebumps raced up her thighs. 'Open your legs wider,' he commanded, and she obeyed, unable to deny him anything when he touched her like that.

Both of his hands cupped the backs of her thighs and then stroked upwards to cup her bottom. He squeezed it gently before trailing around to her hips. She was panting now, biting back a desperate moan of pleasure. Weak and powerful all at the same time.

He kissed the tops of her inner thighs and then moved upwards. She held her breath and cast her eyes to the ceiling, unsure of what he would do next. Surely, he wouldn't...

'Oh!' She gave a strangled gasp as his tongue swept between her folds and lapped at her entrance. She gripped the thick muscle of his shoulders for balance.

A deep masculine groan rumbled from between her thighs and she felt a sudden tightness build within. But before she could gather her thoughts he stood up, gathered her in his arms and carried her to the bed.

A soon as she was laid down his fingers sought her entrance. He knelt at the lower half of her body and moved his thumb over the source of her pleasure, until she began to whimper and press against his hand seeking a release she didn't fully understand.

He lowered, settling his broad shoulders once more between her spread thighs. His mouth was on her, and his tongue swept against her again and again, replacing his thumb and moving in a circular motion as both his hands cupped and squeezed her bottom, drawing her closer to him.

The hot, wet tightness built up. Until all she could do was moan and press herself harder against his tongue. Then all at once a climax of pleasure raced through her body. Releasing in shuddering waves a feverish joy that caused her to cry out his name. She gripped his shoulders and arched her hips against him, panting in shock and amazement.

But... Wasn't he meant to put himself inside her?

'I...I don't think you did it right.' She gasped. Thinking of the lock and key she'd been told about.

He raised his head and grinned up at her wickedly. 'Oh, I did it right.'

Limp against the delicious heat of her pleasure, she sighed with bliss. He laid her hips down gently, almost reverently, and she sank against the fresh straw mattress. Boneless, and so content she couldn't help but smile.

He moved up and over her, kissing at her neck and causing more shivers to race down her spine. Gently he nudged open her legs a little further, and settled himself at the juncture of her thighs. His manhood pressed at her entrance, causing the wonderful ache to begin to tighten once more.

His big body blocked out all light and a little fear tugged on the frayed edges of her nerves as she realised how strong and powerful he truly was. She was nothing compared to his strength, and he was so big in every way. She stared at his shoulder and sword arm as they flexed above her.

So careful with his movements, she noticed, so gentle. The fear retreated.

How strange, to think she would never have experienced this at the nunnery.

Her life had changed in such a short amount of time.

She sucked in a breath and braced herself, for whatever was to come. The distance between them shortened as he moved to lie above her. His every action controlled and considered as he bore the rest of his considerable weight on his arms above her head.

There was a little bit of discomfort as he reached with one hand to position himself. Some light stretching. Nothing she couldn't handle. She smiled to herself, relieved. She could cope with this act of the marriage bed. *Especially* if he did that other thing beforehand.

Still, it seemed an odd thing for men to desire, and she wondered why they fell over themselves at court trying to get women alone so they could do this to them.

Another grunt followed by a flex of his hips which caused a hiss of pain to escape her lips. She realised then that he hadn't been fully inside her before... In fact, he hadn't been inside her at all... Not really, only positioning himself at her entrance. She felt it now, however, as the full length of him pushed inside her and she sucked in a sharp breath.

'I'm so sorry,' he whispered. 'It should only hurt this first time.'

She nodded, her voice a tight squeak. 'I'm fine... Are you done now?'

Jorund muttered something savage in Norse and she winced.

Why had she asked him that?

He moved his hips again, withdrawing, or so she thought, but then he slid forward slowly once more. She tensed, waiting for more pain, but there wasn't any.

'How does that feel?' Jorund asked, his breathing laboured.

Amée blinked up at his face, cast in shadow.

'What?'

'Does it still hurt?' he asked gruffly, his voice deep and rough against her skin.

'Erm…' She shifted beneath him, testing the feel of him inside her. She heard a masculine groan and so she stilled. 'No?'

'Just tell me to stop if it hurts.'

'Erm…I will,' she answered, not sure what she should be feeling or what the correct answer could possibly be.

His breathing became faster and he pressed down against her harder. He kissed her neck and trailed his lips around to hers. He'd not kissed her mouth until now. He'd kissed her intimately, was inside her even now. But he'd not kissed her on the mouth tonight, not yet.

She wanted that more than anything else. To feel the passionate crush of his lips against hers. Like the kiss they'd shared in his room that morning when he'd torn her clothes from her body and made her ache with longing.

She raised her head seeking his lips and when they joined she welcomed it, melting with the pleasure of it. His tongue stroked against hers in a gentle caress that made her mind spin. One of his hands slid between them and stroked over the bud at the top of her entrance. Heat poured from his fingers and pooled between her thighs.

The steady movement of his hips began to cause a tingle of excitement to build. Knowing what those initial stirrings could lead to, she welcomed them. Raising her bottom to meet his thrusts as he moved back and forth inside her. She reached up and touched the flexing muscles of his shoulder, marvelling in the strength and elegance of his big body as it rippled above her.

The tightening began to build again. She closed her eyes, urging him silently with her hips to fulfil what she didn't fully understand herself. One of his hands fisted in her hair, while his other hand had moved to her hip and was squeezing gently with each thrust. Their panting breath mingled. She opened her eyes and found him watching her intently, his breathing hard and his muscles straining.

No one had ever looked at her like that before, as if no one and nothing else existed. She could have lived happily under his sapphire gaze for ever. But the tightness built so high until she could no longer hold on to it and then it shattered within her. She closed her eyes and cried out as ripples of pleasure bathed her from head to toe.

His thrusts became faster, wilder, until he came to his release with a masculine cry of his own. He gathered her body close and groaned against the hot pulse in her neck.

She sighed, her view of the world and her marriage altered for ever.

Chapter Nineteen

Jorund stared up at the ceiling. He waited patiently for
the beat of his heart to steady and his breathing to even
out. Although he doubted he would ever return to the
man he'd been before.

Making love to Amée had been beyond any pleasure
he could have imagined. She'd consumed him body and
soul.

His life now would be split in two.

There was only to be the time before Amée and the
time after. Nothing else had any meaning or relevance.
Not any more.

He turned his head to look at her. She'd been staring at
the ceiling too. Her lips flushed with his kiss, her curls a
tangled cloud around her head. After he'd rolled off her,
she'd moved the furs and blankets to cover them both—
well, as much of him as she could manage. She grasped
the blanket to her chest now, a stunned look on her face.

To think that before they'd met he'd thought himself
condemned to a marriage with a devout and faint-hearted
holy woman. Nothing could be further from the truth.

Responsive and willing to his touch. Innocent but not

prudish. He'd almost killed himself trying to hold back. It had been worth it though, to watch her climax beneath him for the second time that night. Safe in the knowledge that he could please her at least.

It would be difficult to leave, but he had to. Better that than face her fear or pity if he had one of his nightmares. Especially as his nights had been particularly troubled of late and the likelihood of a night terror was high.

He was also dangerously tired, and might fall asleep if he remained much longer.

'I should go,' he mumbled, more to himself than to his wife. 'To my chamber.'

She sat up still clutching the blanket to her chest, an unnecessary modesty that made her seem more vulnerable somehow. 'But…why?'

He fought the instinct to reach out and comfort her. Instead, he stood, the bed creaking as he did so, and went to pull on his discarded clothes. 'I prefer to sleep alone.'

'I see,' came her quiet response.

When he looked up, she'd already turned away.

The curves of her body were outlined by the blanket and furs in the dim light. Her hair, a mass of midnight curls, flowed down her shoulders and back. Covering her skin from his view. But he would never forget what it looked like. He knew the creamy softness of her breasts, the drowsy lavender scent of her hair, the sweet musk that anointed the nape of her neck.

He missed her already.

To stop himself from getting back into bed, he focused on putting on his boots. Maybe she found his leaving her offensive? More likely, she was glad to be rid of his massive bulk from her bed.

Either way, terrifying her in the middle of the night would be too much for both of them to bear.

'Goodnight,' he said as he left.

She didn't reply.

Amée wasn't sure what had woken her, but she sat up with a bolt of fright. Her heart pounding wildly against her chest and the bedding tangled around her as if she'd been tossing and turning in her sleep. The room was dark; the fire had burned down to a reddish glow and only offered minimal light. She searched the shadows but saw nothing.

She was alone.

Rising from her bed she went and threw another log onto the fire. The flames sparked to life quickly, but offered little comfort. Her skin was cold and clammy so she quickly pulled on her shift as well as a thick woollen mantle to ward off the chill. It felt as if she'd been visited by an evil spirit—which was ridiculous.

Despite the clever design of the fire in its niche in the wall, the hole bored into the stone above failed to draw all the smoke away and the room became stuffy and her eyes began to stream. The log must have been damp.

She sighed. Maybe she needed some air. She glanced at the window for a moment, but then thought better of it and walked to the door.

A bit of fresh air—that's what she needed. And by the time she returned to her bed, the room would be warmer and hopefully a little less smoky.

She didn't bother with a candle. She knew the worn steps better than the back of her hand.

As the stairs curved, she noticed a soft flickering light moving beneath Jorund's door.

Amée hesitated. But before she could make a decision,

his door opened with a long-suffering creak and Amée flew behind the curve in the stairwell. She couldn't face him. Not after what they'd just done together. What would he think if he found her creeping around in the middle of the night?

She could still see his door from her position. Without a candle she knew she'd barely be seen in the darkness, covered as she was in her mantle. For some strange reason she waited and watched.

Who knew what made her stay rather than flee back to her room?

Curiosity? Obsession? Whatever it was, she cursed it later.

Valda emerged from Jorund's room carrying a candle. She closed the door behind her softly as if afraid to wake the person inside. She was wearing a linen tunic and not much else. Then she walked across the passageway and into her own room without a backwards glance.

Amée stared into the darkness long after the door had closed. She clutched the stone wall either side of her, as if bracing herself not to fall. The mortar digging into her nails and causing pricks of pain beneath.

He'd been with Valda.

Straight after he'd been with her!

It was one thing to have suspected his infidelity, but to have it confirmed…and so brutally.

It was extremely humiliating, and begged the question: *Would she ever be enough?*

Had he lied to her, broken his promise in less than a day? She replayed their conversation from earlier in her mind over and over. He'd sworn to take 'no other wife.' That there would be 'no rival to her title or their heirs… no humiliation.'

Was this it, then? Secret meetings in the dead of the night. Still keeping his promise to her with twisted logic? Sneaking behind her back. Leaving their bed as soon as his duty as a husband was complete?

Trust a man to follow an agreement word for word without a single care for feelings. Jorund almost rivalled her own father in that—although her father would never have agreed to such terms. Not from a woman.

The stone walls and darkness became too suffocating to bear. She ran down the steps as quietly as she could. Passing their chambers with her breath held tight.

As she stepped out from the rotunda and into the courtyard she sucked in a lungful of air and then let it out with a quiet sob.

She gathered her arms around herself and closed her eyes. Jorund's strong arms had been wrapped around her only hours ago. Caressing her, touching her. Holding her down in such a fiercely possessive gesture it had made her whole body burn with a longing she still felt in the heart of her bones. She ached to be held by him even now, and that knowledge hurt almost as much as Jorund's continued infidelity.

She opened her eyes.

The sun was beginning to rise. It filled the sky with slashes of reds and pinks that were both strikingly beautiful and ominous.

She shivered and turned away.

Chapter Twenty

A small, heavily armed party crested the hill and paused. Jorund was made aware of their presence immediately. He left his morning meal and stood by the gate, watching as it snaked down from the opposite hill and slowly made its way up towards the fort.

The banners and shields of Lothair Évreux were well known. The townsfolk stopped and stared as their once proud lord rode through a land that was no longer his.

Amée came to stand beside her husband. It was the first time he'd seen her that morning. She must have started the day earlier than usual. He turned to give her a reassuring smile, perhaps a welcoming kiss to her cheek. But when he looked upon her face all thoughts of flirtation vanished from his mind.

Her skin was pale, her lips pinched into a hard, straight line. Her hair severely tamed and covered by a veil. She looked nothing like the passionate woman he'd made love to last night.

She didn't say anything to either him or her father as he arrived. Considering she'd hugged over a hundred serfs on her return to Évreux, the coldness towards her father in contrast was telling. But then, he'd always suspected that her father had hurt her as a child. The way she'd behaved in those first few days of their marriage. How she'd cowered after spilling her cup of milk, the secret room she'd confessed to hiding in as a child. All of it, including her mother's ill health, could have been caused by regular beatings. It painted a dismal picture that made his guts twist with rage. No wonder she didn't seem herself this morning.

How could he bear such a man to be near her?

And yet, politically he could not insult a Frankish lord.

Jorund scrutinised him as he approached. He'd not paid much attention to him at the signing of the treaty— of course, he'd not known then that he would be marrying the man's daughter.

Lothair might have been considered handsome once, but would be described as 'distinguished' now. There was little muscle to the man—he'd never been a warrior. Thick wavy dark hair was cropped a little longer than usual for a man of the Frankish court. Possibly it was a small spite aimed at his King's ever-receding hairline. Whatever the reason, Lothair appeared very proud of his appearance. His moustache and hair shone with perfumed oil, and he wore Byzantine silks and jewel-encrusted brooches. Thick rings adorned his fingers as he rode on a chestnut stallion towards the gate.

Lothair's small pebble eyes sharpened at the sight of them, and he cantered to where they stood. From the shortness of the man's thigh bone, Jorund guessed Lothair wasn't much taller than his diminutive daughter. He was probably enjoying the rare opportunity to look down on a man as big as himself. Short, insecure men tended to do that.

'I have come to congratulate my daughter on her recent marriage,' said Lothair with cool disdain, as if Jorund were no more than a serf, and not the Lord of Évreux. That didn't bother him, but he did mind the way his wife stiffened at his side.

'Welcome, Lothair. However, your retinue must remain outside of the gate. Count Rollo is in residence and we are full. If I'd known you were coming, I would have suggested a delay to your visit.'

Lothair's cold eyes narrowed. 'You expect me to leave my guard outside?'

Jorund smiled. 'Yes.'

'Impossible.'

'Nothing is impossible… Look around you.' He paused and smiled broadly. Let that sink into the old bastard. 'You have nothing to fear. The Count's guard, as well as my own, will be plenty of protection during your stay here.'

Lothair glared in response but eventually nodded. He could not question the Count's ability to protect a Frankish noble in his own land.

'You can have your old chamber during your stay here, my lord,' said Amée plaintively, and Jorund frowned down at her. She gave a small shake of her head, as if telling him not to argue with her. Out of respect, he did as she asked. Although she seemed altered by Lothair's presence, he couldn't deny her inner strength still remained. He trusted she knew how to handle her father better than him.

But if her father hurt her, or broke her courage in any way… There would be no secret place for him to hide from Jorund's wrath.

Lothair looked above their heads at the rotunda just visible above the surrounding walls. A slow cruel smile curved across his face, revealing sharp canines. 'Is that where you sleep now, daughter?' he asked mildly.

Amée's eyes hardened as she nodded. 'Yes, it is the best room available. I'd gladly give it up.'

Lothair looked away from the rotunda with a condescending roll of his eyes. 'I'm sure you would, daughter. But one of the lower rooms will suffice. I'll explain the arrangements to my men. I'm tired after my long journey—maybe you could arrange for some refreshments in the hall, instead of standing around idle?' With a flick of his reins, he cantered back to his men.

Jorund turned to Amée to laugh at her father's impertinence, but she was already striding back towards the kitchens.

He walked over to one of his men. 'Watch them,' he said with a jerk of his head to Lothair and his party. The man nodded.

Amée's sudden change in demeanour was worrying. She'd become cold and withdrawn, when only a few hours ago she'd been writhing beneath him, dragging his lips to hers in an embrace that had branded his soul.

He looked up at the rotunda and saw all the shutters were open except the lord's previous chamber. Something in her father's cruel smile plagued him.

Why did she do that, keep the shutters closed? The view was breathtakingly beautiful—why shut it out?

It wasn't as if she had a problem sleeping in the room as far as he was aware... Well, she'd never seemed uncomfortable when they'd had lessons together. She'd rejected the room at first but he'd presumed that was because the furnishings had been in such a poor state. Maybe it had nothing to do with the furnishings? But what, then, and why?

He walked into the courtyard and headed to the feasting hall determined to find his wife and answers.

He wouldn't bother waiting for Lothair, or welcome him into the hall as custom dictated.

The bastard knew the way.

Hunched over a bucket Amée scrubbed desperately at the silver for her father's refreshments. He only liked the best of the silverware for his table and she'd used all of it at the feast the night before; most of it was still dirty.

Beatrice and Emma were running around the pantry trying to rustle up some form of refreshments that would suit his exacting requirements. Perfect, unblemished fruit, mature cheeses and wine—she didn't have any wine. She brushed aside a tendril of hair that had escaped her veil.

Why was her father here? Why now? What could he possibly want?

Fear for her already precarious future grew like a vine around her heart, squeezing the strength from her body.

'What are you doing?'

Amée stiffened at the sound of Jorund's voice and slowly straightened her spine. She didn't have time to explore her wretched past. She needed to find something to drink that was as good as the wine at court…which was impossible.

'You do not have to fear him any longer—I am here.' Jorund's words were quiet but sincere. Did she really have nothing to fear? Jorund still didn't know about the contract.

She sighed and stopped scrubbing. 'I think…I just fell into old habits.' She hated herself for it, but as soon as she'd seen him again, the old fears had returned. Why else was she pandering to her father's demanding tastes?

Jorund stepped around the table to face her. When he spoke, it was a gentle statement rather than a question. 'Because he used to hurt you.' His fists were clenched at his sides, as if he were struggling to control himself. She should hate him after seeing Valda leave his room last night, and a part of her did. But another part of her wanted him to understand, and longed for his comfort.

However, if Jorund confronted her father, it would only make matters worse. 'Not very often.'

'And...your mother?' Big hands covered hers and lifted them from the bucket of water. 'Beatrice and Emma can deal with that. Come sit with me.'

'He's right, mistress,' said Beatrice thumping a basket of fruit on the table confidently. 'I'll deal with your *guest*. We'll be fine.'

Jorund led her by her wet hands to a small table with two stools in the darkened corner of the kitchen. Emma handed Jorund a cloth and then went back to work. He gently pressed it into her hands, and she began to dry them.

Did he think her mad?

'He has no say here. Do not feel as if you have to run around after him.'

She laughed lightly. 'I know... I... He'll leave soon. He never liked to stay here long. Sometimes it's just easier to do as he asks, although my mother never learnt that lesson.'

He sighed and leaned forward. 'Tell me.'

She stared at the wall and shrugged. 'My father likes order, and at times my mother could be difficult.'

'What do you mean by difficult?'

Shame clawed at her throat. Dare she confess it?

Last night, she'd thought they were close, in both body and spirit. Then she'd discovered the truth.

But…maybe if she explained her past to him, he'd realise the pain his infidelity caused her? Maybe he would understand, and stop?

Besides, she supposed she should explain anyway. Her father would probably torment her about it at some point. He liked to do that sometimes.

At least if she told Jorund now, she could explain it in her own words. 'It's difficult to explain… My mother… There was an imbalance in her moods—as if her mind had a constant fever. She could be extremely happy sometimes, and hopelessly sad the next. She was rarely…balanced. It was why my father avoided us for the most part. When she was happy, she adored my father, and he enjoyed her devotion. But then her darkness would always return at some point. Her ardour for him would cool and, frustrated, he would take other lovers. She took those affairs…badly. Sometimes she would become violent and attack him, and he would respond in kind. Theirs was not a happy marriage.'

How many times had her father called her mother mad and tried to beat the darkness from her?

Which had only made her worse.

She caught Beatrice's eye and the older woman gave her an encouraging smile as she finished plating up the large wooden tray and carried it out. Emma joined her, carrying two large jugs. A choice of drinks…that was wise.

Not for the first time she thanked God for the goodness of her people. It was one of the many reasons why she loved them. They knew everything, and protected her when they could.

If they hadn't been so kind… She shivered.

'That must have been hard for you.'

She shifted with guilt under his probing gaze, but she couldn't let him think she was innocent in the treatment of her mother.

'I avoided her, too, sometimes,' she confessed. 'I wasn't as good a daughter as I should have been, Jorund. You need to know that. I found her shifting moods... unsettling. Unlike my father I didn't enjoy her days of extreme joy. There was always something...*desperate* about them.' She shrugged helplessly, realising her words didn't make any sense.

Who wouldn't love the overwhelming love and affection her mother had shown her on those days?

Except, of course, she hadn't...because it hadn't felt real.

She sighed. 'I loved my mother—very much. Please know that. Especially on days when she was more settled, when her moods were balanced and she felt herself again. When she was peaceful. But then my father would arrive and she would be giddy with excitement. Constantly talking, and arranging feasts that I knew would never take place. Dancing and singing at all hours. Waking me up in the middle of the night to pick apples or skip stones across the river. I could never predict what she would do or how she would behave. When my father was home, I sought solace in books and parchments to avoid them both. When he was away, it felt as if we were free. I should have spent more time with her, but I was so lonely and I loved playing with the town's children, and I couldn't do that when he was here.'

She searched his face hoping he would understand her. The sympathy and lack of judgement in his eyes gave her the strength to continue. 'I hated when she was sad. She would keep to her rooms with only Beatrice for

company and I would not see her at all for many days...
sometimes weeks at a time. I tried to help her, but nothing I did seemed to help. We just had to wait for the darkness to pass and the cycle to begin again.'

She looked down at her fingers. There were crescent
moons embedded into her skin from clasping them too
tightly.

'You were a child,' Jorund said softly, taking her hands
in his. The touch was warm and gentle and reminded her
of his caresses from last night. Heat flowed through her
and she felt as if she were falling. Was she just like her
mother after all? Ruled by passions she couldn't control?
A wave of nausea washed through her and she pulled her
hands away.

How could he be so kind when he'd bedded another
woman straight after being with her?

'And yet, I still wish I'd done more...' She shrugged
and spread her hands over the table, finding comfort in
the solid wood beneath her fingertips. 'But we cannot
change the past.'

'It was your father who should have done more, not
you.'

'Yes.' She nodded sadly. 'But he didn't. He enjoyed her
adoration and love but he never returned it. My mother,
despite her changing moods, was a very beautiful woman
who loved him desperately.' *Unnaturally*, thought Amée,
remembering how her mother had been obsessed with
him. She never wanted to be like that, but she could feel
herself inevitably drowning in the intoxication of her
own husband.

Did all women lose themselves this way? Possibly it
was no longer solely admiration she felt for Jorund, nor
was it a passing fever like her mother's. Instead, it was

deep and enduring, carved in solid stone. It was terrifying, but also…thrilling, in a strange way. If only he felt the same way back.

'He manipulated her moods to suit himself,' Jorund said, snapping her thoughts back to the present.

'But I knew she was unwell. I should have kept a better eye on her. Looked after her better…'

Jorund draped an arm around her shoulders and pulled her close. 'How did she die?'

'An accident. It was no one's fault.' The lie slipped so easily from her mouth she didn't have time to think. How many times had she said it? Over and over, until it had become a truth all of its own.

'In your father's room?' he asked, and she shook her head.

'It wasn't a beating, it was an accident. She fell…while riding.'

It was too late to retract it, although she doubted Jorund would care in the same way the church and crown would. They would have denied her mother a Christian burial, not to mention the trouble it would have caused Beatrice. Loyal Beatrice, who had found her mother and cut her down from that tree. She had lied, and together with Amée they'd burned the rope.

Jorund might think badly of her if he knew the truth, and she could not risk Beatrice's safety.

Her father had his suspicions, but he was happy to perpetuate the lie—as it only made life easier for him. The secret, however, weighed heavy in her own heart. It smothered her voice and stopped her from confronting Jorund about Valda. It whispered to her that *some things were better left alone.*

What good could come from speaking of it?

'We should go see to him. He's been alone for a long time. It's rude of us.'

Jorund eased back in his chair and shrugged. 'I don't care. Do you?'

Amée smiled sadly. 'No. But I'm the Lady of Évreux now, and I have a responsibility to my guests.' She stood, her back straight and proud as she went to see to her father.

To her surprise Jorund followed.

Chapter Twenty-One

The day after Lothair's arrival, Jorund, Amée and all their guests went on a hunt.

It went well. Two stags and three boars had been flushed from the deepest undergrowth of the forest and they'd ridden hard to catch them. Jorund had brought down the stags and Valda had helped him with the boars they'd cornered.

The Princess had tired easily, however, and most of the hunting party had returned to the fort before midday. Lothair had left with them, and Jorund couldn't help but wonder if that was why Amée had insisting on staying behind with him, when he'd suggested he and Valda check some of their traps first before heading back.

Even after their talk in the kitchens Amée still appeared more reserved than usual. Colder somehow around him. Gone was the teasing, flirtatious friendship that had begun to blossom between them. In its place was something far more polite and distant.

Where was the woman who'd challenged him about the state of their supplies with clenched fists? The beautiful lady who'd sighed wistfully over dusty old books?

Who called her horse Luna and spoiled it with apples every day?

All the light within her seemed suffocated and diminished somehow.

It had to be because of her father.

Amée's revelations about her parents' relationship had answered so many questions he'd had about her childhood and her subsequent choice of joining the church. But there were also so many more questions that remained. He felt as if he were missing something vital still, but he couldn't think what.

He'd purposely not gone to her room last night, thinking she might need time to herself after the stress of dealing with her father. Had he been wrong to do that? To allow further distance between them, when she'd only just accepted him in her bed?

He sighed, unsure if there was any correct answer, except to give it time.

They should head home.

He'd sent too many men back. Firstly, to guard the others' return, and then to take their prizes back.

But doubt fogged his mind when he looked at Amée. Her eyes were closed, her face tilted to the light. She seemed at peace for the first time since her father's arrival and the day appeared to shine a little brighter because of it. Her face was flushed from the fresh air and exercise. Her hair was uncovered today, parted down the centre and plaited into two thick braids. An embroidered headband encircled her forehead, matching the russet colour of her mantle. She wore one of her new gowns in forest green with gold embroidery. Every inch the Lady of Évreux in her finery. Jorund was proud to call her his wife.

'Should we head back?' he asked lightly. Despite his

earlier thoughts he would gladly stay in the woods forever if she willed it.

She squinted at the sky and sighed. 'Yes, I suppose so. I'll need to begin preparations for the evening meal soon, and we're quite far out as it is.'

Jorund frowned.

Yes, they were... Almost at the borders of his land, in fact.

Amée turned Luna around with an easy click of her heels and a gentle tug on the reins. She'd grown into an experienced rider over the past three weeks. Managing to keep pace with them even when they'd caught sight of their prey and had had to charge forward.

As they made their way back through the forest towards the orchards of Évreux, a strange silence descended like a shadow on the land. As if even the birds were holding their breath. Awareness pricked along his spine.

Many years of experience had taught him never to ignore his instincts. His hand moved to his shield, and his eyes searched the trees. Hopefully, he was simply seeing threats where there were none. Even so, it was always better to prepare for the worst. He rode his horse closer to Amée's and signalled Valda, who silently flanked her on the other side.

A bush shivered; an arrowhead glinted in the sunlight. With a yell Jorund covered Amée with his shield.

Jorund's warhorse was seasoned in battle. But Amée's was not.

Luna screamed in pain and reared, throwing Amée off and onto the ground. It stumbled a few more steps before it, too, collapsed. Two arrows had struck home in its flank and neck. It was alive but badly wounded and breathing rapidly.

Jorund jumped down from his horse, his sword drawn, and he covered Amée with his shield again. Stunned by the fall she stared up at him with shocked wide eyes, but otherwise unharmed.

He knelt beside her, shielding her as best as he could. It was not an action that came naturally to him. A man as big as he was an attacker, not a defender.

Another arrow flew, but the aim was terrible, as if their assailant was panicking, and…alone.

'There!' He pointed towards the bushes with a roar. 'Take him alive!' Valda burst into action with the rest of his men.

Amée groaned as she looked up at him, her eyes unfocused as she struggled to gather her wits. She glanced around her as if in a daze.

Then she saw her horse, and she choked on a sob as she struggled to stand.

'Luna!' she gasped. It hurt him to do it, but her safety was far more important than her feelings. He held her down with a firm hand against her belly. 'Wait!'

He glanced around, to check if they were safe. By the sounds of his men, the assassin had already been captured but he scrutinised the surrounding trees to be certain. After a moment, he released her with a nod, and she ran to her bleeding horse. He covered her as she ran, just in case.

Bile churned in his stomach as he took in the bloody scene before him. He'd seen worse, but he knew how it would affect Amée, and that's what was the hardest to stomach. The horse's eyes were wild with pain and fear, its breathing irregular.

This could have been Amée.

She wept as she patted the animal's neck and whispered into its ear. Ripping at her finery to create bandages to pack the wounds.

The blood loss was great, the mare weak. Slowly its head slumped to the ground. Defeated it stared at Amée with pained, trusting eyes, as its breathing began to slow. Either at the calming sight of its mistress or in acceptance of its possible death, he couldn't be sure which. Perhaps both.

Amée looked up at him, her eyes awash with tears. 'Jorund, she won't stop bleeding. Please help me! *Please!*'

He swallowed the lump in his throat and nodded.

'We need to cauterise the wound… Build a fire,' he ordered one of his nearby warriors, who immediately pushed together a few sticks and leaves at his feet and began to strike on a flint. Valda emerged with a struggling youth at the end of a rope and tied him to a nearby oak.

'Valda, ride to the town. Bring back a cart, big enough to carry her horse.'

After tying up the prisoner she began to cross the clearing. He met her halfway. Valda glanced at the state of Luna and then looked at Jorund. There was a grim sympathy in her eyes, which he always hated, especially when it was combined with an 'are you mad?' stare.

'Wouldn't it be better to put it out of its misery?' Valda asked quietly.

'No!' he muttered, also keeping his voice low, so that Amée wouldn't hear their arguing. Jorund pointed at the animal with a frustrated stab of his finger, and whispered through clenched teeth. 'Even if I have to carry that *damned animal* back by myself it's going to survive! You hear me?'

With a nod she mounted her horse and galloped away.

Valda could not understand. To her this was not even a skirmish; the death of a horse would mean nothing on the battlefield. He'd never even named his own horse, despite having it for years.

Jorund cursed and spat on the floor, desperate to relieve the bitter taste in his mouth from all the blood and fear that had raced through his veins moments earlier.

Not for himself, of course. But for Amée.

When the small fire was hot enough, he plunged his dagger into the flames and waited for it to glow. Instructing his men, they held down Amée's horse. It screamed and jerked as first he pulled free the arrows, then the red-hot blade touched its flesh. The rancid smell of burnt hair and muscle singed his nostrils and made him cough, but he ignored it, working to close the wounds as quickly as possible while Amée comforted the animal.

Afterwards she curled up on the ground beside its head, oblivious to the filth. She stroked Luna's velvet muzzle with soothing words even as tears poured down her cheeks.

He'd not been exaggerating when he'd said he'd do anything to ensure her pet's survival. He would have happily pressed the glowing blade into his own flesh if it would have eased Amée's torment.

Cold rage swept through his muscles, causing them to bunch and tense. He refused to look at their assailant until he was satisfied of the horse and Amée's wellbeing. But he knew where he was. Tied to a tree. Waiting. The darkness inside of him smiled; he would take great pleasure in hurting him later. Usually, dark thoughts like these frightened him—they reminded him too much of his father—but today he welcomed them.

It didn't take Valda long to return. A harvest cart entered the clearing pulled by two heavy workhorses. They pranced and strained at the smell of blood in the air. But the driver urged them forward with a crack of his reins. Several burly serfs, more than was needed, sat in the back of the cart. They hopped off before the cart had fully stopped and pushed out planks of wood to create a ramp.

It was not often that he was surprised, but today he was, and grateful. He raised an eyebrow as Valda jumped down from her horse.

She shrugged. 'They insisted on helping… Once they knew who it was for.' She nodded over at Amée, who had leapt to her feet and was already instructing her people in tying the ropes around her horse. As he was no longer needed, he walked over to the tree where the lone archer was bound.

The archer was young. Painfully so. Some of the fiery rage eased within him.

The hair on the boy's chin was more like dirty clumps of fluff than a man's full beard. His pale grey eyes were red and frightened.

He would have looked like this.

All those years ago, when he'd rode with his father.

'My wife loves that horse,' Jorund said mildly, and the youth's breathing quickened. His eyes darting pitifully to the activity, and then back at his bound hands that trembled miserably.

It was then that Jorund remembered he was still carrying the knife in his hand. He played with it lazily as he squatted down to face the boy. The small apple of the youth's throat jumped with every panicked swallow as he watched the blade dance.

'Why did you attack my wife?' asked Jorund. The boy looked away, his jaw remaining firmly closed.

Should he start cutting off his fingers, one by one? Something held him back... Maybe it was because he was so young.

What would Amée think?

His need for vengeance cooled even further.

No! He would have answers. He grabbed the boy's bound hands and pulled them forward. Then he prised open two fingers from the clenched fist and moved the dagger into place. The blade kissed the skin just below his knuckles. He could take them with a quick slice—the blade was sharp enough...the fingers thin.

'If you lose these fingers, you'll never use a bow again.'

The boy broke with a whimper. 'There's a pound of silver for the man who kills her.'

'A pound of silver?'

Such a pitiful amount. Although people had been killed for less...much less.

'All of the war bands in Cotentin have heard of it.'

'Who *dared* put a price on my wife's head?'

'I...I...don't know.' The boy's face paled, as if there was a greater threat to fear than the blade at his fingers. Suspicion bloomed inside Jorund's chest, making his stomach churn.

'Who?' he roared, grabbing the youth by his throat and pressing him into the tree until the boy winced and wheezed.

'I...I swear... I do not know him... Only that we should kill her and report it to our chief.'

'And who is your chief?'

'Erik Blacktooth.'

The boy crumpled into tears as soon as Jorund released his neck. Nothing more than a fearful child ordered to do the bidding of lesser men. Bitterness soured in Jorund's gut and he tasted blood and soot in the air. Grabbing the boy's wrists, he pulled him forward and raised his blade.

The boy flinched and then relaxed as Jorund cut him free of his bonds.

'This ends *now*. Tell Erik to meet me at the lone apple tree that stands on the crest of the hill overlooking Évreux. I will pay double to know who ordered these attacks. Is that understood?'

The boy scrambled to his feet with a fearful nod and ran towards the woods.

'And, boy!' he snapped, and the boy stumbled a few steps before turning to face him. Jorund stared him down, willing him to listen. 'After you have delivered my message... Some advice for you. Choose your friends more wisely in future. A life with raiders is a short one.'

The boy's head bobbed and then he fled into the forest without looking back.

By then, Luna had been loaded onto the cart and Amée was sat beside her.

He mounted his horse and followed beside the cart. Amée looked up at him with confused and despairing eyes. 'You let him go? I mean—I'm glad you didn't hurt him... He was just a boy after all. But why would he attack us?'

'It was a mistake—he thought we were raiders, and then he panicked.'

Amée frowned at his weak answer, but with a nod she turned back to comfort her horse.

Jorund hated to lie to her. He had his suspicions regarding the attacks, but he refused to upset her any more than he needed to without further proof.

Chapter Twenty-Two

Luna was sleeping peacefully in the warm straw of her spacious stable. Amée had insisted she have the largest one, as well as all of the hay and apples she could possibly want. It still didn't satisfy Amée's need to comfort her, though, and she'd refused to leave the horse's side even when Beatrice had begged her to take some rest. She'd known she couldn't leave her, not at such a critical time after her injuries.

Fever and infection could still develop, but at least Luna was a little stronger now and had a greater chance of survival. She'd applied herbs and honey to the wounds to ward against disease and covered them with boiled cloths. It was the treatments the abbess had always sworn by for wounds, that combined with a watchful eye.

Which was why Amée had resigned herself to a night in Luna's stall. Hand feeding her water and oats to keep up her strength, while she regularly cleaned and dressed the wounds as often as she dared.

Beatrice had insisted on making the stable as comfortable as possible for her mistress. She'd sectioned off a small area of the stable with hay bales to keep out the draft, as well as a pile of blankets and furs for Amée to rest on when she needed to. There was a small iron brazier by the door offering heat and a small amount of light.

'Have you eaten?' asked Jorund. He stood hesitantly in the open doorway of the stable, a pile of logs in his arms which he dropped beside the brazier. Beatrice must have told him her plans. She was glad that he didn't question them. Her father would have mocked her for caring so deeply over an animal.

'Yes, thank you. Gisla came and brought me something.'

A flash of surprise crossed his face and Amée chuckled. 'She's not the type to get her hands messy, so she didn't stay long. But she's got a good heart.'

Jorund closed the door behind him and walked over to her side. 'As have you,' he said, nodding down to the sleeping Luna. 'She looks a lot better.'

'There's no fever yet.'

'That's good.'

She nodded in agreement, and wondered why he was here. He swayed on his feet, a telltale sign of indecision.

'Is something wrong?'

'No,' he answered quickly with a shake of his head, a little too quickly for Amée's comfort.

She swallowed the knot in her throat and looked away.

'I promised you my protection and my devotion,' he said in a rush.

His words tore at her heart—was he about to confess his relationship with Valda? A part of her couldn't stomach it. For the admission to pass his lips and become a solid weapon in her world. She dared not speak.

'I know I can be...private at times. But I do care for you, and today... If you'd been hurt...' He paled, his eyes burning with torment.

'I'm fine.' She took a step towards him. Interrupting him before he could say another word. 'You've kept your promise to me: I'm safe and unharmed.' It wasn't the love she craved but it was enough.

'I swear…' He took her hands in his and lifted them to his lips. Kissing them gently, one by one. Then he leaned down, his back curving as he bowed down to her. Letting go of her hands, he cupped her face next, caressing her cheeks as he pressed another kiss to her lips.

Each kiss felt like a promise. A vow to keep her safe from harm and cherish her always. He pulled ever so slightly back, opening his mouth to say something more. To swear an oath that she knew he wouldn't keep.

She didn't want his lies. She couldn't bear it. Her hands wrapped around his thick neck and pulled him to her lips.

After the terrifying events of the day, all she wanted was to feel alive again. To be reminded of the pleasure and excitement only Jorund could give her.

Passion ignited between them, and she clung to him. Desperately wanting his promise of love and devotion while knowing his heart was already divided. The overwhelming lust they felt for each other could not be denied. No matter how much it hurt her in the future, she couldn't untangle her heart from her desire, or deny the pleasure of his touch.

She still wanted him. She was afraid she always would.

Unable to resist, Jorund instinctively deepened the kiss. He'd wanted to reassure her that his sleeping away from her was only to ensure her safety, that it wasn't because he didn't want to be with her… Far from it—he couldn't seem to keep away from her.

But then he would have to explain why he was concerned for her safety in bed... How could he explain that? After swearing to protect her? He would have to confess that he wasn't always in control of himself. That in his sleep he sometimes became wild and as frightened as a little boy. It was too humiliating.

Amée's urgent kisses made him forget his thoughts, and he became lost in her passionate responses.

'Untie your hair,' he said. '*Please*, I long to see it. It's so beautiful.'

A becoming blush flushed her cheeks, and she unbound her hair, casting aside the leather ties and headband onto the straw beneath their feet. She shook out her mass of ebony curls. The soft clouds bounced with abandon around her shoulders. He reached out and tugged lightly on one of her midnight coils, watching in fascination as it sprang back into shape.

Resilient, soft and beautiful, just like Amée.

She closed the distance between them. Delicate fingers clawed at his tunic, and he obliged her by shedding it quickly. The amber flecks sparked in her eyes, and she quickly tugged at the ties behind her neck to loosen them.

Then she moved away from him, and his chest tightened at the loss. She lay down on the little pile of bedding amongst the straw, her eyes never leaving his face as she offered herself to him.

'Lie with me,' she asked sweetly, biting her lip with the uncertainty of her request. As if he could refuse her anything.

He knelt down at her feet in the thick straw, placed both palms on her bent knees to steady himself. As he leaned forward to kiss her, Amée raised herself up on her elbows to meet him.

Revelling in the touch of his skin, her hands smoothed gently over his chest and shoulders, running up and down his muscles with long caressing strokes. He rocked forward, settling himself between her thighs, pressing himself close so that she could enjoy the hard length of him against her core.

'I love...your...body,' she panted between the hot kisses he pressed against her mouth and neck.

The innocent admission took his breath away and he groaned as fiery lust raced through his veins. His hands urgently tugged at the neckline of her gown, dragging it down past her shoulders. Thankfully, she'd loosened the ties enough that the material didn't rip. Pale breasts and dark nipples were revealed to the cool night air and he kissed them with greedy lips.

She moaned as his tongue swept over the tight bud, gripping the sides of his head with her hands and arching her spine to meet him. She rocked her hips against him, her gasps of pleasure desperate and needy, as he lost himself in her luscious body.

She squirmed violently beneath him, and he raised himself up onto his arms, worried he might be crushing her. The hands that had been clutching his head dropped to her skirts, and he stared in wonder as she used the sudden freedom between them to quickly yank them up to the tops of her thighs.

Brown eyes, splashed with gold, stared up at him, her face rosy. A few strands of golden straw stuck in the thickness of her curls. 'I need you now,' she gasped, her hands feverishly working on the ties at his waist.

He swept a hand down her thigh and sought her entrance beneath her skirts. Hot and wet she pressed against his fingers with a pleading moan. He couldn't hold back a moment longer, and shoved down his trousers with eager impatience. Gathering up her hips in his palms, he positioned himself at her entrance and then pushed inside her with a hard thrust.

Tight, warm heat washed over him and he dropped his head into the curve of her neck with a heavy moan.

'Yes!' Amée cried out beneath him, grabbing first his hips and then his buttocks as she squeezed and pushed him harder against her. No longer in control of his own thoughts, he allowed her to work him. She controlled his thrusts with panted commands and squeezing hands. Their lovemaking was wild and desperate.

She watched him as he climaxed, her own pleasure rushing forward in a wave as she saw him unravel beneath her pressing hands. She moaned beneath his sweating body, rubbing against him with the last ripples of delight as he poured himself into her.

His body and his soul were hers to command.

When Jorund finally regained his wits, he realised Amée was already falling asleep beneath him. He took a moment to adjust both their clothing, and then covered her in blankets for warmth. Then he left, shaken by his desperate longing to stay by her side.

He waited outside until dawn, and then ordered a guard to watch and follow her from now on. He no longer trusted her precious safety within the walls of the fort, or anywhere.

Amée awoke to a velvety, whiskered nose pressed against her face.

'You're standing! What a clever girl,' she gasped. Stumbling to her feet, the hay of the stable floor sticking to her in big clumps as she walked over to greet her pet.

Thankfully, God had been kind. There was still no sign of fever.

Amée grabbed an apple from a nearby sack and offered it. To her delight Luna chomped happily on the apple and a surge of relief flooded through her at the sight. She rubbed Luna's head and kissed her nose in praise. Luna dipped her long head and nuzzled her in thanks.

'At least you're pleased to see me,' whispered Amée with a sigh.

Where had Jorund gone?

After their lovemaking last night, she was sure he would have stayed with her. But no...he was already gone. Disappointment sat heavy in her stomach like a stone.

Still, she couldn't deny that he cared.

Maybe not in the romantic way she longed for, but there was passion and kindness there. He'd been quick to arrange the sealing of the wounds, as well as their transport back home. Most men would have slit Luna's throat and considered it an act of mercy. Jorund had never even suggested it, and for that she'd always be indebted.

He was a good man. He respected her as his wife and had acted accordingly to ensure her happiness. That didn't mean he owed her anything more... Did it?

Luna began to snuffle at her head, and she realised with a giggle that she was eating straw from her hair. It was probably for the best Jorund hadn't stayed. She definitely wouldn't look quite so ravishing in the hard light of day. She still wore the same gown from yesterday. It was torn and covered in blood, hay and sweat. She was exhausted and probably smelt far worse than she looked... which was bad enough.

'I think I should go and bathe,' she said to Luna, who snorted in apparent agreement. She gave one last scratch behind the animal's ears before she left.

A young man was waiting on a stump outside the stable. He jumped to his feet with a smile. 'My name is Birger, my lady! I've been ordered to guard you.'

'Oh!' she replied, confused and more than a little surprised.

Then she saw them. Jorund and Valda astride their horses, heavily armed and riding towards the gate. They'd emerged from a stable further ahead and hadn't seen her.

Surely they didn't need to go hunting again?

Part of her was glad he'd not seen her—she did look a fright.

Another part, a far louder and wounded part of her, cried out at the injustice.

How could he forget her so easily? When every day she longed for him even more than the last? Maybe he thought her behaviour ridiculous and wanton? She'd been so intoxicated by her desire for him last night that she'd practically ravished him. Maybe he'd left in disgust straight after?

Either way, it seemed as if his relationship with Valda was stronger than whatever fleeting moment of lust he'd felt for her. Whatever growing intimacy and feelings she'd imagined between them must have been in her mind.

She lowered her head and hurried forward in the opposite direction, feeling as lowly and as wanted as a rat in the kitchen. Her guard following like a shadow.

Chapter Twenty-Three

'Would you please fetch us some more flour, Birger?' Amée asked sweetly between gritted teeth later that day. He'd followed her everywhere, even waited outside her chamber door while she bathed and dressed.

Birger frowned from his position by the door. 'I am tasked with guarding you, mistress. I should not leave your side.'

Amée scowled at him. Birger had been under her feet ever since she'd left the stables earlier that morning. She was certain Jorund only meant for Birger to guard her if she left the fort. But Birger had disagreed—his instructions were apparently to 'guard her with his life, wherever she went.'

Another chain on her freedom. Resentment bubbled under her skin every time the well-meaning Birger got in her way.

Which unfortunately was often.

She couldn't relax around him. Even Emma and Beatrice appeared affected by his presence, regularly glancing at her faithful hound nervously.

Amée let out a long-suffering sigh and placed her hands on her hips to confront him. She was still exhausted from her long night tending Luna and not in the mood to deal with overzealous men wishing to impress their master. 'We have important guests to look after, and many jobs to do before yet another feast tonight. I could do with your help, Birger. I'm sure when Jorund gave you the task of protecting me, he didn't expect you to be standing around idle watching me work!'

At the mention of Jorund, Birger lifted from the wall with surprising speed. 'How many sacks?'

'Just the one will suffice. Next we'll need plenty of wood for the fires.'

He left quickly, with a renewed vigour in his step. As soon as Birger left the kitchen, Beatrice shuffled closer towards her and spoke with a hushed voice. 'Mistress, please be careful… We're worried about you.'

Amée stared at Beatrice in surprise. Was this why they'd seemed so nervous of Birger's presence? 'Don't worry about the attack yesterday,' she reassured her. 'I'm fine, honestly, and Luna is recovering well.' She flicked her wrist to the doorway, adding with a barely concealed jeer, 'Look, Jorund has left me with a *helpful* guard to keep me safe.'

Amée turned back to the bread she was kneading and gave it a hammer with her fists. She was so tired. But it wasn't entirely because of Luna. She was tired of the uncertainty and the unspoken half-truths between Jorund and herself. He'd said he would not shame her with another wife, but was Valda always going to be a silent third party in their marriage?

He'd bedded her after he'd been with Amée that first time. He spent most of his waking day with Valda and not Amée. Even after the attack he'd gone riding with *her.* Had possibly even left his wife in the stable last night to sleep with *her*!

Beatrice reached out and held her wrist firmly, causing Amée to pause in her torrent of unwelcome thoughts.

Beatrice's eyes glanced fearfully at the door before she whispered in a rush, 'One of the villagers has heard news from the south. There's a price on your head. Someone has offered the Norse raiders a reward for your death! There is talk that your husband may have ordered it. His father once ran with those raiders…he would have the connections. We're afraid for you, mistress.'

'A reward, for my *death*?' Amée stared at Beatrice in horror, before shaking her head. 'It can't be Jorund. He wouldn't…'

'I agree,' said Emma with a firm nod. She'd had a soft spot for Jorund since the incident with Skarde. 'The raiders are evil men. They may be looking for any excuse to unseat Jorund from his position before they invade. It might even be one of their strange customs—to kill the wife of their enemy?'

Amée nodded, grateful for an explanation. 'Yes! That must be it. We all know how some of the Norse raiders were unhappy with their share in the treaty. They must be trying to steal what they cannot claim honourably.' Although she felt more unsettled by the second.

Had Jorund learned of the contract? Thought to kill her rather than wait for a child that may or may not arrive in time?

Did he want Valda for his wife instead?

Was that why he'd let the lone archer go? But then why bother protecting her at all? He'd saved her life twice now. It didn't make sense.

She shook her head. No, he would never do such a thing!

But maybe Valda would?

Nothing Valda had done so far implied such an awful thing, but she couldn't think of anyone else who would want her dead. One thought glanced across her mind, but the idea made her sick to her stomach and she pushed it aside.

'Don't worry, Beatrice,' Amée eventually answered. 'Why would Jorund give me a guard if he didn't want to protect me?' She went back to working on the bread, pounding it with her fists, as yet more questions raced through her head like wild horses.

'I hope you're right, mistress,' said Beatrice.

She didn't say anything more, as at that moment Birger walked in with the sack of flour.

The three women worked in silence.

A walk!

That was what she needed to clear her mind. All the preparations were under way for the feast and she couldn't stand the strained silence of the kitchen a moment longer. Beatrice and Emma's worry pressed in on her as if she were already in her grave.

It was late afternoon, but there was plenty of time before the evening meal. Her thoughts were too chaotic for her to sleep, and she would rather do anything else than keep her father company.

'I'm going for a walk. I suppose you will insist on joining me?' she said to Birger as they left the hall. He gave a grim nod, and she began walking. Birger followed a few paces behind.

At the gate of the fort, she noticed two dark blemishes on the opposite hill. It looked as if two horses were tied to her mother's tree. Usually, she avoided looking in that direction but for some reason—that she could not fathom—today she looked.

Maybe she'd seen them out of the corner of her eye and instinctively her gaze had followed?

It was an odd sight to see anyone lingering at that tree. The locals all avoided it as much as she did. There was darkness and sadness soaked into every grain of it and no one liked to linger in its presence for long. There was a superstition that its darkness would seep into a person's blood and destroy them from the inside out.

So, who could it be?

It only took her a moment to realise.

Jorund and Valda.

He does not love me! How many times had her mother wailed those words in her father's absence? Fallen to the floor and wept in despair, screaming those same words over and over. Was that to be her fate too? Was the boot against her neck not one woven with violence but an equally deadly one poisoned with…love?

She was tempted to run to her chamber and lock the door. Hide from everything that threatened to control and hurt her.

No!

She would not run away from her fate a moment longer. She would face it, better to know than suffer this purgatory of uncertainty!

She looked towards the heavy limbs of the tree in the distance and the shapes beneath it. This time she wouldn't shy away from the truth and pain. Anger warmed her blood and she shouted for a horse, her head held high.

Jorund and Valda faced away from Évreux, watching for the approach of the lone archer's chief.

Soon he would have answers.

Unfortunately, he didn't notice Amée's arrival until it was too late.

'Take her home immediately!' he shouted, glaring at Birger as they arrived on horseback. He was surprised Amée had been brave enough to ride a horse unfamiliar to her. He would have felt proud of her, if he'd not wished her anywhere but here at this moment.

How could he meet with a vile raider in the presence of his wife? Especially one who'd made at least one attempt on her life. Someone who'd known his father, and the disgusting history of his youth.

Tiredness fuelled the rage within him. Birger paled at his expression as he and Amée dropped down from their horses.

His stomach churned. What if his suspicions were correct? What if he was right about the person behind the attacks?

Birger swallowed noisily under the weight of his livid gaze. He reached to take Amée's arm to draw her away. But she threw it off with a smack of her hand and strode towards Jorund.

A wrath he'd never seen before burned behind her eyes. 'I must speak with them!'

He glanced back to the tree and the awaiting horizon. Still no sign of the raider, but he might not come from the fields. He might arrive from the wood or the orchard, might even now be watching them with an arrow nocked at the ready.

He tried to block her body from the orchard with his own. Oblivious of the possible danger, Amée tossed the reins of her horse at Birger and strode towards Valda, who sat beneath the tree. She rose as Amée approached, equally as confused by her anger and presence as Jorund.

'I can see your tryst from my room! Have you no shame, no honour? Or do you have even more wicked plans in mind…other than bedding my husband?' Amée shouted, breathless with anger.

Jorund felt trapped in a cage that he could neither see nor feel. Her life could be in danger at this very moment. And she thought…

'What?' he whispered.

Amée's head swivelled between them with equal censure. 'I will not be shamed openly. *Not here!*' She stabbed her finger towards the tree with disgust, and Valda blinked. He doubted he had ever seen Valda afraid, but she looked it now. Her face had paled, and she stared at Amée as if she were about to be whipped to death.

'No… My lady, it is not what you think.'

Jorund frowned at Valda's strange words and snorted in amusement at the ridiculousness of the situation. 'Valda has no plans to bed me. What nonsense is this? Go home immediately. We will speak of this later!'

He gestured for Birger to take hold of her, and to his credit he took a hesitant step forward before he lost his nerve under her fiery glare. She turned on Jorund next by thumping him in the belly with her fist.

'How *dare* you? I am not blind!' She spun back towards Valda with an angry hiss. 'Are you behind the attacks? Are you the one who wants me dead? Not content with stealing him, you wish to take my life as well?'

'I would never harm you, my lady. I swear it!' gasped Valda, horrified.

His own anger and impatience flared. 'Are you *mad*? Valda would never hurt you. And as for stealing me from you—I have told you already. I have had, and will have, no other wife but you! Valda is like a sister to me—don't be so ridiculous!'

Amée's glare hardened and she took a step towards Jorund, her face tilted up to look at him, rage and defiance burning in the gold flecks of her eyes. Her voice was low and deadly. 'I see the way she looks at you! I do not care what you do with her in your chamber, but you will not humiliate me in public! *Don't* ever call me mad.'

The wind rushed from his lungs. *Damn!* He'd been so thoughtless with his words. 'I only meant... This is ridiculous! Tell her, Valda.'

He turned to Valda and she opened her mouth, but was quickly silenced by Amée's next words. 'I saw her leaving your room! I'm not as naive as you believe. So, stop treating me as if I am stupid!'

His heart contracted and his vision blurred for a moment. There was only one reason she would have seen Valda leaving his room, and it would be after one of his nightmares. Disgrace crawled up his spine and he felt sick with dizziness.

Valda took a step forward, her voice helpless as she struggled with what she'd sworn never to discuss. 'But... But it's not what you think! I...'

All the dark secrets that he'd fought so hard to keep hidden were attacking him at once. His shameful past, his nightmares! Like a pack of wolves, they threatened to tear him apart until nothing remained. He could not breathe, or think clearly.

Before Valda could say another word, he turned and roared at Amée like a wounded animal. 'It is *nothing* to do with you! Now, I *order* you—*go!*'

Amée faced him without any fear, and it only made

him feel more despicable for shouting at her. Still, he would rather she thought him a beast than know the truth of his real weakness.

Her eyes met his, and she looked at him with an empty, cold stare. As if he'd broken her heart and now lived as a stranger in her eyes.

'Finally,' she whispered, her voice sharp with bitterness, 'the *truth*.'

His soul cracked under the weight of her disappointment as she rode away.

'*Why!* Why would you not tell her?' Valda sighed with exasperation as she watched Amée leave.

'She's being ridiculous. It does not concern her. As it does not concern you!' he growled, turning away to search the fields and trees for the raider.

The real threat.

He'd thought she wasn't going to say any more, but after a long silence she spoke, her voice soft with pain. 'She's right.' When he looked at her, she shrugged, crossed her arms and stared out into the horizon. 'About the way I look at you. She's not being ridiculous.'

Was every woman in his life going to turn on him today?

'What are you *talking* about?'

Tears appeared in her eyes, and he felt the ground tilt beneath his feet.

Valda didn't cry.

'I thought I hid it so well.' She smiled weakly. 'But I suppose another woman would see it...' Horrified understanding must have dawned across his face because Valda gave a hollow laugh. 'Don't worry, I know you don't feel the same way.'

He wasn't sure what to say. Valda loved him? The woman who'd fought by his side for years? Who he'd always loved…but like a sister? He hated to be the cause of her pain, and yet he knew there was no comfort he could offer.

'I'm sorry.'

She shook her head and dipped to pick up her bow. 'I know. But do not be angry at her for misunderstanding our relationship. She had cause. After tonight I will leave. If my fate is not to be with you, then I will go and search for my sisters. I have spent too long away from them as it is.'

He shook his head, dazed and confused. But what could he say? There was no way Valda could stay with him, not now. 'Well, all I can say is that you have terrible taste in men,' he grumbled.

The scouts he'd sent out into the forest returned and Jorund untied his horse from the tree and mounted it. 'I must go and speak with my wife. Wait here for the chief. I'll send you more warriors immediately.'

Jorund cut the bags of silver from his saddle. They fell with a heavy shiver as the silver bounty within shifted and clanged inside. 'This ends now. If they give up the name of the culprit behind the attacks, then pay them. If not, kill them all.'

Chapter Twenty-Four

'There you are, Amée. Always hiding from your responsibilities.' Her father's voice froze the blood in her veins.

She looked up from her chair by the fire wishing she was mistaken. She couldn't stomach her father, not so soon after her confrontation with Jorund. She half wished she hadn't threatened to castrate Birger if he continued to follow her. At least then she wouldn't be alone with her father.

But there he was. Stood in the doorway of her bedchamber. Walking in as if it were still his room.

I am no longer a child, and this is my home, not his! she reminded herself quickly as she rose to face him.

'I was resting before the feast tonight. It's about to begin… You go ahead, I'll join you shortly.'

She'd hoped he would leave. She hated to be alone with him. With the shutters closed and the fire low she could barely see him now that the door was half closed. Why had she left it open? Had a part of her hoped that Jorund would have followed her? Begged for her forgiveness? But he hadn't; she'd sat alone in her misery, praying that she'd somehow been mistaken.

Maybe she *was* mad.

Lothair came to stand in front of her. He took out a small bottle from a pocket within his mantle. 'I don't have much time. Soon we will be free of your husband… one way or another. If ever you miss your monthlies, you must drink a tea made with four drops from this vial.' He thrust the bottle in her hands and she fumbled with it. His other hand snapped crushingly around her wrist. 'Why must you always be so clumsy? I'd hoped your time at the nunnery would have given you some grace at least!'

A spark of defiance lit within her and she twisted out of his hold. 'What is it?'

He hissed a curse. No doubt he'd presumed she'd have accepted it without question. 'Your freedom! You saw my contract with King Charles, you know my plan. If there are no heirs within two winters the land reverts back to me. You will be free to accept your calling to God. No longer burdened by the shame of this marriage. It will be as you wanted it to be.'

She stared at the bottle in her hands, horrified. 'It's an abortive?'

He shrugged dismissively, 'Your mother struggled to conceive. I'm sure you will too. But this will *ensure* the alliance fails. Even if something should happen to…stick.'

Amée shivered at her father's callous words.

He leaned forward. 'You want an end to this miserable marriage, don't you? To go back to the nunnery, where you're safe. You're not safe with him here. The attacks by those raiders only prove it. They are savages that live only for death and destruction.'

Dare she defy him? He was right about one thing at least. Her marriage *was* miserable.

She stared at Lothair, searching his face for any sign of compassion but found none. He only cared for power;

he'd never loved her or her mother. It was a truth she'd always known, but it still ached as if it were a broken bone badly set.

What she did now had to be for her and her future alone.

She stared at the vial as if in a daze.

Jorund turned away from Amée's door and walked down the stairwell feeling as if his heart had been ripped from his chest.

He'd heard enough.

He'd been mad to think that a woman as sweet and as gentle as Amée could ever want a beast like him. She'd been biding her time, scheming with her father to end their marriage as soon as possible.

Two winters...

Hadn't she asked him if he could wait that long?

But she hadn't waited... What had caused her to change her mind? Unless she'd already used something to hold off pregnancy. She'd been keen to grow her herbs in the gardens... Women were knowledgeable in such things, weren't they?

He was in the courtyard now and he stared at the neat rows of freshly turned soil. The gardens were tidy. Sprouting with an array of herbs and young vegetables in the summer sun. There wouldn't be much to harvest this year, but there would be plenty the following. This was not the work of a woman who didn't plan to stay to see the fruits of her labour. After all of Amée's hard work, why would she willingly leave it all behind?

He paused, and turned back to the rotunda with its shuttered windows.

Idiot! He was letting his own insecurities get the better of him.

Amée was afraid of her father. She'd been bullied by him most of her life. He knew in his heart that if she did obey him it would only be out of fear. It wasn't as if she could rely on Jorund. She'd thought he'd betrayed her with Valda—of course, she would feel vulnerable and long for her old life. The question was, would he give her up?

No, he loved her too much.

The realisation hit him like a bolt of lightning. Followed quickly by another darker thought that stole the air from his lungs.

He'd left her alone with that evil man...

Amée continued to stare at the vial in her hand.

Wasn't this what she wanted? A chance to go back to her old life—to live in peace at the nunnery once more?

The thought no longer filled her with hope. She imagined a life away from her home, away from the people she loved. Even the thought of a life without Jorund hurt, when by all reason it shouldn't.

To go back to the nunnery would be like being buried alive. A slow suffocating death with no light, no pleasure, no pain...a grey, drab existence like the habit she'd once worn. The same habit Jorund had ripped from her body, his eyes filled with lust.

He'd made her feel alive again. She was grateful for that at least.

No matter how miserable Jorund's rejection today had made her, the sad fact was that she still didn't want their marriage to end. He was a far better man than Lothair could ever hope to be. Jorund had her people's best interests at heart. He wanted a future for them. It was more than Lothair could ever offer.

He lied to you! He's an unfaithful liar who could never love you.

But could she kill his child? Could she abandon her people? Could she abandon him?

No.

It didn't make sense, but she knew that what was left of her broken heart still loved him. And she would remain by his side. Never could she welcome him in her bed again. So, she only hoped she did carry his child. Otherwise, she wasn't sure what would happen in two winters' time. She only knew that she and Jorund would never give up their land willingly.

Lothair would have to fight them for it.

She stared hard at her father and raised her chin in defiance. 'You have no heirs with your new wife *either*, Father. Maybe my mother wasn't the issue—'

The slap cracked across her cheek in a flame of pain. It did not shock her. A slap was inevitable whenever she was alone with him. But this time she refused to cry or run away.

She lifted her face and stared back at him. With great satisfaction she threw the vial into the fire, enjoying the smash and hiss as the poison was consumed by the flames. She was no longer his daughter to control and threaten.

Her father's face boiled with rage as he raised his arm for another strike, this time with a closed fist. She did as Jorund had shown her. She grabbed Lothair's arms and threw out her knee. She rejoiced when she hit soft flesh and Lothair screamed out in pain. Releasing him, he crumpled to the floor, clutching his groin and wailing.

Her hands shook, but she refused to run. She picked up her skirts and strode calmly from the room, pausing at the doorway to say in a voice full of command, 'You will *never* lay a hand on me *ever* again.'

As she walked down the spiral stairs, the enormity of what she'd done struck her hard. She clutched at the walls, taking comfort from the age and strength of the stone beneath her fingertips.

Had she *really* done it? Stood up to her father?

Tears pricked at the back of her eyes, but it wasn't because she was frightened or felt guilty for what she'd done. They were tears of relief. She took another step and another, her shaky breath releasing a little easier the further she moved away from him.

What had possessed her of late?

First, she'd confronted Jorund and Valda. Now, she'd challenged her father. It was as if she enjoyed throwing herself against the rocks.

She paused on the second level of the rotunda and closed her eyes with a sigh.

No, she didn't enjoy it. But she was tired of hiding from the truth. No matter how bitter and painful it was.

She didn't love her father and would never allow him to bully her again.

Sadly, she loved Jorund. But she knew now that she was not like her mother. She was stronger, and could weather the pain without letting it tear her apart... She had to.

To think that she'd thought she could find peace only by running away. When all she'd really needed to do was face her fears.

She took her next steps down the stairs with greater purpose in her stride.

A thunder of boots rushed up the stairwell, and Jorund almost trampled over her in his haste. He grabbed her waist and pressed her against the wall to stop them both from tumbling down.

'I heard a scream!' he gasped, his eyes and hands searching her face and body for any sign of injury.

'It wasn't me!' she snapped, thrusting him away from her. 'Now, get out of my way. I've guests and a feast to attend to.' He put a hand on her arm to stop her and she shrugged it off with a jerk.

Her father emerged from the stairs above, clutching his groin and wheezing pitifully. He took one look at Jorund and then limped into his room, slamming the door shut behind him.

Jorund looked back at her with amusement and admiration in his eyes.

She huffed in response and continued down the stairs. Jorund hurried after her out into the courtyard. 'I need to speak with you, Amée. You're wrong about Valda. Let me explain—'

'Not now, Jorund. Let me do my duty as *your wife* and see to our guests. You can speak with me after.'

'But—' pleaded Jorund.

She spun round to face him. 'After the feast!' she shouted, her fists clenched at her sides. He stopped walking and stared at her, his mouth hanging open as if he were about to say something more but could not find the words.

Valda galloped in on her horse and his eyes flew to her. 'I must speak with you!' she gasped as she rolled down from her horse.

With a snort of disgust Amée walked away.

Life was not perfect, but she would make the best of it. At least she knew she could.

Chapter Twenty-Five

Jorund knew what he had to do. Now that Valda had revealed the true villain behind the attacks, Jorund had no choice but to act.

But the revelation would hurt Amée, deeply. Even more so than the *other* secret he'd kept from her. The weakness of his mind. After what she'd told him about her mother, how could he admit to a similar flaw?

But there was no denying the truth. Valda had heard it directly from Erik Blacktooth's putrid lips. Her father—the man who should cherish and love his daughter—had offered money to any swine willing to kill her.

It went against human nature, against all decency. Jorund couldn't understand it, although he suspected it was to do with the contract Lothair had spoken of with Amée. He needed to find out the details, see how extensive the plot was.

Lothair entered the hall and sat stiffly at the lord's table, oblivious to Jorund's disgust. Lothair sighed as if he were dismayed by his surroundings. 'I miss the finery and amusements of court. I think I will leave for Paris in the morning.'

Amée looked at her father with hard unforgiving eyes. 'That might be for the best.'

'You want amusement, Lothair?' snapped Jorund as he stood up. Rollo, Gisla—in fact, everyone in the hall—stopped their conversations and stared curiously at the sudden change in Jorund's demeanour.

Lothair was startled by the aggressive tone of his voice and mumbled, 'I'm feeling tired, maybe I shall take supper in my room.'

The man began to stand, but Jorund was already behind his seat. He thrust the man back down on the bench with one firm hand to his shoulder.

'Stay. I have an amusing dance I could show you,' Jorund said, nodding to a nearby warrior who quickly replaced his position behind Amée's father. He moved to the front of the table, picking up a nearby stool as he went. Amée reached out and grabbed his arm as he passed her seat.

'What are you doing?' she whispered.

'What has to be done.'

It was true: he had to teach Lothair a lesson. But he also had to find out why he wanted to kill his own daughter. None of it made sense, and if he didn't discover the truth, then the threats to her life would never end.

'Have you heard of knife dancing?' he asked, although he knew his answer already. There was no such thing as 'knife dancing.' Jorund smiled at the uneasy shake of Lothair's head. 'It's a Norse tradition. Hold out your hand.'

'I don't—' At a nod from Jorund, the warrior behind grabbed Lothair's hand and pushed it down on the table, hard.

Jorund pulled out a wickedly long dagger from a sheath at his hip. It was smoothly curved on one side with sharp teeth on the other. He held it up so that Lothair could see it more clearly. Lothair swallowed back any words he might have said with a gulp, and his complexion turned sallow.

'If I were you, I'd spread your fingers wide…and keep them nice and still… I wouldn't want to nick you by accident.'

Lothair paled and looked at Rollo, who smiled coldly back at him. There was no hope for him there—Jorund had already told his overlord about his suspicions regarding his father-in-law before he'd been able to confirm it.

Lothair spread his fingers wide.

'Good. Let's start slowly. Build up my concentration…' He began to stab the point of the blade into the wood between Lothair's fingers slowly. Each fall of the blade causing the older man to flinch.

Jorund gave an icy chuckle. 'Don't be so jumpy! I'm very good at this. Why, I only nicked Gunnar once last time,' he said, casually nodding at the warrior who held Lothair's wrist.

His father-in-law glanced up at Gunnar, who held up his free hand with a lopsided grin. He gave a little wave of his three remaining fingers, and Lothair looked as if he were about to be sick. Of course, Gunnar had lost those fingers in battle, but Lothair didn't know that.

'My father used to be a lawless raider. Did you know that?'

'What?'

Lothair followed the movement of the blade obsessively and frowned at the odd change in conversation.

'His name was Ragnar Halvorson, and I hated him,' continued Jorund, the beat of his blade weaving without hesitation through Lothair's trembling fingers. 'He killed without mercy, honour or respect. He forced me as a young boy to witness the terrible crimes he committed.' He began to stab with more speed until the blade became a blur between Lothair's fingers. Sweat poured from both their brows, despite the fact Jorund's voice remained calm and light. 'So, you see. I know what it's like to have a father who is…unnatural.' The blows of his knife became harder. Bitter words landing with each stab of the knife. 'A man with… No honour! No heart! No decency!' He looked away from the knife and stared into Lothair's terrified eyes, the blade still falling. 'Who would even order the death of his own child for wealth and power? You do not deserve *my Amée.*'

Jorund paused and held the blade up high. Lothair's eyes locked with his and widened with dread.

How many times had Amée been afraid of her father like this? Even once was too many.

'I know of your plans. You are behind the attacks on my wife. What is your deal with King Charles?'

'I have no idea what you are talking about!' spat Lothair. 'Count, what is the meaning of this?'

Rollo's voice was cold and menacing. 'What games does your King play with me?'

Amée stood. Her voice clear and confident despite the pale pallor of her skin. 'The marriage contract…it states that if there is no heir within the first two winters of our marriage the land of Évreux will return to my father.'

Lothair's eyes turned wild with rage, and he sprayed spittle as he wailed. 'The King is a coward and a fool! He had no right! No right to give away *my* land. It is mine! I will have it back! The contract—'

Of all people to speak at this moment, Jorund was surprised it was the Princess Gisla who interrupted Lothair's ranting with a pretty laugh. As if Lothair were a pitiful creature dancing for her amusement. 'Oh, stop, Lothair! Your contract is meaningless! I know my father—he likely only agreed to it to pacify your overbearing pride. Nothing he promised you is legally binding. The treaty negates it.' She placed a reassuring hand on Rollo's arm. 'He would never risk war.'

The room fell silent as the news filtered through Lothair's conceit and arrogance to the coward beneath. His eyes narrowed on Jorund, a twisted smile spreading across his face. He had one last arrow. 'One day you will wish I'd succeeded in killing her. She is as weak in mind and body as her mother before her! I could have saved you from that *madness*—from that shame. She killed herself, you know, hanged herself. She'll be as mad and as jealous as that bitch of a mother before her...' He smiled cruelly. 'You've probably already started to see it...her imbalance.'

Jorund raised the blade high, and Lothair's eyes turned black with fear as he prepared to plunge it into the back of his hand.

It was Amée's voice that stopped him. 'As I recall, *Father*, you were not the one to find my mother's body. *I was*—do not speak of things you do not understand... like contracts.'

Lothair turned purple with rage, but he didn't dare move or speak with Jorund's dagger held high in threat.

'Don't,' she said, her eyes shining in the firelight of the hall. 'We are better than them.'

He knew what she meant. That they were better than both their respective fathers.

She stood and stared hard at her father. 'You are to leave Évreux now, and never come back. You are no longer my father and have no right to be here. You are *ban-ished* from our land.'

Jorund removed his blade from above Lothair's hand. 'If you ever threaten even a lock of her hair again, I will hunt you down and slit your miserable throat.'

As soon as he was free, Lothair ran from the hall. The jeers of both the Norse warriors and Amée's loyal people followed him out into the night.

'I will ensure he leaves,' said Jorund, calling to several of his men.

Outside he watched Lothair scramble to gather his men and leave. Jorund followed at a leisurely pace. Glad that it didn't take long before they were on the road.

Soon they were at the lonely apple tree on the crest of the hill. Lothair spat at it as he passed.

Jorund stared at the tree, and sucked in a sharp breath. He halted his men with a raised hand, and they watched the torches of Lothair and his men fade into the night.

I can see your tryst from my room! Have you no shame, no honour?

Amée's words from earlier hit him like a shower of arrows, one after another.

Not here!

Was this the same tree her father had cruelly mentioned? The tree of her mother's death? The same tree she could see from her window?

He thought of the closed shutters. The stifling air of her room regardless of the time of day. The apple tree perfectly framed in its view.

That was the reason why she always kept the shutters closed. It was so she wouldn't have to see it. His fingers bit into his reins and his horse danced with a moment's confusion.

He settled it with a soft murmur, his mind unfurling like a serpent casting off its dead skin until it was born anew. He'd hoped to leave his past behind, but it still haunted his dreams. He would not allow Amée's past to haunt her too.

Maybe Valda was right: instead of hiding from his past he should face it.

Secrets could not fester in the light.

After Jorund had left the hall, Amée looked at Gisla and gave her a weak smile. 'I'm sorry. I think I may have to go to bed…'

Gisla patted her hand kindly. 'Of course.'

As usual Beatrice had lit the fire in her room to warm it. The air was stifling and smoky. After everything that had happened over the last few days, hiding from the tree suddenly seemed childish and pointless. She could not hide from her past; this was her home and she would not let the past torment her any longer. She went to the window and pulled the covers down from the shutters. A speck of light caught her eye and she opened the shutters wide.

Fresh night air bathed her skin. A balm for her soul.

There was a flaming serpent making its way up the opposite hill. Her father's departure.

'Go,' she whispered. 'And never return.'

Jorund was one of the torchbearers, although she could not see him from this distance.

She'd expected to see the serpent of torches either continue on into the darkness or return. It did neither, and she found herself watching in fascination as the torchbearers stopped for a few moments and then formed a ring of flames. In the centre of the torches stood her mother's tree, a twisted and gnarled spectre.

She couldn't be certain but she thought she saw the massive figure of her husband dismount and walk towards it. Nothing happened for several moments and she wondered what they were doing. But then she saw movement from others in the ring. Some of the torches were brought to the tree and lowered at its base.

A fire had been made.

The apple tree was being cut down branch by branch and its wood burned beside its trunk. The flames of the fire grew stronger, lighting up the entire hill.

A single torch moved away from the gathering and rode back towards the fort.

She knew who it was even before his horse came galloping into the courtyard.

Jorund.

He'd burned her mother's tree. There was no doubt in her mind that he'd done it for her. He must have realised why she covered the window and had thought to remedy it. Her heart filled and then overflowed with bittersweet love.

Below the tower he stopped and dismounted. Swinging from his horse as he looked up at her window. A torch in one hand and an axe strapped to his back. He stopped at the bottom of the steps, and for once she had to look down on him.

'He's gone, and you no longer have to cover your window,' he called up.

'I saw, thank you.'

'May I speak with you?' he asked, his voice uncertain.

'Yes,' she said, and then realising that her voice had almost been a whisper, she called down a little louder, 'Yes!'

***

There was a moment when he thought she might have refused his request, and his heart had almost burst out of his chest it had been beating so hard. But then her voice carried down to him, a simple, 'Yes.'

He ran up the stairs, taking two or three at a time. At her door he stopped breathless and waited.

Could he really admit the awful truth?

He pressed the palm of his hand against the oak door. It swung open with surprising speed. Amée must have opened it at the same time as he'd pushed.

'I hope I did the right thing,' he gasped, his air stolen by fear and indecision. Unsure if he was still talking about the tree or himself.

Amée smiled tenderly. 'I am glad it's gone. But... It no longer disturbs me quite so much as it did.' She took a deep trembling breath. 'She was ill, and what happened to her...' Tears dropped from her eyes as she whispered, 'It wasn't my fault.'

He pulled her into his chest and held her tight. 'How could it *ever* have been your fault?' he murmured into her hair, his body wrapping around her, drawing her close. He wanted to bundle her up and protect her from the world, so that no one could hurt her ever again... Even himself.

'Valda is leaving. She wishes to follow her own destiny—she knows I could never love her.'

Amée pulled away from him, and he let her go, unsure if he had the strength to continue. She still refused to look at him, her face cast in shadow and only half lit by the dying fire. 'I see. She got tired of waiting for you to choose.'

'No! We grew up together, she's like family. She and her sisters were the children I played with when my mother was still alive. I should have stayed with them after my mother's death. But I joined my father…and I've regretted it ever since. But I swear, she is like a sister to me, nothing more. I never imagined that she would think of me as anything other than her brother.'

Amée turned on him with bright amber flames in her eyes. 'She goes to your bedchamber in the middle of the night. That is not *sisterly*!'

Desperately he pleaded for her to understand, to trust him. While knowing he had no right to ask such a thing. 'I *swear* I have never been unfaithful to you. Either in body or thought.'

The pain in her eyes made him realise that he couldn't keep his shame from her a moment longer. It wasn't about her trusting him any more. It was about him trusting her to accept who he really was. The light as well as the dark.

'She came to my room…because…I'd probably screamed,' he said, his voice barely above a whisper.

'What?' She stared at him in complete shock. She had not expected that answer.

He sighed. 'That night—did something wake you? Is that why you left your own bed in the middle of the night?'

Bewildered at the turn in conversation she tilted her head in thought. 'I…I'm not sure… Possibly.'

He moved towards the window and looked into the darkness beyond. The tree still burned, casting its light across the hill. 'It's why I prefer to sleep alone. Like most warriors, I have been in many battles. I have seen death and suffering. But nothing compares to…' He paused, unsure if he could say anything more. She came towards him and took his hands in hers.

'Go on,' she urged.

'When I was with my father…terrible things happened—things I should have stopped.' The words sounded pitiful in comparison to the horror he'd witnessed. He couldn't look at her as he spoke. He needed to tell her everything, but the shame was like a blade in his gut, seeping poison into his blood. 'I wanted him to be proud of me… He thought me too sensitive, too emotional. That my mother's influence had made me weak. He was going to make a man out of me. *Pathetic!*' He spat the last word in disgust. Angry at his father for using him, angry at himself for wanting to please such a worthless man. 'His raiders lacked all honour. They attacked the weak and the helpless, they destroyed everything in their path. They were a plague on the land. But worst of all was my father—he *enjoyed* the violence and the suffering. Took pleasure in…torturing and humiliating people. Those are the memories that torment my nights. When I sleep…sometimes I dream of them…the victims…and I scream, or shout, or lash out. When I'm like that, Valda sometimes comes to wake me. She wouldn't tell you why because I made her swear never to speak of it.'

When he finally allowed his eyes to drop to her lovely face, Amée was looking at him with kindness in her eyes. 'You are a good man, Jorund. That's why those days haunt you.'

Her pity only made him feel more wretched and he thrust her hands away so that he could get more air. 'Don't call me that!' He moved to the window and breathed in huge gulps of air as if he were drowning. 'You don't know what I'm capable of. You have *no idea* what I've done in the past. I hold myself to higher values now, but there was a time when I didn't… Don't call me good. I'm not.'

'You were a boy. You told me yourself…not much

older than I was when your mother died.' She came to stand beside him, her warmth offering a candle of hope.

He shook his head. 'I didn't look like a child. I was taller than you are now and had already fought beside my mother in battle.'

And yet…he'd felt like a child. He'd helped clean his mother's armour and weapons; he'd shielded her back, passed arrows when she'd needed them. But he'd never seen brutality…not *real* brutality, like the kind his father dealt. 'I should have killed him—fought back at least. Instead, I ran away, like a coward.'

'You were a child, and it wasn't your fault.' She turned him towards her with a gentle tug on his arm. Then she reached up and caressed his face with the palm of her hand. He leaned into it and closed his eyes. Starved of her touch and unable to resist.

She smiled. 'We are not our parents and we cannot control the choices they make. But we can choose to be free of them. We can acknowledge both the light and the dark within ourselves and move forward.'

He must have leaned down a little, because when she spoke her lips brushed against his.

'Take me to bed,' she whispered. 'And… Stay with me. Please. I don't want to wake another day without you by my side. I love you.'

He opened his eyes, and stared into hers, not quite believing what he'd just heard. 'You love me?'

'Yes. It doesn't matter if you don't—'

He grasped her by the waist and pulled her close. 'Of course, I love you. I would give you everything, all that I am, and all that I have, if you asked it. There is nothing I want more in this life or the next than for you to look at me and be glad I am your husband.' He choked on his tears as he clasped her to him, pressing fevered kisses on her face and neck. Then he pulled away. 'But I'm afraid. I'm not myself during those dreams. I could hurt you…'

'You could never hurt me. And I am stronger than you think—remember? I will simply get out of bed and…throw a log at you to wake you up,' she teased, and he chuckled.

When he opened his mouth to say more, she shook her head and pulled his lips to hers. She kissed him deeply, her tongue mimicking the passionate way he'd kissed her that first time in his room. He groaned into her mouth as he struggled to unstrap the axe from his back and remove his tunic at the same time. Impatient, Amée grabbed the soft linen tunic between her fists and ripped it down the middle, baring his skin to her eyes and mouth.

'You're a fierce woman!' he said with a wink, and she laughed.

Amée felt overwhelmed by love and joy.

There was nothing to keep them apart now. No past or torment could stop her from loving Jorund with all her passionate heart.

They stumbled to the bed shedding clothes and fumbling with ties. Their lips constantly seeking one another. Only reluctantly releasing to focus on loosening a belt or a ribbon, before claiming each other once again.

Jorund was naked first and lay down on the bed, propped up by the rolled furs at its head. He reached for her as she stood in her shift above him. He cupped the back of her head with his big palm and gently pulled her down to his lips. She followed gladly, offering her mouth as she climbed on top of him to sit on his stomach.

Knowing that he loved her filled her with a confidence she'd never before tasted.

He kissed her, his touch slow and sensual as he savoured every curve, every hitched breath and every sweet kiss. She responded, willing and eager for his touch.

As he seduced her lips, his hands made quick work of pulling down her shift to reveal her breasts. She moaned as a large hand cupped and then lightly squeezed her flesh. Her own fingers exploring his body greedily as she rocked her hips against him, desperate for more, knowing that she needed him as much as he needed her. Reaching between them, she eased herself carefully down onto his manhood. He threw back his head with a hissed curse, and her body shivered with power. Taking his hands in hers she held them tight. Bracing herself against the strength of his arms as she began to move above him. She took him slowly. Sliding up and down carefully until she'd adjusted to his size.

The muscles in his neck strained with the effort of holding himself back. She increased the movement of her hips with every stroke until they were both wild with longing. When he couldn't take it any more, he swept her up and rolled her body beneath him. Unable to control the raw lust that rushed through his body as he held her close.

She shattered beneath him and he followed soon after, holding each other tightly as their bodies and hearts became one.

They fell asleep cradling each other. No darkness or secrets between them, only a peaceful sleep, followed by a brighter morning and a beautiful view.

Epilogue

Less than two winters later

Jorund walked into their bedchamber and smiled at the sight in front of him. His wife lay on the bed, their twin boys asleep in her arms. On her back and propped up by a rolled fur, each of her arms supported and protected her babes even as she slept. He knew that she wouldn't move a muscle. The instinct to nurture so deeply ingrained in her heart and soul that she obeyed it even while sleeping.

He took off his boots and walked tentatively across the room to the open windows. He considered shutting them. But the summer breeze cooled the room and he suspected Amée would be very warm with both boys pressed up against her.

The births had been long and difficult, but she was doing surprisingly well only a few weeks later. Last night William and Robert had seemed to insist on constant feeding. They'd all been up most of the night, including Beatrice and Emma, who considered themselves to be the boys' aunts. He had to admit he loved that, especially as he and Amée had no real family to speak of… Except, of course, each other.

He sank into the chair by the window and looked out at Évreux. All of the gods, Christian and Norse, had been generous to him. He wasn't sure he deserved it, but like all Norsemen, he would take it regardless of whether he deserved it or not.

He closed his eyes, exhausted, and allowed himself to sleep. He couldn't with the boys in bed with them, and he'd taken to sleeping in the chair most nights.

Amée had been right when she'd insisted he would never hurt her, unknowingly or otherwise. But sometimes the dreams of the past still haunted him, but never as badly or as cruelly as before he'd opened up to Amée about them. If he did have a nightmare, she was usually soothing him before he even knew what was happening.

However, he still did not fully trust himself with the boys…maybe that would change over time. She complained about it, but allowed him to do as he wished. 'Only until the babes are weaned, and then you'll be back where you belong!' she'd growled at him with a hard look.

She was fierce, and he would never underestimate the power of his wife's love.

When he woke it was to the sound of a baby's hungry cry. He looked over and smiled as a weary Amée patiently finished feeding one babe, only to have to juggle to feed the other. 'Let me take Robert,' he said and picked up his milk-drunk son, gently tapping his back until he brought up a burp.

'It amazes me that you can tell the difference. I still have to look closely,' Amée said with a wince as William latched on.

'Lucky guess. Robert's always the hungry one.'

She chuckled and then sighed. It sounded a little despondent, so he went to sit on the bed beside her. 'What's wrong?'

'Oh, nothing. Just a bit sick of lying in this bed.'

'The birth was arduous. You need time to recover.'

'It wasn't that bad, especially considering we had twins. Honestly I'm feeling much better.'

He searched her face to be certain, and then nodded. He trusted her more than he trusted himself, and always would. 'Well, if you're feeling up to it, there is something I would like to show you.'

She looked up at him with a glowing smile. As if he were an illumination in one of her precious books. He would never tire of seeing that look.

Amée's heart fluttered with excitement. 'Ooh! How intriguing!' She was desperate to see something other than these four walls and she was grateful for an excuse, any excuse, to leave her bed. She loved her new babies dearly, but the last few weeks had been exhausting. She was either asleep or feeding. Jorund had been her rock throughout, comforting her when she struggled with the initial pain of nursing. Soothing, changing or rocking the children so that she could sleep, and generally ensuring that she had no worries except for the care of herself and the feeding of their family.

There was a light knock followed by Beatrice's head popping round the door. It was almost impossible to keep the woman away for long. 'They're awake!' she exclaimed brightly, bustling into the room with a fresh bowl of water and a washcloth, which she set on the table by the bed.

'Could you please get my gown from the chest, Beatrice? I'm going to stretch my legs once William's done.'

'Of course, take your time. I'll be fine with the little ones until you're needed.'

'Thank you.' Yes, she would love some time alone with her husband. Jorund only left her side during the day to manage the estate, but it would be nice to spend time alone without the babies. She was beginning to feel more like a prize cow than a wife.

After a long feed William was finally finished and Amée quickly handed him into Beatrice's care, practically jumping from the bed when she was done. She dressed and washed quickly, hoping the gap between feeds would be a long one.

What could Jorund's surprise be? The repairs to the fort were complete. Amée had managed the reconstruction work and had saved all four halls. But she'd certainly kept Jorund busy with her next lot of plans. As well as more accommodation for their people, she'd also designed a small building for her collection of books and papers. She hoped to build it into a place of learning eventually, although she had her hands full at the moment with the boys. Still, she was always optimistic about what they could achieve. The fort was becoming more impressive by the day. She and Jorund had built a strong base that reflected the growing pride of Évreux and its people.

He stopped at the entrance and turned to her. 'I have added a new stone above our threshold.'

Sure enough, when she looked up, she noticed the central stone above the doorway had been prised out and replaced with a new one. 'Was there something wrong with the old one?' she asked, confused as to why he would replace a perfectly fine stone with a new one. Then she noticed it. 'Did you carve something into it?'

His shy smile was enough to make her heart burst with affection. 'Lift me up so that I can read it better.'

He picked her up, gently raising her high with his usual ease. Carved with careful precision were the words:

Home of Jorund Évreux, his beloved wife, Amée Évreux, and their children, William and Robert Évreux, born 914 AD.

'I thought we should use your family name as I do not have one. And I've left space for more children. I can carve their names after...' he said, his breath warm against her cheek.

She turned her head to face him. 'You wrote this?'

'Yes...while you were resting. It will not burn or rot like paper. But it will last longer than a saga. And all who cross this threshold will know of my love for you, and for our family.'

She kissed him hard and passionately, pausing to gasp, 'I love you too. My sweet, kind giant!'

'One flesh and one spirit,' he replied, quoting the Norse marriage vow.

'Yes.' She smiled, and wrapped her arms around his neck. 'My beloved.'

* * * * *

*If you enjoyed this book
why not check out this other great read by
Lucy Morris?*

The Viking Chief's Marriage Alliance